"*Laws of Depravity* by Eriq La Salle should be on a fast track to Best Seller status. It is the story of good vs. evil where it's not always clear who are the good, and who are the evil. *Laws of Depravity* may be the most engrossing book you read this year, bar none."

—Lee Ashford, *Reader's Favorites*

"Eriq La Salle, in *Laws of Depravity*, has written an utterly compelling and riveting thriller with echoes of the dark master, Thomas Harris. Here, La Salle also adds a surprising twist by weaving in a spiritual component that raises the narrative to lofty and thought-provoking levels. It's a wonderful accomplishment."

—Leonard Chang, author of *Over the Shoulder* and *Crossings*

"Actor and director Eriq La Salle's intense debut is a modern day parable cleverly masquerading as a crime novel. A muscular, gritty and spiritual thriller."

—John Shors, bestselling author of *Beneath a Marble Sky*, *Beside a Burning Sea*, *Dragon House*, *The Wishing Trees*, and *Cross Currents*

"*Laws of Depravity* will take you on a heart-pounding ride of vengeance, murder and atonement, never letting you rest until you've reached the final page. Eriq La Salle deftly draws unforgettable characters who tangle with good and evil and seek spiritual understanding and forgiveness for some of the most dastardly deeds human beings are capable of committing. Drawing on his talent as an acclaimed actor and director, Mr. La Salle digs deep into his characters' psyches, delivering a group of bruised and tarnished individuals you won't soon forget."

—Neal Baer, coauthor of *Kill Switch* and former Executive Producer of "Law and Order SVU."

"The surprises keep coming in La Salle's twisting debut thriller, in which good and evil aren't always black and white. In addition to the absorbing, fast-paced plot that will keep readers guessing until the end, each wonderfully sculpted character has a distinct, lifelike personality. The plot offers catalysts for change while raising spiritual questions and blurring the line between good and evil, which propels the story upward from being merely a solid, entertaining thriller to being a gripping must read that could have readers pondering right and wrong long after they've finished."

—*Kirkus Reviews*, Starred Review

"A serial killer known as the Martyr Maker is on his final round of murdering 12 clergymen once every ten years. Two New York City detectives and the FBI are on his trail, but maybe the dead clergy aren't as innocent as they appear. A gritty crime thriller, spiritual quest, and love story all woven into one compelling tale."

—*Publishers Weekly*

LAWS
OF
DEPRAVITY

ERIQ LA SALLE

EBONY
MAGAZINE PUBLISHING

Poisoned Pen
PRESS

Published by Poisoned Pen Press in association with Ebony Magazine Publishing
P.O. Box 4410, Naperville, Illinois 60567-4410
(630) 961-3900
sourcebooks.com

Originally published in 2012 in the United States by 4 Clay Productions.

Library of Congress Cataloging-in-Publication Data

Names: La Salle, Eriq, author.
Title: Laws of depravity / Eriq La Salle.
Description: Naperville, Illinois : Ebony Magazine Publishing, [2022] |
    Series: Martyr maker ; 1 | "Originally published in 2012 in the United
    States by 4 Clay Productions."
Identifiers: LCCN 2022019579 (print) | LCCN 2022019580 (ebook)
Subjects: LCSH: Murder--Investigation--New York (State)--New York--Fiction.
    | Clergy--Crimes against--Fiction. | Serial murderers--Fiction. | LCGFT:
    Thrillers (Fiction) | Detective and mystery fiction. | Novels.
Classification: LCC PS3612.A2435 L39 2022 (print) | LCC PS3612.A2435
    (ebook) | DDC 813/.6--dc23/eng/20220420
LC record available at https://lccn.loc.gov/2022019579
LC ebook record available at https://lccn.loc.gov/2022019580

Printed and bound in the United States of America.
SB 10 9 8 7 6 5 4 3 2

For such are false Apostles, deceitful workman, masquerading as Apostles of Christ.

And no wonder, for Satan himself masquerades as an angel of light.

It is not surprising then if his servants masquerade as servants of righteousness. Their end will be what their actions deserve.

—2 CORINTHIANS 11:13–15

God had surely forsaken him. How else could he justify the pure evil that held him captive? Everett Deggler was committed to God. He passionately dedicated his entire life to serving and pleasing his Lord. Everett converted souls and spread the Gospel. He had instilled in both of his sons a fear of and the need to worship God, even if at times he had to physically beat those principles into them. Deggler made the necessary sacrifices. Whatever was required of him to gain God's favor and protection he did without question. In the fall of 1981, the city of San Francisco was on edge with the murders that had played out in the news for the past month. Everett heard about the eleven victims but never doubted for a moment that God was always watching over him.

Everett's hands were tightly bound behind his back and his eyes blinded by the cloth that had been securely placed during his abduction. As he was roughly led from the van that he had been thrown in earlier, he was aware of the cool trickle of urine that ran down the front of his thigh. Fear and absence of sight made him stumble and fall even under the firm guidance of strong hands. He tried to pray, but every new sound brought a greater distraction and sense of fear and dread.

It took some time, but the two men found the perfect spot to kill Everett. It was an abandoned church on the outskirts of San Francisco, in the Sonoma suburbs. Small and in the middle of nowhere, it offered them the type of privacy needed for the things that were planned. The men were brothers, the younger one named Abraham and the other Noah. Abraham, at twenty-three years old, was tall, extremely muscular and the leader of the two. He had not involved Noah in the eleven prior murders, but he wanted him here now as a spectator and not a participant. Unlike Abraham, Noah didn't have the stomach to inflict pain, but observing it was a different matter. Besides, he had many reasons of his own for wanting to be present.

Everett was still blindfolded as one of the men forced a large plastic capsule in his mouth and made him swallow. He was then attached to an old pulley device. Slowly he was lowered into a vat of boiling water. He was pulled out just as his skin blistered and he was being asphyxiated by the steam, which was scalding and constricting his lungs. He was only immersed in the water for a few seconds, but the pain was searing and excruciating. Everett wasn't sure if he had passed out or not, but suddenly he felt the presence of one of the men just in front of him pouring ammonia on his raw skin. As Everett screamed he felt the man's hand loosen his blind-fold. It took a moment for him to gather his bearings and vision. The blurred image of two men standing before him finally became clear. It was the recognition of the men that terrified him even more than what he had already endured. Everett was desperately trying to make sense of the sight of his two sons standing before him when Abraham stepped closer and smiled as he whispered, "Hello, Father."

1

New Yorkers were enjoying the warmest fall that they had seen in several years. The weather of 2011 would be remembered for a few things: Namely its schizophrenic last two months of summer—the blistering heat of August and the unseasonably cool September. October was supposed to have been much colder than it actually was, but it was two weeks before Halloween and many people still weren't even wearing sweaters. Unlike the hot days of August, when the streets of Manhattan were thick with the stench of garbage and car fumes, the air now was light and clean. New Yorkers were still cordial and not yet made introverted by the winter months. Even at night the streets were more populated than usual for this time of the year, with people taking full advantage of the surprisingly warm weather.

Northeasterners knew better than most the brutal potential of winter. They made it a point then to squeeze what they could out of agreeable autumns. Even though most of them didn't want to admit it, they all knew deep down that the winter storms would soon be upon them. 42nd Street was gone. It no longer existed. At least not to the silver-haired man who slowly cruised the Times Square district. He remembered the real 42nd Street. Pre-Disney. The 42nd Street of the '70s, '80s and early '90s. The peep shows and prostitutes and the ever willing hand job from a stranger in the darkened X-rated theaters. It was easier then. Everything was so much more accessible when the urges came and he decided to give in to them. These days though, it required a little more effort. He only indulged his temptations once or twice a month, but still he was constantly aware of the effort. When he needed the release, he drove to the city from Staten Island. He needed to be far away from his own community. He could never risk compromising his good name and reputation. No one that knew him could possibly understand the pressures of his job. He understood more than anyone that the value of his work far outweighed any minor indiscretion that he occasionally allowed himself.

He got off on so many different things. For him it wasn't just about a sexual release. It was just as much about the cruising, the spotting, the danger and fear. The buildup and foreplay was equally important and pleasurable. He got off most on the sense of abandonment. The letting go and submitting to his most primal urges. Ninety-nine percent of the time he was who people expected him to be. Who he was supposed to be. But once or twice a month, he allowed himself to be whoever and whatever he needed to be. He had rationalized this over thirty years ago as a small price to pay after his first encounter with a prostitute.

He had been in the city a few hours now and had lost track of time. The availability of good hookers in the surrounding areas of Times Square had become more and more sporadic with slimmer pickings. Still, he usually started his hunt there, more so because of the overall energy and nostalgia. One of his new favorite cruising spots was in the lower 30s on the East Side. The warm weather had allowed the streetwalkers the luxury of wearing a wide range of scandalously revealing outfits. They paraded up and down the street in lace, fishnets and thongs. Some flashed their breasts at passing cars while others negotiated with prospective clients. The man sat in his car at the end of the block for over an hour watching all of the activity. For the last twenty minutes, he found himself staring at a raven-haired Latina in six-inch heels. She wore a sheer mesh outfit which impressively showcased her curvy ass and large breasts. She wasn't by any stretch of the imagination the prettiest or sexiest of the bunch, but she had an edge and sass that turned him on. He had enough experience with hookers to know that certain personality traits were more important to him than physical attributes. When he was in this mood he needed a woman who was aggressive and strong and who could take the power from him that he was more than ready to relinquish.

She didn't speak much. One of her talents was reading the various men she had sex with. She was very clear as to why they came to her. Some needed permission or validation to be who they really were. Others, like the silver-haired man she was with now, knew exactly who they were and came to her to indulge and celebrate that acknowledgment. He paid and tipped her in advance. He gave her double what they had negotiated, doing so because he wanted them both to be clear on the rules of engagement. In the hour or so that they would be together, he needed to own her. He was paying as much for her mind and imagination as he was for her time and body. He needed the closest thing to truth that she had to offer. He paid her well because tonight he didn't want to be hindered by any limits. His or hers.

By the time he left the hotel on 38th Street it was almost 4:30 in the morning. The hooker was better than he had anticipated. She brought him to the places he wanted and needed to go. More than once. He had planned on leaving no later than 3:00 to make sure he was back in time for work. Unfortunately he wouldn't have time to get back for a shower and clean clothes even though he still had the smell of the prostitute and the pissy scent of the hotel room on him. Fortunately he had brought a change of clothing and left them in his trunk. Nothing could ever interfere with his work, especially not his own weaknesses. He stopped at a gas station on the way back to Staten Island and brought the clothes into the men's room with him. He gave himself a whore's bath in the tiny porcelain sink, changed his clothes and emerged from the bathroom in his black suit and white priest's collar.

Father Montrelle hurried back toward his car determined to be on time for 6:00 a.m. Mass. He was in such a rush that he never noticed that the same van that had been following him all night was parked not too far from his car. As he looked up he saw the silhouette of a large man standing thirty feet away. The man's hands were at shoulder height and he was holding a large object that the priest couldn't quite make out. Father Montrelle heard a short whooshing sound just before something hit his leg. He let out a yell as he felt the pain and noticed the blood and a long wooden arrow protruding from his right thigh. Before the priest went down, the large man reloaded his crossbow and put a second arrow in Montrelle's left thigh. The pain sent the priest into immediate shock. He fought as best he could to stay conscious. As he fell to the ground he made very little sound and movement. A look of confusion and fear washed over Father Montrelle's face at the recognition of his tormentor. The large man quickly moved toward Montrelle, picked him up and placed him in a nearby cargo van. The vehicle sped off just as the station attendant came out to investigate the noise.

From the time he was a small boy, Father Montrelle had a fascination with sunrises. Even as a child they represented new beginnings and possibilities to him. Just before the door of the van was closed, Montrelle saw the first hint of the day's sunrise. As the van pulled off, the priest lay helpless and terrified, certain that this would be his last.

2

I f your right eye causes you to sin, gouge it out and throw it away. It is better to lose one part of your body than for your whole body to be thrown into hell."

Father Conner was a gregarious man. Short and round with an infectious smile. He was revered and popular here at St. Jude's, in lower Manhattan. Here at the church he was known for many things. His knowledge and command of the Bible was impressive even to those who had been ordained long before him. He was a favorite among the older parishioners for both his candor and accessibility. He was referred to by many in the congregation more as "Uncle Conner" than Father. He was regarded as much for his unwavering devoutness as he was for his wit, humor and acts of kindness. To him it was God, not the Devil, who was in the details. Various items of interest were littered throughout the office. There seemed to be something for everyone. Sports memorabilia for the men. An impressive collection of home design and furnishing magazines for the women. Filled candy jars and random toys for the children. Father Conner was gifted at making people feel comfortable, disarmed and receptive to him.

As he quoted scripture to the younger man that sat across from him, his voice was steady and even. "…and if your hand or foot cause you to sin, cut it off and throw it away. It is better for you to enter life maimed or crippled than to have two hands or two feet and be thrown into eternal fire," Father Conner continued.

"So you really accept all of that as the law of God?" the younger man questioned.

The man's name was Quincy Cavanaugh. He was lean and fit. He carried with him a certain gravitas that demanded attention and acknowledgment. His most noticeable physical traits were his sharp features, sea-green eyes and olive complexioned skin. The dark hair and green eyes were attractive collisions of his Irish-Italian lineage. He was strong, attractive and charismatic. Quincy absent-mindedly played with an autographed Babe Ruth baseball that he picked up off the priest's desk.

Father Conner smiled as he responded to his question. "This is the law of the Old Testament. We subscribe to the laws of the New. Mr. Cavanaugh, do you belong to the Catholic Church?" Father Conner asked.

Quincy returned the priest's smile. "More out of habit than anything."

"Do you believe in God?" Conner pressed.

"I'm assuming you mean in the traditional way."

"It's a pretty straightforward question," the priest persisted.

"Do you really think that one's belief in God is that straight-forward? Assuming I do believe, in your opinion, does God control our destiny or do we?" Quincy asked.

Having been asked that same question numerous times before, Father Conner offered his patented response. "I think the destiny of the individual is the will of God for the better of the collective."

"And what of our sins, Father?"

"Have you sinned, Mr. Cavanaugh?"

Quincy laughed. "We've all sinned, Father. I was just asking hypothetically."

The slightest hint of irritation began to creep into Father Conner's tone. "The salvation of your soul should not be a hypothetical proposal. Are you seeking religious rationalization or confession?"

"I don't know, Father. Maybe both."

Father Conner saw in that moment the one thing that he had somehow overlooked earlier. He was disappointed in himself that his preoccupation with scripture and lecture had blinded him to the man's affliction. The priest looked past the man's clear, sea-green eyes and saw in that moment the brokenness. It wasn't temporal or isolated, but rather something much more consuming.

"Why don't you tell me what's troubling you," Father Conner gently asked.

Quincy fidgeted a bit before responding. "It's not me. I know someone who's suffered a horrible loss. I guess I'm just trying to figure out why God chooses to turn his back when He's needed most."

Father Conner had pretty much heard it all before. These types of queries were, more or less, variations on a theme. But there was something so basic and unfiltered in the man's line of questioning and reason that made the priest want to respond likewise. "Death has a way of making us want to blame someone. That someone is usually God," Conner said.

Quincy was quick to clarify. "This wasn't just a death, Father; it was a suicide. A boy. Just a little boy. What kind of loving God lets a little boy feel so much pain that the only way out for him is death?"

Father Conner sighed, partly out of sincerity, partly out of habit. He needed his response to have weight and clarity. He spoke even more deliberately. "Man is responsible for most of the pain in the world, not God. We can tolerate the injustices of the world if we accept that man is liable to God. Spiritual accountability."

Although he wasn't quite sure what it was, the priest noticed something different in the man's eyes.

For the first time during their conversation, Quincy stared directly in the priest's eyes without blinking or turning away. "Do you really believe that?" he asked.

Although a bit unnerved by the man's stare, Father Conner refused to be the first to break contact. "Not just as a man of God, but simply as a man," he said confidently.

Quincy carefully placed the baseball back on Father Conner's desk and looked at him rather seriously.

"Do you believe in hell, Father? I'm not talking about it as some existentialist exercise, I mean a tangible hell. I'm talking physical torment for physical evil."

The priest shifted slightly in his chair to better engage Quincy. "What you seem to be referring to sounds more like physical retribution than…"

"That's my point. Can an evil act befalling an evil person be considered hell? For instance, let's say a man who was in a position of power and trust so abused his title that it caused irreparable damage. So now if that man suffered physical pain or even death because of his abuse, wouldn't that be considered a hell by his own construction?"

Father Conner rose and extended his hand, a not so subtle hint that the conversation no longer interested him.

"I'm not sure I have the answers you're seeking. Catholicism is not a religion of hypothetical rhetoric."

As Quincy stood, he seemed oddly lighter, as though some unseen burden had been, at the very least, partially lifted.

"Well then, maybe you can answer this one last question for me, Father. Do you think there is a special hell for priests who rape helpless children?"

Father Conner panicked as Quincy opened his jacket. The priest immediately noticed the light catching the metal gun handle at Quincy's side.

3

The autumn air invigorated Elena. It felt light and pure in her lungs, even slightly medicinal. She loved the feeling in her chest as it spread throughout her entire body. As she jogged throughout the city, she took in every detail. Old buildings, new buildings, cars, trees, squirrels, birds, nothing was overlooked. Since she had left her watch on the nightstand, she had no idea what time it was, or even how long she had been running. She just ran. She ran with no particular route or destination. On this beautiful autumn morning, her only thought, her only preoccupation was…one foot in front of the other. As she finally began to tire, Elena found herself in Battery Park. For so many reasons, this quickly had become her favorite park in all of Manhattan, not just for the still verdant trees and foliage it offered, nor its endless vistas. She loved this park most because of the water that surrounded it.

Water always spoke to Elena. It calmed her and gave her assurances. She was by nature a water baby. As a child, she sat quietly for hours at a time on her native Colombian shores and enjoyed the water's mystery and power. Beaches, lakes, ponds, they all spoke to her. If she stayed away too long, they called her. When she needed centering and order, they called her. The water still made her feel like a child, filled with curiosity and wonder. She had been fortunate to have passed this trait down to her son before he died. She came to the water now, as much for him as she did herself.

Joaquin had been dead for two months now, but here, she still felt his presence. Each day she came, Elena embraced both the joy and sadness that awaited her. And though each moment held the possibility of either laughing or crying uncontrollably, she was equally appreciative of them both. It was here that she felt the most connected to her son. It was here that she felt she could tell Joaquin the things she hadn't when he was alive. Whether He was listening or not, Elena still thanked God for the water. As she watched the gentle currents, she became oblivious to everything other than the water. Oblivious to her accelerated heartbeat. Oblivious to the tears that began to fall. Oblivious even to the man who sat on a nearby bench studying her intently.

Quincy had arrived at the park an hour or so ago with the hopes that she would be there. After confronting Father Conner, he needed to see her, even if only for a minute or two. As he watched Elena with her eyes closed facing the water, he saw in her something kindred and familiar. He saw great beauty and pain. A soul older and heavier than her twenty-something years. As Elena got up to leave, she sensed Quincy's presence and turned toward him. He was a bit uncertain how best to respond so he offered up a smile and hoped that she would receive it as a noninvasive gesture. Just seeing her left him feeling "light." No other woman had done that before. He had wanted to tell her many things, some about himself, some about Father Conner, but he couldn't. For now, he would just have to enjoy the simple high that she had left him with. As she walked off, he wondered many things about her.

It was strange, considering that Elena hadn't really met that many people since she'd been in New York, but still she had thought for a second the stranger looked familiar. She saw in his brief smile something sad and incomplete. She knew that look well. She knew firsthand the gift and curse of being fractured and could easily identify it in others. Just as a soldier out of uniform inherently knows the presence of another soldier, so too did the fractured sense their own kind.

4

Quincy drove up to the Heights after he left the park. As he sat in the small, dark confessional booth at St. Augustine's, he couldn't help but feel young and mischievous. Hearing the sound of someone entering from the other side prompted him to sit up a little more erect with a simple smile slowly creasing his face. As the small partition was slid open, Quincy cleared his throat and spoke softly using an exaggerated Irish accent that altered the identification of his natural voice.

"Bless me, Father, for I have sinned. It's been at least two years since my last confession and lately I have had impure thoughts."

"What type of impure thoughts?" the priest asked.

"Well, lately I've found myself lusting after another man, but he ignores me and pretends that I don't exist."

Quincy listened and smiled as he heard the priest exhale a long and weighted sigh. The next time the priest spoke, his tone was considerably different. It was much less formal and sanctimonious. "You do realize that there is a special place in hell reserved for idiots like you?"

"Yeah, I know. But as long as they have free cable and unlimited porn, I'll be okay," Quincy retorted.

Both men exited their respective booths and warmly embraced each other. As the two separated, the resemblance between them was obvious. The priest was an inch taller and two years older but they were unmistakably born of the same clan. Quincy's older brother Liam was considerably more handsome than most people's preconception of what a priest should look like. He held a squishy stress ball in his right hand, a habit that he had picked up long ago that helped him get through the countless confessions that he heard on a daily basis. Quincy looked down at the small ball and laughed at his brother.

"Maybe you should find a less stressful profession," Quincy said teasingly.

"Yeah, you're one to talk. What are you doing here?" Liam asked.

"Since you don't bother to come see anyone, I figured I'd come harass you here," Quincy responded.

Liam looked at his younger brother quizzically, sensing there was more. "How's Ma?"

"Same ol' same. You know Ma. I stopped by and saw her the other day. She asked about you," Quincy said with something resembling a smirk.

"The Church has had me swamped lately. I'll try to swing by sometime this week to see her," Liam said apologetically.

Quincy laughed as he looked directly at his brother. "No you won't. We both already know that. Guess when they were teaching you how to forgive the whole world, somehow your own mother didn't make the list."

Liam could always tell when his brother was deflecting attention from himself by playing the guilt card. They were so close that their most basic strategies were often transparent to each other.

"Did you really come here to give me a hard time about Ma?" Liam quipped.

"No. I just...I just wanted to talk," Quincy shot back at him.

Both men loved their mother, Colette, but neither was particularly close to her. They had always felt that although she was physically present, she had in all other ways abandoned them after the death of their father. Even though Quincy and Liam were much too young to comprehend or begin to articulate their mother's condition, somehow they intrinsically knew that she had become emotionally immobilized by their father's passing. They quickly learned to depend on each other much more than anyone else. Unlike his brother, Quincy had at least found a way to forgive her. He felt that she spent enough time and destructive ways punishing herself far more than he or Liam could ever do.

Both Quincy and Liam had been violated physically, sexually and emotionally as children. Colette had chosen denial when her sons needed her most, partly because of the fact that it happened at the hands of a local priest whom she had encouraged to assume a surrogate father role after the death of her husband. She turned a blind eye and deaf ear to her sons' pleas for help because her need to believe in the goodness of God was greater than the needs of her own children. Both Quincy and Liam had only fragmented memories of Colette being happy and vibrant. When their father was alive they remembered her laughing and being more like the mothers of their normal friends. There were the rare occasions when they remembered her as a woman who was still trying to win at life.

Over the course of his life, Quincy had often thought about his father. If he had survived his cancer, how different would all of their lives have been? His father was only thirty-two when he died and had by no means reached his full potential. From what Quincy could remember, his father was soft-spoken and kind. He was all things baseball—specifically, his beloved New York Yankees. Quincy took great pride in the fact that this same passion had been instilled in and passed down to him. Quincy remembered his father as being handsome and funny. He couldn't help but wonder what would have been the accumulative effect of his father's existence had he been around to raise his boys to become men.

"You wanna go grab an early lunch?" Liam asked.

"Yeah, that sounds good," Quincy said smiling.

As Liam started removing his collar, he led his brother in the direction of the rectory. "By the way, it's three."

Quincy looked at his brother confused. "Three what?"

"Three years, two months and seventeen days since your last confession, but who's counting?"

"Well let's just say that God and I reached an understanding."

"Oh yeah, and what's that?" Liam asked.

"I don't bother Him, and He returns the favor."

Quincy playfully shoved his brother as the two laughed and headed toward the exit.

Considering how close they were, it was odd how much the brothers' life paths diverged. They had both been molded and stamped by the horrors of their early childhood, but in very different ways. Whereas Liam was now dedicated to and obsessed with the redemption of man's soul, his younger brother was much more preoccupied with the destructive nature of it. The irony was that Liam had been the wilder of the two in their youth. His anger often led to violence. When he was thirteen, he did a three-month stint in juvie after splitting a bully's head open who had made the mistake of picking on Quincy. After Liam was released, it was Quincy who first noticed the changes in his brother. They never talked about what happened during his stay, but it was shortly afterward that Liam became serious about God. Quincy surmised that Liam had somehow made his peace with the Devil. It was one of the many things that Quincy both admired and envied in Liam.

He also accepted the fact that it was a type of peace that he would more than likely never find.

5

Father Conner's eyes looked upward. Frozen and fixed in the hereafter. His head was lying in a puddle of sticky blood. His nude body had been completely flayed. The priest was 98 percent exposed muscle and tissue. Both of his hands and feet had been severed and neatly placed next to his body. There were noxious scents in the room. In the seconds before his death, Father Conner's body had the time to register fear. A ring of urine and feces stained the white oak floor beneath his skinned body. His arms were extended to the east and west, wrists facing upward. The positioning of the priest's body closely resembled the large, brass crucifix that hovered nearby. New York's finest milled about, inspecting the scene and trying to make sense of it. Even the most hardened cops made an effort to avoid looking directly at the body. Two beat cops had already vomited in separate corners at the gruesome scene.

The fact that such sheer savagery and barbarism had been committed against a "man of God" was a sobering testament to the cops of how much of a godless city they actually lived in.

One detective knelt over the body. If he was disturbed by the carnage, he hid it well. He was African American, late thirties, attractive and muscular. His name was Tavares Freeman, but most people, cops included, only called him by his childhood nickname: Phee. It was short for "Phenomenal," a name he earned at eight years old during his Pop Warner days. The nickname had many incarnations along the way to adulthood. "Phenom," "Phenomenal Freeman," "Phee-Man," and then of course, simply "Phee." The name and myth grew throughout high school, college and his eight years in the NFL. He was widely considered to be one of the top five free safeties to ever play the game. The main reason he had excelled in his position was the same reason he excelled in everything he did. His countermoves. Rarely did Phee instigate or initiate. His innate talent was his incredible ability to counter. The combination of his impressive instincts as a cop and his father's many connections made his promotion to detective one of the fastest in the city's history.

Phee hunched over the dead priest's body, taking in everything and contemplating his next move. All the other cops were happy to give him a wide berth not just because of the horror committed, but also because of the things they knew about him. They knew he was in a zone. They knew he and his partner were the best closers on the squad, and most importantly, they knew Phee didn't fear evil. Not even the pure evil that butchered the priest. Ironically there was an eerie calm to him. His only concern was gathering details and dissecting even the most mundane aspect of the crime scene. One of the things that made Phee such a good detective was that he saw nothing as insignificant, and the word minutia wasn't a part of his vocabulary. Everything at a crime scene told him something, either about the perpetrator or the victim. This scene in particular told Phee many things, but as he looked at what was left of the priest, he focused on one empirical fact: There was an animal out there somewhere that needed to be put down.

"Started without me?" a familiar voice broke Phee's zone. Phee turned to face his partner, Quincy Cavanaugh. Quincy looked around and walked the space as though it were his first time. As he looked down at the skinned body, there wasn't even the slightest indication that the detective had laid eyes on the priest before, that just a few hours earlier he had sat in this very office confronting the now deceased Father Conner. Quincy played his role well. He knelt on the opposite side of his partner, positioning Father Conner's body between them. This was their routine. Kneeling over corpses, one looking east while the other looked west. One surveying the north while the other scrutinized the south.

"You wanna bring me up to speed?" Quincy asked.

"Father Conner, seventy years old. Janitor found him after he didn't answer several calls from his assistant, who was out sick. Supposedly everybody loved him."

"Not everybody," Quincy quipped. "Anything on the security cameras?"

"No. Janitor said somehow the system was disabled last night."

"Our killer?"

"A kill this clean doesn't make me think it was a coincidence."

Quincy's eyes darted around the room. It was more of a defensive impulse than a visual documentation of anything in particular. In this moment he needed to avoid his partner's eyes. Quincy pretended to be doing his job, but more than anything he was just trying to keep it together. He went through the motions of asking questions. He had to feign professional concern for the victim. Quincy was the only person in the room with the inside knowledge that Father Conner wasn't worthy of the sympathy that fellow officers and the rest of the city would so abundantly bestow upon him. He felt Phee looking at him and deftly deflected with another question. "What's the closest you have on a T.O.D.?"

"The coroner's office put final expiration around 9:30 this morning."

"Final expiration?" Quincy was slightly confused by Phee's choice of words.

Phee clarified. "He died bad and long. Took at least an hour to be skinned this methodically."

Quincy felt claustrophobic. There was a weird pressure on his diaphragm that challenged his breathing. The sudden pressure on his diaphragm caused his breathing to become dense and staccato.

It was at that moment that he regretted having had brunch with his brother. Keeping the food in his system was a challenge. As he stood from his crouching position, there was a sudden onset of vertigo. Had it not been for Phee, Quincy would have gone down. Fortunately none of the other cops saw him stagger and he was able to play it off.

Quincy walked the crime scene for an hour or so, sometimes with Phee, but mostly alone. He needed room to think, to recover, and most importantly, to maneuver. He had already shown weakness at the scene. He couldn't make any more mistakes that might compromise him in the eyes of his colleagues. Quincy had to retrace his every move to make sure that there was no way to link him to Father Conner. As he looked for the baseball that he had played with earlier, he was surprised to discover that it had disappeared. He tried to control his growing anxiety by playing back as many details as he could of his earlier visit. More than likely the ball's absence was insignificant, but Quincy's mounting paranoia had him working overtime in his mind. He saw himself playing with the baseball and eventually placing it back on the desk. The last thing he needed was for his prints to show up at a murder scene where every cop in the room saw him wearing gloves. As he thought back to the ball, he remembered in detail the conversation that he had with Conner. He remembered the hatred that he felt for him. He especially remembered the dark place that his hatred had brought him in his mind. Quincy remembered coming here to kill the priest.

6

A couple of months before, Quincy and Phee had investigated the possible homicide of an eleven-year-old boy whose handcuffed body was found hanging in an abandoned building. After a short investigation and the discovery of a hidden note, it was determined that the boy had handcuffed himself and his death was quickly downgraded to a suicide. Quincy had only met the boy's mother, Elena, once. But in that brief meeting, he knew he would remember her for the rest of his life. She was the only woman who had ever transported him. Her eyes alone moved him in ways that he had never even contemplated. On one hand she left him feeling awkward and shy, and on the other she emboldened him with thoughts and feelings that had been foreign to him. She arrived in New York from Colombia a day after her son's death. Quincy and Phee met with her the following day. It was Phee who ran point on the interview and officially briefed Elena on the police findings. Quincy relegated himself to a background position because from the moment he first saw her, job or not, he refused to be the one who directly brought her anything resembling more pain. As he listened to her talking to Phee, he learned a few random things about her. He found out that she had an obsession with water, and since her arrival in New York, had spent the entire day and a half in Battery Park because it was the only thing that could calm her. Through the course of the interview two things stood out most to him: Her love for her son and her oft-repeated belief in God. He wondered whether or not she had ever entertained the thought that God had nonchalantly turned His back on her and her son. Joaquin had committed suicide on his eleventh birthday. Quincy believed in God, but for very different reasons than his brother and Elena. He believed there had to be a Higher Being, because who else could orchestrate the twisted symmetry of an eleven-year-old boy ending his life the same date he had begun it? Who but God could put so much pain in the heart of a child that his natural sense of optimism became nothing more than hopelessness and defeat? Quincy believed without a doubt that there was a God. He was convinced that pain and loss were a constant reminder of His presence. Of His omnipotence. God giveth and God...

Quincy felt a connection to Elena immediately. Beyond the obvious physical attraction, there was much more. Something deeper and more visceral. In the two months since he had met her, Quincy had kept his distance. He respected her need to mourn and simply kept an eye on her from afar. Earlier in the park that day was the closest he had been to her since they first met. What she didn't know was that Quincy had occupied some of his free time by looking into her son's suicide. After talking to Joaquin's best friend, Alberto Guzman, Quincy started putting pieces together which led him to the source of the boy's pain. It was more about what Alberto didn't tell Quincy than what he did. Like Joaquin and Alberto, Quincy and his brother Liam had both been raised as altar boys and molested for years by their local priest. From his own childhood molestation, Quincy instinctively felt that Alberto was hiding things. He remembered when he was a boy how deeply the culture of fear, shame and protection was inculcated. He saw firsthand the open secrets protected in the name of Church and God. When he was a kid back in the '70s, victims like him and Liam were overwhelmingly surrounded by enablers, by people who existed in the shadows of denial and moral hypocrisy. But in this day and age, there was no reason or excuse why Joaquin and Alberto had silently endured the horrible crimes perpetuated against them. Quincy remembered the helplessness he had felt as a young victim. He carried that feeling with him even to this day. Even eighteen years on the force—twelve of those being considered one of the best homicide cops in the city—didn't completely erase that sense of helplessness.

Quincy's informal investigation led him to Father Conner and the revelation of his pedophilia. The discovery of the priest's crimes had brought it all back to him. The fear, the anger. The hate. He wanted to kill the priest. He wanted to do what he lacked the courage of doing to his own tormentor years ago. But when he had sat across from Father Conner and confronted him earlier, he came up predictably short. His desire and need for vindication was somehow supplanted by some convoluted moral code. He had killed men before, but always in the line of duty. No matter how monstrous or reprehensible he found the priest, Quincy was simply unable to kill anyone in cold blood. The best he could muster was an ultimatum. He took the priest's passport and gave him two hours to turn himself in and confess to his crimes. He chose to do it this way because a year ago Quincy had been brought up on disciplinary charges for physically assaulting another priest who had been arrested and subsequently convicted of raping a two-year-old girl. He had to be strategic in how he handled the Conner situation because his past bias could easily compromise the very justice he was seeking. This was the main reason for his invisible investigation. No one could know that he was there or played any part in Conner's arrest. He didn't want to risk arresting him only to have some lawyer get him off on a technicality. He needed the confession to appear as genuine and unsolicited as possible. There could be no room for coercion or retraction.

Quincy lied to Conner and told him that he had at least four people who were willing to come forward and give damaging testimony against him. He told him the only reason he didn't arrest him on the spot was that he wished to spare the victims and their families the additional pain that a public trial would bring. Conner accepted the terms. Even though Quincy lacked the apathy and temerity to kill the priest himself, he was ultimately fine with the two options that he thought would unfold. Either the priest would take his own life or he would end up in prison, where more than likely someone would take it for him. When Quincy left Father Conner at his office, he never in a million years thought that a third option would take place. How could he have imagined that, minutes after leaving the priest, someone would actually do what Quincy had only fantasized about doing?

7

Kravitz, the coroner, had called Quincy and Phee an hour after
they left the crime scene and asked them to come over right
away. As they stepped into the elevator, Phee hit the down button
and then turned and smiled at Quincy.

"I'm not gonna have to worry about you fainting in the
coroner's office am I?" Quincy quickly shot back. "Kiss my hairy
Irish ass. I already told you, it was just some bad Chinese. You
know I've handled worse than the priest."

"It doesn't get much worse than that. Makes you think. This
city's got some sick motherfuckers walking around. I mean, who
does something like that? Especially to a priest?"

Quincy halfheartedly hunched his shoulders and offered no
other response as the elevator doors opened and they exited.

Kravitz was a heart attack waiting to happen. At 5'8" and 370 plus pounds, he and his health were always the proverbial and literal elephant in the room. He looked like a Botero sculpture, round and exaggerated. But whatever his appearance or physical limitations, he more than made up for it with his vast knowledge of the human body. He was universally regarded as the best coroner on the East Coast, and arguably in the entire country. Quincy and Phee had never met a man so pleasantly fascinated with death. The more creative the cause of death, the more pleased Kravitz was to dissect and analyze. He had single-handedly solved some of the most unsolvable cases in the tri-state area. He had consistently been a potent witness for the prosecution in some of the city's most high-profile murder trials. Defense attorneys hated to see him coming, because if their client was in any way linked to a cause of death, Kravitz easily connected the dots for the jury.

Quincy and Phee were both surprised to find Kravitz hunched over the corpse of Father Conner. He didn't normally start cutting the body of murder victims until he ran extensive lab tests. Early in his career, his approach had been criticized as being backward, but he soon proved his critics wrong. Kravitz was already removing organs by the time the two cops entered.

"Damn, Kravitz, so is your new thing now cutting them while they're still warm?" Phee jokingly teased.

Kravitz was much too preoccupied with dissecting the priest to even look up as he responded. "Wasn't my idea."

Quincy quickly chimed in. "Then whose was it?"

"Mine." A disembodied female voice floated in from somewhere deep in the corner of the room. As the two cops turned in the direction of the voice, they discovered a dark-haired woman sitting at a small desk in the corner. She wore an off-the-rack pantsuit that was tailored to make it look more expensive than it actually was. Her black pumps were much more focused on function than style. She wore her hair in a basic bun, and her only attempt at wearing makeup was a little foundation to minimize some residual acne scars from her teenage years. She had an iPad and several files in front of her.

"I smell a fed," Phee smirked.

"Special Agent Maclin," the woman said, finally looking up from her files. Agent Janet Maclin could best be described as an overcompensation. Her life was a series of unpredictable and radical strategies. Her mother died when she was five years old and she was raised as an Army brat by her father and three older brothers. The perpetual moving from base to base and school to school relegated her to "the new kid status" that kept her a constant target for repeated teasing and bullying. At her older brother's urging, they developed a strategy for her first days of school. He had her seek out the kid with the toughest reputation, approach him, and without provocation or warning, release a barrage of punches on her unsuspecting classmate. Sometimes she won; sometimes she lost. But always in the grand scheme of things, she became both feared and respected.

There was the time when she paid a beautiful Russian escort to attend a new recruits' Christmas party with her. As the night wore on, the two women made out in a corner, both to the delight and intimidation of a few of her colleagues. She was neither lesbian nor bisexual, but knew if played properly, she could establish a reputation that would serve her well throughout her tenure at the Bureau. The rumors of her being a "bush-licker" kept her from the unwanted advances of her fellow agents. She had neither the time nor interest in such distractions. Agent Maclin had one goal, and one goal only: No matter what it took, she would become the first female director of the FBI.

Phee looked at the agent, unimpressed. "Feds always crawl out for the big cases."

"Technically I've been on this case much longer than you and your partner."

"How's that?" Quincy asked.

"Because if my hunch is right, your killer is serial. This isn't his first, and trust me, it won't be his last."

"Agent Maclin, I think I found it," Kravitz interrupted.

Maclin and the two detectives crossed over to the coroner and surrounded him and Father Conner's body. Kravitz used an elongated scalpel to finish a long incision on Conner's now detached stomach organ. The priest's torso was a large open cavity with many of his major organs removed and displayed on a nearby table. As Kravitz finished opening the stomach, he removed a tiny plastic capsule among the undigested food. The item was slightly larger than a medicine sized capsule, with a fortune cookie-sized paper rolled in its center.

Kravitz placed the paper on a light board and used a magnifying screen to better read the tiny letters written on it. Mt 5:30.

Agent Maclin was the first to speak. "Same MO. It's a Bible passage."

Maclin wanted to read the entire verse and make sure nothing was missing. The queasiness that Quincy had experienced earlier was now coming back. As Maclin grabbed her iPad and typed in the Bible passage, Quincy steadied himself in anticipation of the referenced verse. After she found what she was looking for, Maclin read aloud.

"It is better for you to enter life maimed or crippled than to have two hands or two feet and be thrown into eternal fire."

Although Quincy believed in coincidences, the odds of this being one was impossible for even him to accept. The fact that this was the same passage that Father Conner had recited to him earlier left him feeling certain that something much more deliberate and ominous was at play. He supported himself against the gurney, not because of weakness or nausea, but rather because he found himself terribly unbalanced by the knowledge that the killer was in the church at the same time he was.

8

After the autopsy, Quincy and Phee met back at the station with Agent Maclin. They took over a conference room and made it clear that no one else was allowed in. Maclin had requested to work with the two detectives, but beyond them and their captain she was paranoid of too many cops being in a position to possibly compromise her investigation. Quincy was the first to agree with her. It was a sad fact and widely known that many cops were willing to leak leads to the press for a little extra cash. Cutbacks and limited overtime had everybody feeling it. The recession had affected people in various ways. Sadly, a loss of integrity was often collateral damage.

As Quincy and Phee looked on, Agent Maclin opened a file on her iPad. Her screen was soon a slideshow of grisly photos of murdered victims. Some of the men were crucified, beheaded, hung and even skinned like Father Conner. As the two cops looked on, Maclin stood and addressed them.

"We call him the Martyr Maker. He emulates the killings of Jesus's disciples. The first known killing occurred thirty years ago almost to the day. A priest in California was crucified. The autopsy revealed a small, plastic capsule with a Bible passage in the victim's stomach. As you can see, the methods of killing have varied but the MO is always the same. All victims were respected leaders of the Church. Various denominations. In '91 he resurfaced in Chicago and killed twelve and disappeared again. Ten years ago he was in Boston. Killed another twelve then vanished until today."

Phee shook his head. "A thirty-year killing spree. Any chance of it being a copycat?"

"Unlikely. We found matching hair samples in the first and third sprees. Also, from day one, the Bureau limited certain specifics of the murders from the press, and yet all thirty-seven killings have the exact same pattern and details. The only thing he changes is his method of execution," she said.

Quincy interrupted. "Earlier you said that the first murder was almost to the day. What did you mean?"

"The first three murder cycles all started October 17."

"Today's the 19th, which more than likely means one thing," Phee blurted.

"There's at least one other body out there that we haven't discovered yet," Quincy added, finishing his partner's train of thought.

When dealing with other law enforcement officers, Agent Maclin wasn't above testing her colleagues to quickly determine their skill set and instincts. The good and bad about Maclin was that she definitely didn't suffer fools lightly. She was smart, crafty and unorthodox. She consistently sought those same traits in others. The minute she determined who the lead detectives were, she pulled as much info on the two as she could find. She had to know if they would be an asset or liability.

Maclin didn't enter situations unprepared. Both Quincy and Phee had outstanding records and were highly regarded in the department. She needed whoever she worked with to know how small a window of opportunity they had to catch the person responsible for the murders. Maclin had both personal and professional reasons why she needed to stop the beast, not the least of which was the likely possibility that solving this case would immortalize her with the Bureau, and greatly enhance her chances of one day becoming its director. There was no way that she was going to risk the most important case of her life with a couple of inept local yokels. She needed the best and nothing less would do. Maclin liked the fact that these two detectives listened and processed the information she gave them. The thing that had impressed her most so far was not the fact that they had passed her first little test of their attention to detail, but that she could tell from the way Quincy looked at her that he knew they were being tested.

"Updated profile and hair samples puts him in his midfifties, red hair, Caucasian, highly intelligent, religious and athletic." Maclin rattled off the information.

"So exactly what kind of timeline are we looking at?" Phee asked.

She looked at both men and responded. "Once he starts, he kills three times a week for four weeks."

There was an interesting thirty seconds of silence when the three simultaneously accepted the burden and responsibility of stopping a "midfifties," "highly intelligent" animal before he finished and disappeared for another ten years.

Maclin looked at her watch and quickly started gathering her things.

"I've printed out separate files for the both of you. Go over them and we'll meet back here at 6 o'clock. I've gotta call DC and let them know that they were wrong in thinking that we had seen the last of him." She handed the two cops their files and then quickly exited.

They were going to have to pull an all-nighter. Quincy knew he had only two hours or so to catch a nap, grab something to eat and familiarize himself with a case going back some thirty years. Being an insomniac, he could easily forgo the nap, so he decided to grab a sandwich and study the files in the park. If he was lucky and she kept to her routine, he would see the one person that could lift him above the horrors of his day.

9

B y the time Elena made it to the park, the October sun had begun setting. Large cumulus clouds served as the canvas to the amazing spectacle. Elena had always found autumn sunsets to be the most dramatic and breathtaking. Coupled with the picturesque foliage and the eastern light, there was nothing more beautiful. Unlike this morning, there were other people there. Some stood around, while others sat at picnic tables or improvised seating. There were couples, mothers and children, even a few singles scattered about, enjoying the evanescing sunset. Elena looked around and saw a familiar form sitting and reading a pile of papers from an accordion file. As the sun completely disappeared, many of the spectators left. Elena, bundled against the dropping temperature, was determined to stay a few minutes more. She closed her eyes and soaked in the stillness as though it would be possible for her to save and ration it in later times. Times when it was more needed.

A deep voice momentarily startled her. As she opened her eyes and turned around, she discovered the stranger she had seen earlier.

Out of reflex, Elena stammered. "Excuse me?"

"I was just wondering if you had a preference. Sunrise or sunset?" Quincy asked.

Elena smiled and turned away from him in an effort to dismiss him as politely as possible. "No," she said.

He picked up on her intent and quickly blurted. "I'm sorry if I disturbed you. I met you a couple of months ago when you lost your son. I was one of the detectives investigating his death."

Elena looked at Quincy blankly as he continued speaking.

"I don't expect you to remember me. We only met once and it was a very difficult time for you."

As he stared at her, Elena became increasingly uncomfortable. His stare unnerved her a bit. Not in any kind of lascivious way, but in a way she had never been looked at before. Even in the absence of sunlight, she saw great detail in his eyes. It wasn't so much how he looked at her, but rather how he looked through her. She felt raw and exposed under his stare. She knew he saw her. Really saw her. Beyond her grief and defensiveness. She became insecure. Afraid that all the things she had spent the better part of the last couple of months trying to hide he would uncover in just a matter of moments. She was the first to break the stare, turning back toward the water. She heard his deep voice again, but refused to face him.

As he realized that he had made her uncomfortable, he turned and headed away. "You shouldn't stay out here alone. It's not safe."

When she looked around she realized that everyone else had left. She had always hated being told what to do and when to do it. But she also wasn't a fool. New York was New York, and she had no interest in becoming a morbid statistic. She walked about twenty-five feet or so behind the cop as he headed toward the park's exit. He walked at a pace that allowed her to both keep up and keep a comfortable distance.

She studied his walk. She tried to figure things out about him. He looked to be in his mid to late thirties. He moved with a certain grace and confidence. The thing that stood out most to her was his weight. Not his body weight, but rather the weight of his presence. There was a strength and depth to him. As he reached the park's opening, he slowed a bit but never turned around. Once he felt that she was safely out of the park, he crossed the street, got into his car and disappeared around the corner. Elena turned in the opposite direction and made her way toward her father's building.

Elena's father Romero had just gotten out of the shower when she walked through the door. He wore a wife-beater and oversized sweatpants. There was evidence of a once athletic man beneath the years of challenge and hardship. In his day, Romero was quite the ladies' man. He was born in a small town just outside of Cartagena in Colombia. His biological mother had died when he was eight and his father ended up remarrying a woman he didn't love, who was the daughter of a successful pig farmer.

When Romero was a junior in high school, he had spent a

night out with friends drinking and partying. They had all passed out in a local park on picnic tables. He remembered being the first of his friends to wake the next morning and witness the incredible sunrise over the water. By the time the others had awakened, the moment had passed and they had missed it. At sixteen, that sunrise had molded him. As Romero watched it unfold, he wanted nothing more than to capture those breathless moments that life was so filled with. That sunrise changed his plans. Or more specifically, his father's plans for him. His father was a state assessor, and like many fathers, had hoped his son would choose the same profession. His father found stability and consistency in numbers, because unlike people, numbers never lied. But at sixteen, Romero realized that he was born to create. The only reason his father supported him was because there was no denying that once his son discovered a passion for art, there was an impressive shift in his focus and maturation. Romero had always wished that when he had children they would appreciate nature and beauty as much as he did. He hoped that they would be inspired by and passionate about the things most people overlooked and took for granted.

Romero met Elena's mother during an exchange semester at NYU. while pursuing his master's degree in art history. Her name was Christina Slotnick and she was a dance major and art minor who took great pride in being more talented than most of her peers in both departments.

He first met her at a student exchange orientation the day after he arrived in New York. She was pregnant a month after they started seeing each other. Christina came from a wealthy family and for all of their purported liberalism, Romero quickly found out the hard way that he wasn't quite white enough for her family to ever truly accept him or the child he had fathered. It was the first time he had ever found himself on the receiving end of such racism and classism. It was very ironic considering the fact that back in Colombia his family were the fairer-skinned Latinos who, following a long line of perverse intraracial prejudice, often looked down their noses on their darker-skinned fellow countrymen. Romero's father had made it abundantly clear from an early age that his son was not allowed to date "Negritas." They were okay for sport and recreational dalliances, but not much more.

Although Christina's family had passionately urged her to abort her pregnancy, Romero successfully convinced her to have the baby and put it up for adoption. He had only pretended to favor the idea of adoption to buy time and ensure that Christina wouldn't abort the child that he was determined to raise.

From the time that Christina found out she was carrying a girl, a strange uneasiness overtook Romero. The thought of being a single man and raising a woman terrified him. Everyone knew the relationship a daughter had with her father became the barometer by which her relationship with all other men would be measured. With a son it was different; all he would have had to do was be a man. With his daughter he couldn't settle for anything less than Godlike status. Even before she was born, he was afraid that he had failed his "Angelita." Failed her long before he welcomed her into the world. Long before he held her and cried at her beauty and innocence. From her first breath and subsequent cry she turned his fear into purpose. Through prayer and diligence he fully embraced all the things that he needed to be for her. He wanted to elevate her above other women. He wanted both a princess and a tomboy. He secretly dreamed that she would be the artist that he had hoped to be. That she would pick up and continue the journey that he was forced to abandon in order to raise her. He needed his daughter to have substance and integrity. In spite of all the young women that he had toyed with and disappointed in his life, he needed his daughter to be his redemption.

Elena moved like her mother. Romero had never seen a child who so intrinsically understood the laws of space, time and movement as his daughter did. Sometimes he would watch for hours on end as she danced and played in their backyard or trips to their favorite park. When music was unavailable she danced to the beat of her own imagination. Just like the sunrise from years ago, when he watched his daughter move, she reminded him of why he had wanted to become an artist in the first place.

Romero brought his daughter back to Colombia and raised her as a single parent. He did the one thing that he knew would get him back in his sire's graces: He abandoned his dreams of being an artist and went to work with his father. His need for security far outweighed any and all other desires or priorities. Being a good father to his daughter was all that mattered to him.

When Elena was seven years old, Romero forced himself to have a very difficult conversation with her. It was on her birthday that he sat her down and told her how her mother had been killed in a car accident shortly after her birth.

Elena and Romero had, for the most part, always enjoyed a close father-daughter relationship. The first major rift between them happened when an eighteen-year-old Elena unexpectedly became pregnant. Surprisingly, Romero had more issues with Elena's desire to marry Carlos, the boy who had impregnated her, than the actual pregnancy itself. Elena was not in love with the father of her child, and she would more than likely never be in love with him. In Romero's opinion, Carlos was beneath his daughter. The last thing Romero wanted as a consequence of her pregnancy was for her to settle when it came to love. Carlos was much too simple for Elena to ever imagine a lifetime with. His idea of planning for the future was knowing in advance the time and whereabouts of the next hot party. He died of a heroin overdose three years after Joaquin was born. Like Carlos, all of Elena's suitors either failed her or never quite measured up. It broke Romero's heart that Elena had never been in love. Not even close.

10

Jesus's death wasn't the worst of the persecution of the Martyrs. Both the greater and lesser known Apostles died equally horrible deaths. James was beheaded. Philip was scourged, imprisoned and crucified. Matthew was chopped to death by a halberd-like weapon. Mark was killed as he was dragged by horses through the streets of Egypt. Bartholomew was flayed. Peter was crucified upside down on an X-shaped cross. Paul was beheaded. Luke was hung from an olive tree in Greece. Jude was crucified at Odessa. Thomas was speared to death. Simon was crucified. John, who was called the beloved disciple, was put into a cauldron of hot, boiling oil. By a miracle of God, he was taken out without any injury. After being banished to the Isle of Patmos, John wrote the book of Revelation. He died as an old man. He was the only Apostle to die peacefully.

The largest wall in the conference room was filled with crime scene photos of thirty-seven victims whose deaths emulated that of the slain Apostles. The space smelled heavy and stale with the lingering scent of old coffee and human interaction. It was well after 10:00 p.m. when Maclin looked up at the clock on the wall. She and the two cops had been so immersed in their work that none of them were aware of how fast time was passing. Agent Maclin preferred to work alone and had for the better part of the last ten years managed to do just that. Her last real partner, Agent Edgar Willington, was the closest thing she had ever had to a mentor. He was a good twenty years older than her. He was smart, fearless and analytical with a wicked sense of humor and adventure. Willington was the best agent she had ever known. He was killed three weeks before he was set to retire while working the case he had dubbed the Martyr's Murders. Little did Maclin know at the time that ten years later she would still be pursuing the same case that had cost Willington his life.

Maclin stood and stretched as Quincy and Phee debated, bantered and scrutinized every detail they could about the case. She quickly noticed that Quincy was normally the one to ask the first question or offer the first hypothesis. It seemed to her that Phee's job was to counter with either a barrage of disconfirming questions or dissect the things that he agreed with to make sure they'd covered every angle. Although she hadn't bothered to consider whether or not she actually liked the cops, she definitely respected them. Each man seemed to know and accept his most productive position in the relationship. She heard them ask questions that she and other agents had asked a million times before. But periodically they would throw in a few that she hadn't thought of. They were good. They had a system, and damn good instincts. She respected them because they reminded her of something that Willington had taught her a long time ago: If you wanted good answers, then you had to ask great questions.

"What if the profiles were wrong?" Quincy turned and asked Maclin.

She quickly responded. "Over the years we've had him profiled eight different times by eight of our best profilers. They all came up with the same thing. We may not know everything about our killer, but what we do know is solid intel."

Quincy looked at her for a beat before replying. "I wasn't talking about the profiles of the killer. I was talking about the victims."

"I'm not following you," Maclin said.

Quincy made a gesture toward the mountain of files. "Every report you have on the victims talks about what upstanding members of the Church community they were. What if they weren't? Jesus was crucified alongside two thieves."

"What's your point?" Phee tossed out.

"The violent and public methods by which the Apostles were killed were the same methods used on the lowest and most despised criminals long before Jesus and his crew showed up. I think our guy is killing his vics for their crimes, not their beliefs. Just a hunch."

Unfortunately at this point, he could only sell it to her as a hunch. He couldn't tell her that he knew horrible secrets about

Father Conner. He couldn't tell the FBI that he confirmed those dark secrets under duress and without a warrant or even an authorized investigation. And with the previous mark on his record, he most certainly couldn't tell her that he was with the now deceased priest only minutes before he was skinned alive.

As Maclin mulled over what Quincy said, there was a quick knock at the door followed by a detective sticking his head in the room and announcing:

"Another body was found in a hotel up in the Bronx."

As Quincy turned to Maclin he blurted, "Looks like we found our missing corpse."

11

The Brandstrum Arms Hotel had a long and storied history. It started off as a modest family-run hotel in the early part of 1916. Ezekiel Brandstrum and his brother Holland struggled for years to turn a profit when they found unexpected success with the arrival of Prohibition. The basement of the hotel was turned into a very lucrative speakeasy, while the upstairs rooms were used for a variety of decadence and sin. The thirteen years of the dry law were very good to them. People came from all boroughs to indulge their vices at the Bronx's most famous house of ill repute. Ezekiel was murdered by a Bronx gangster named Billy Olives when the Brandstrum brothers had started to believe they had gotten too big to continue paying protection fees. Holland spent his final days in prison on tax evasion and racketeering charges when Mayor Fiorello La Guardia, a.k.a. Little Flower, clamped down on the rampant corruption that plagued Manhattan and her adjoining boroughs. By the early '70s, the Brandstrum Hotel was a shooting gallery for the ever budding population of heroin addicts and weed pushers. In the late '80s and mid-'90s, it was a whore's den. For all of its vice and scandal, however, the Brandstrum Arms would be remembered by most of this generation as "the place where they found that murdered priest."

Father Aidan Montrelle's body was tied to a makeshift cross in what used to serve as the hotel's lobby. The corpse was impaled by twelve large hunting arrows, each one strategically targeting a major artery. Father Montrelle looked like some freakish, life-sized human pincushion. In addition to the awful stench in the hotel, there were various signs of decomposition.

Phee pulled out a tiny jar of mentholated salve and smeared it just above his upper lip before handing it off to Quincy and Maclin, who did the same. The minute they were told another body had been found, Maclin had called ahead and demanded that no one be allowed in the hotel until after their arrival. At this point she didn't even trust the CSU. If she was lucky, the crime scene was not yet contaminated. If they had any chance of stopping the madman, who had at least ten more victims to kill, they certainly needed all the luck they could get. Luck to a good cop was always the result of smart work. There were no magic wands or genies in lamps. Intelligence, instincts and work ethic produced more lucky hits than anything else.

Willington had often told Maclin that "every crime scene was its own bible." If read properly the answers would come. There was a three-foot diameter pool of blood that surrounded the dead priest, keeping the three cops at a measurable distance. Quincy and Phee had never seen anything like this, but Maclin clearly remembered the same type of execution ten years ago when she first pursued this madman. Quincy and Phee started their investigation of the crime scene fifteen feet from the corpse and worked their way in. Maclin pulled out an ultraviolet glow light as she moved closer to the body. The light would detect hair, lint or the smallest clue that might have otherwise been stepped on. As she stood two feet from the corpse, she used her camera to take multiple pictures from every conceivable angle. For the first twenty minutes, no one said a word. The three of them worked in concert as meticulous technicians combing through every detail and square inch of the lobby. Maclin had brought her own forensics kit and ran preliminary tests on anything resembling evidence. After nearly two hours, the three cops had individually arrived at the same frustrating conclusion: The killer hadn't left behind anything useful for their investigation. It was that same frustration that caused Maclin to nearly snap the head off a uniformed cop who entered without their permission.

"What part of no one in here did you not understand?" she barked.

"Sorry Agent Maclin, but we just got a call from Brooklyn," he said.

"What is it?" Quincy asked.

"A couple of homeless guys found a body in an abandoned church in Red Hook. Cops from the Seven-Six say it looks like another one of ours," the cop said.

Maclin quickly looked at Quincy and Phee with equal parts of confusion and alarm. Phee eloquently verbalized what all three were thinking in that moment.

"Oh shit," he sighed.

They arrived at the old abandoned church in Brooklyn. Over the years, the building had changed names and at one time or another housed various denominations. It had been officially closed for a month or so, but the extensive decay and neglect made it feel like it had been shut down much longer. It was apparent that even when the church was operational it was not a well-maintained house of God.

As Quincy entered with Maclin and Phee, he was the first to see the body. The naked victim had been crucified in an upside-down position and stoned to death, as evidenced by the severe damage to the body and the dried blood on the various bricks that laid nearby. The dead man's one remaining eye was open and permanently fixed upward. What was left of his face was horribly swollen and disfigured. Maclin and the two cops stood on the periphery of the room. Quincy used the ultraviolet glow light that she handed to him to carefully map out a clear path to the body. After clearing a path, Phee and Maclin joined Quincy.

Phee made his way to the opposite side of the dead man as he and Quincy flanked the body in their usual way. In thirty years and thirty-nine victims, the most compelling evidence was a few foreign strands of hair that had been found on four of the dead bodies. Although the hairs were determined to have belonged to the killer, the national database had never yielded a DNA match.

The two cops focused much more on the history and method of the killing as Maclin focused much more on the forensics of the scene. Quincy and Phee followed the trajectory of the dead man's one-eyed stare to a broken stained glass window on the second floor. The painting depicted on the glass was that of a small flock of worshippers standing in front of a humble but beautiful church. The two cops felt that it wasn't a coincidence that the victim had been placed in the perfect position for this to have been the last thing he saw before he died. Quincy glanced at Maclin and saw not just the usual determination on her face but something even greater. He saw the need. It was a given that protecting the public from a crazed serial killer was the obvious motivation for her. He even surmised the more pedestrian reasons she needed to break this case: the career ascension, the dismantling of the glass ceiling that he was sure she had encountered, and even the silencing of voices of discouraging naysayers. But as he looked at her now, meticulously examining every square inch of the dead man's body, Quincy saw something more.

Ninety-four minutes had passed when Maclin called out, "I think I found something."

As the two cops approached her, she held up a single hair with a pair of tweezers. As she put the light on it, they could all see that the hair was a couple of centimeters long and unmistakably red.

12

P hee called Kravitz around 3:00 a.m. He said they needed an analysis and comparison of a hair sample as soon as possible. Nothing got the big man up and moving like a "middle of the night body call." Phee was adamant that even though it wasn't conventional, Kravitz was the only one who should handle the analysis and autopsy on the two incoming bodies. With time being of the essence, it didn't make sense to any of them to send the hair sample back to the labs in DC when Kravitz and his skills were so readily available.

Phee and Quincy agreed with Maclin, that the fewer people running point on this investigation the better. They didn't have time to check or recheck each other's work. Not only were they up against the clock, but they were up against a calculating killing machine, the likes of which none of them had ever imagined. It meant much more toil and time for the four of them, but with their collective talent and work ethic, this was their best shot at closing the case.

Phee had left Quincy and Maclin at the crime scene. They were still sifting through evidence and searching for even the tiniest of details. Phee had been designated to get the hair sample to Kravitz personally and to also get him started on Father Montrelle's body.

Phee beat Kravitz to the lab by twenty minutes, which allowed him time to steal a much needed power nap. Working cases with these type of hours had taught the good cops to get it in whenever they could. Vets knew never to just stand when you could sit, never just sit when you could lay, and never just lay when you could sleep. Phee was sleeping on a desk outside of Kravitz' office when the large man came lumbering out of the elevator. Kravitz still had sleep in his eyes and unfortunately hadn't even bothered to brush his teeth. He pretended to be grumpy. The more inconvenienced he could depict himself as having been, the greater the favor he might be able to negotiate somewhere down the road. Second only to politicians, law enforcement was big on quid pro quo. Kravitz was neither above nor beneath exploiting the demand for his impressive talents. He was quick, thorough and none too shy about reminding people that he was simply the best.

"Good morning, Sunshine," Phee teasingly greeted him.

Kravitz barked back some incomprehensible response and took the plastic baggie that contained the hair sample from the outstretched hand of the annoyingly chipper cop. Father Montrelle's body was just being delivered as the two men addressed each other.

As Kravitz pulled out his keys and unlocked his office door, he looked over his shoulder at Phee and said, "I'll have something for you in an hour on the hair, and a prelim on the body half an hour after that. When you come back, hopefully you'll be accompanied by three Egg McMuffins and a coffee."

"Only three?" Phee shot back.

"Believe it or not, I wasn't born with this beautiful body. It takes work. What can I say?"

13

Phee's father was a Joe Kennedy-type. Like Kennedy, Clay Freeman was a resourceful and smart man. He was a visionary who figured out how to build a fortune off the illicit needs of people, and then turned around and matriculated that criminal start to a political juggernaut. Clay ran New York City. To the general public and politically naive, he was anonymous and nonexistent. But to those that really mattered, Clay Freeman was one of the most powerful men in the New York political infrastructure. He wielded bipartisan control over every conceivable level of the city and state government. He made mayors, owned senators and destroyed governors on a whim. It was widely rumored by those in the know that it was Clay who actually brought down Spitzer. The range of speculation was everywhere from the amusingly absurd to the darkly plausible. There was the one report that the two had gotten into a heated argument over who was the better all-around player, Kobe or LeBron. Then there was the slightly more credible offering that Eliot had broken a golden rule of politics. Not only had he started reading his own press, but he'd tragically started believing it. Clay Freeman was not the kind of man one said no to. Unfortunately that was a lesson that some had to learn the hard way.

Clay was born and raised on the unforgiving streets of Harlem in the '40s. He first made a name for himself at the age of nine, when he threatened to kill his stepfather for beating his mother. Coincidentally or not, two days after the threat was made, Clay's stepfather disappeared and was never heard from again. By the time Clay was sixteen, there was no mistaking who he was and what he was capable of. He ran with a gang called the Sugarhill Cobras. One day he and one of his boys got jumped by a rival gang on 147th and St. Nick. When the other boy ran off, Clay was forced to face his enemies alone. He was no match for the three older boys and suffered a brutal beating. A week later, not only were the three rival gang members dead, but the boy who had abandoned Clay was hospitalized with two broken legs. One of the dead boy's uncles was a former bagman for the legendary Harlem gangster Bumpy Johnson. His name was Alton Slopes and he was a rising star in the Harlem underworld. His young nephew was a knuckle-head who Slopes always knew was going to end up dead before he turned eighteen. But still he was blood, and somebody would have to pay for his death.

After Slopes asked around, he got wind that Clay was likely

responsible for the murder. When Slopes arrived at Clay's home, the boy politely invited him in and said he had been expecting him. As he served the older man some stale cookies and juice, he confessed to everything. He told him how he alone had tracked down the nephew and his boys and shot them with a gun he had stolen from a shop on 125th Street. He told him how he broke the legs of the coward who had abandoned him. Unprompted, he even told Slopes how he had killed his own stepfather several years earlier. As Slopes looked on he was surprised not just by the calm manner in which the teenage boy was confessing his crimes, but more so by the fact that Clay showed no fear of him even though it was obvious why he had come. Clay looked Slopes straight in the eye and told him, "Do what you gotta do. Death ain't nothin' but part of the game."

Slopes had shown up at the apartment to exact revenge, but by the time he left he ended up offering him a job. By the age of twenty-one, Clay had been a numbers runner, bagman, extortionist, enforcer, pimp and all-around problem-solver. The burgeoning drug trade in Harlem was in many ways akin to the prohibition era. It was a time that afforded endless possibilities to a young, enterprising criminal. Slopes had taught Clay that the best way to control a person was to control what they coveted or needed. This simple philosophy would later make Clay Freeman one of the most influential men behind the scenes of New York politics. By the time he was in his late twenties, Clay was smart enough to know when to leave the 'hood life. Toward the end of his gangster days, he had secretly acquired his GED and even started taking business courses at City College. When heroin took over in the early '70s, Slopes was killed by a young upstart trying to make a name for himself. Avenging his mentor's death was Clay's final act of violence. In doing so, he committed an unspeakably heinous crime that would haunt him for years to come.

It was at City College that Clay met a beautiful Dominican girl who was enrolled in his economics class. Her name was Dolicia Delarosa and she and her family fled to New York after her father, who was a politician in the Trujillo regime, had publicly lost favor with the Dominican dictator. After several months of asking her out, Dolicia eventually acquiesced. On their first date he told her everything. He talked in detail about his upbringing, his life of crime and his plans for the future. She was equally fascinated by and afraid of who he was. Ironically, it wasn't his criminal past that scared her the most. It was his ambition. He had the same type of ambition that her father did. Men who dreamed of being kings were always in danger, and so were those closest to them. Regardless of her reservations, the two were married four months after their first date. Once he received his degree he invested half of his sizable fortune in legitimate business ventures and real estate and vowed to his new bride that his life as a gangster was behind him.

Despite the egregious misfortune that he wasn't Dominican, Dolicia's father still took an immediate liking to the young man from Harlem and quickly became a great father figure to Clay. In almost no time at all, Clay came to realize that his hustle in the streets had prepared him well for the treacherous but much more lucrative life of politics. He never ran for office, he never held a title and he never swore his allegiance to any particular party. Dolicia's father had always taught him that those who held office and considered themselves to be the public architects of policy were really nothing more than impotent symbols and exercises in vanity. The real power was always behind the scenes, controlling the puppets that thought they controlled policy.

Clay and Dolicia had two sons. The boys enjoyed the benefits of their father's wealth growing up as the only family of color at that time in Greenwich, Connecticut. Their summers were a different story. At the end of each school year, Phee and his older brother AJ were ceremoniously dumped in Harlem to stay with Clay's cousins on 129th and Fredrick Douglass Blvd. Clay was determined that his sons would not be weakened by their privileged upbringing. For five weeks each summer they had to learn to survive the streets that had molded their father. Aside from keeping them clear on remembering where they came from, it also helped the boys to better understand their father. It was no secret that Phee was Clay's favorite. Whereas AJ was more introverted and sensitive, Phee was outgoing and athletically gifted. His early success in sports only added to the unbreakable bond between him and his father.

After Phee left Kravitz, he had an hour to kill. Not enough time to go back to the crime scene, but too much time to just hang around the coroner's office. A 4:00 a.m. drive on the quiet streets of Manhattan would help him think. Ironically, this was always his favorite time of the day. Peace and quiet were hard to come by in the city, but at this time of morning there was still something pure and hopeful about the day. In these moments of solitude, Phee found himself thinking of his mother. She died four years ago of a heart attack. But her birthday had just passed, and lately he found himself thinking a lot about her and his father. He missed his mother terribly and could feel that a major part of his father had died with her. There was an unassailable love and devotion that existed between the two of them. Her birthday was one of several holidays that sent his father into a deep depression.

Phee had been planning to drive to Connecticut to spend some time with the old man, but with the urgency of breaking this new case, it would have to wait. The guilt made him restless. He grew angry at his mother's death and also at what he blamed as the cause. He cruised midtown until he ended up in the lower 40s on the West Side. As he had done several times before when his anger led him here, he pretended that his arrival was a coincidence and not his destination. When he found himself in this place (both emotionally and physically), his sense of awareness was heightened. Phee parked the car and counted the various delivery trucks starting their day. He heard in the distance a lone street sweeper making its rounds. As he sat in his car, he watched the cross-dressing sex workers hawking their wares in four- to six-inch heels and trashy lingerie. Within the one block stretch, he studied the geographical caste system that existed in this subculture. As the John's who frequented the areas would say, there were three types of walkers for rent: Mannies, Trannies and Rabbits. The eastern part of the block was populated with the Mannies. These were burly men in dresses and wigs who could never be mistaken for women. In the middle of the block were the Trannies. These were men who took hormones and other measures to better look like women. They were often a fifty-fifty call. Some were easier to spot as men, but a few of them had shattered many a straight man's illusions of his heterosexuality. At the western tip of the block were, last but not least, the Rabbits. Their name was derived from the Jessica Rabbit character because of their cartoonish curves and exaggerated sexuality. These were prostitutes that were born male but surgically reassigned their gender status. Many were from Brazil or Colombia, where with the help of the right plastic surgeon, they could sculpt their bodies into that of the most voluptuous of women. They were all dick-less and most sported double Ds, tiny waists with big hips and ass implants. The Holy Grail for this particular group was to ultimately find a rich, married boyfriend and retire from the game as a "kept woman." Until they reached their goal, working a tiny piece of real estate in the West Forties would have to suffice.

Phee parked his car a half block away where he had a clear view of the prostitutes. As he spotted a tall brown-skinned T-Walker in a platinum blond wig, he moved his car a little closer to get a better look. Phee felt his anger increase at the prostitute's every move. As he continued hawking the hooker, there was something dark and predacious in his stare.

14

Quincy and Maclin had thoroughly run the scene before turning it over to CSU. It was possible that they missed something, but not likely. Their only miss at this point would be something microscopic. Quincy was impressed by the way Maclin ran a scene. She reminded him of Phee. The most that an investigator could ever hope for at a murder scene was that the absent suspect or murdered victim spoke to them. What was different about Maclin and the two cops is that they didn't hope for the communication, they expected it. The scene would tell them things before they even set foot inside. Although she never said anything, Quincy noticed a slight shift in Maclin's approach. Her focus was more on what the victim might tell her than the suspect. On the drive back to her hotel he could tell that she was playing back every detail she had seen at the church.

"So, is this your oldest open case?" Quincy asked.

"It's my only open case."

"Anything different about these last three murders?"

"I don't think it's a coincidence that one was killed in an old whore hotel and that the last one was positioned to face the stained glass windows."

"Neither do I."

"Okay, so what about Father Conner?" she pressed.

"On his back, eyes open, looking up. Ceiling had a bunch of clouds and cherubs painted on it," Quincy listed.

Quincy already knew the implications of Conner's death. He had been killed for defiling innocence. Quincy was careful not to lead too much with his assessment of the murder. He felt more comfortable in simply nudging Maclin and having her arrive at the necessary conclusions. Maclin was sharp. If he pointed her in the right direction, she would easily put the pieces together. He was happy that she had arrived where he needed her to, of her own volition. Unlike the previous thirty-six murders, the current three bodies were all positioned in a deliberate manner. The killer was definitely sending them a message. It was his way of speaking to them.

Quincy had no doubt that somewhere along the way some of the feds had learned of the victims' shady pasts. Whatever crimes the victims had been guilty of, someone had to know about them. His problem was that for various reasons that information was only an element of the investigation instead of the focus.

Maybe the reason was as simple as not wanting to indict the

victims, especially because of who they were. The victims' reputations and lofty standings in the church community had publicly pretty much been placed above suspicion or reproach. He understood that as a mindset thirty, twenty, maybe even ten years ago. But it certainly wasn't valid today.

The lie of who these men really were was one of the many problems Quincy had with the Church. He felt that in many ways, religion was nothing more than a fraternity, with its governing body shrouded in secrecy and protection. To him the word faith was synonymous with control and manipulation. It was the oldest hustle in town, and the only way to keep it going was to protect the product at any and all costs. This deluded notion created a host of problems. Top of that list was the demoralizing concept that those representing the very foundation of so-called righteousness were sometimes the most heinous and wicked.

15

By the time Phee made it back to Kravitz's office it was almost 6:00 a.m. The most recent victim's body had been sent over from the crime scene an hour earlier with specific instructions from Maclin for Kravitz to start an autopsy immediately. Since the stomach content of the victims was one of the things they were most concerned with, Kravitz had started by opening up the bodies and removing those organs first. He deviated from normal protocol because it was the quickest way to confirm that it was the work of their killer. Phee had been in a foul mood ever since he returned. He certainly didn't win any points when he showed up sans the triple order of McMuffins. Kravitz couldn't care less that Phee was obviously distracted and preoccupied with something. A deal was a deal. As promised, Kravitz had run the hair sample and had the results waiting for Phee when he got back. Phee decided to wait for the second dissection. If there were capsules in the stomach, as they all assumed there would be, then he would save valuable time if he were to bring them back to the station with him.

Phee was restless and fidgety, still agitated from his earlier drive. As much as he needed to be focused and sharp, his mind kept wandering. He really didn't care that his pacing was irritating Kravitz. Phee was trying to get out of his funk. He was trying to escape the dark place he had been in for the last hour or so.

"Got em." Kravitz caught his attention. As Phee turned around, the detective saw the coroner holding up two small capsules with bloodied forceps.

16

Maclin had decided to switch hotels to be closer to the precinct, so they swung by her current spot on West 32nd and picked up her things. Quincy dropped her off at the small hotel that she had picked out just a few blocks from the station. He wasn't surprised by her choice. Quincy felt she chose the boutique hotel just off Broadway for its location and because, based on what he could tell about her, it was an obvious fit. Like her, it was simple and efficient with no frills. The very traits he liked about her. After bringing her suitcase into the lobby, Quincy waited downstairs while Maclin went up and took a quick shower and changed her blouse. Quincy used the time to call four detectives that he both trusted and respected and who had no problems keeping their egos in check. The idea was to use them for some of the legwork that he, Maclin and Phee just wouldn't have time to do. Even though they had each run point on several cases, they could come in and accept supporting roles. When Maclin came downstairs, the first thing Quincy noticed was how much she had looked the same as when she went upstairs. Her blouse was changed and her hair was still damp from a shower, but there was something about her that still looked tired and worn. Quincy had only seen her under the artificial glare of fluorescent lighting and under the harsh work lights of the crime scene. But now, in the natural light of early morning, he saw things in her that he hadn't bothered to see before. He saw tension creases in her forehead and on both sides of her mouth. He hadn't noticed earlier the loose skin under her chin, or the hint of acne scars just beneath the thin layer of her foundation. She was by no means an unattractive woman, but Quincy saw that her physical beauty was somewhere very low on her list of priorities. As they quietly walked to the car, the thing that stood out to him most was the deep-seated weariness that she carried with her. He had seen it in both cops and victims before. A premature aging brought on by stress or tragedy. In the right light, Maclin looked ten years older than she was.

Three minutes after they got back to the station, Maclin stood before the team.

"Based on the chronological discovery of the victims, we've ID'ed the three of them as follows. Father Joseph Conner, seventy, of St. Jude's, here in Manhattan. Father Aidan Montrelle, fifty-four years old, Catholic priest from Staten Island. And the last one we discovered was Bradford Higgins, sixty years old. Runs a Protestant church out of Brooklyn," Maclin spouted off.

She stood in front of the large dry-erase board facing Quincy, Phee and a few other detectives that Quincy had recruited.

Maclin continued as she read from her iPad. "The scripture found in Conner's body was: 'It is better for you to enter life maimed or crippled than to have two hands or two feet and be thrown into eternal fire.'"

Maclin pulled up a second chapter and continued to read to the assembled cops. The Biblical reference found inside of Montrelle's stomach was Matthew, Chapter 26, Verse 41: "Watch and pray so that you may not fall into temptation. The spirit is willing but the flesh is weak."

Maclin scrolled down to the final verse and read to the cops. "The scripture from Higgins's body was from the book of Haggai, Chapter 1, Verse 9: 'You expected much, but see, it turned out to be little. What you brought home I blew away. Why, declares the Lord Almighty. Because of my house, which remains a ruin, while each of you is busy with his own house.'"

Everyone in the room was attentive as Maclin presented the most current intel. As usual she was detailed, yet concise. Her mentor had taught her early on how to command a group's attention with even the most mundane information. Several years ago, Willington had made her watch an interview with the famous boxer Sugar Ray Leonard Jr. In it, he credited his effectiveness as a boxer to what he referred to as "an economy of movement." Minimal movement with maximum results. She adopted that approach early on and tried to apply it in everything she did, particularly her communication.

"The coroner is putting Father Montrelle's T.O.D. at four days ago, which means of course that not only was he killed before Father Conner and Pastor Higgins but that the killer has kept to the same start date for thirty years. All indications are that Conner and Higgins were both killed on Thursday. One of the things that worries me the most is that he's never killed two in the same day before. Up until now his MO has been to kill one victim every three days. For some strange reason he's killing a lot faster. As the Bureau rechecks any leads in the prior cases, our job is to find new leads in our recent murders. Detective Cavanaugh believes, and I agree with him, that we need to find out what people aren't telling us about the victims. Despite his recent unpredictability I still think we can assume that he targeted these victims for specific reasons. We've gotta find out what those reasons are. Detective Cavanaugh…" She stepped aside as Quincy stood and addressed the room.

"Bernie and Alvarez, you take Father Conner. Stan, you take Father Montrelle and Asif will take Higgins. We need some good old-fashioned street pounding. I know it's grunt work and we appreciate you guys coming on board. I want every door you knock on to lead you to three more. Habits, routines, vices; we need to know everything we can about our vics, especially the stuff that people are uncomfortable saying about their clergy. You need to slip somebody twenty bucks to talk off record; we'll get the feds to reimburse."

Everyone in the room laughed, including Maclin. Everyone except Phee. Quincy got serious again as he continued.

"All jokes aside. Whether he's targeting the victims for a specific reason or not, the scary thing that we need to keep in mind is that since he's not even following his own rules anymore, we have no idea what to expect from him. It's bad enough he's killing clergy, but if for any whacked-out reason at all he decides to expand his targets, nobody in this city is safe. Nobody. If we're gonna stop this son of a bitch, it's not gonna be by playing by the rules. Do whatever you gotta do. Everything that's said in this room stays in this room. Phee, you got anything to add?"

"No," Phee said absentmindedly.

As the meeting broke up, Maclin turned to Quincy and said, "How's your Bible analysis?"

"The word pitiful comes to mind," he shot back.

"Should I call my guy in DC?" she asked.

"No. I've got someone local that can help us."

"Your brother Liam?"

"Been doing your homework?"

"Always. Do you think he'll give us a good perspective on the verses?"

"Better than your guy in DC. I'll give him a call and see if he'll come down and enlighten us."

"Thanks," Maclin said as she walked out.

Phee was in the back of the room finishing up a phone call.

"I'll see you at two. Yeah, me too," Phee said into his phone. As he hung up, Quincy approached him.

"Everything cool?" Quincy asked.

"Yeah, why?"

"I don't know, you just seemed a little... Nothin', forget it."

"I'm good. I just caught a headache dealing with Kravitz."

"Yeah, well I have a feeling before this is all over with we're gonna be seeing more of Kravitz than either one of us wants to."

Quincy knew his partner. They'd been working cases together for over four years now. Every detective worth his salt believed that once you found a good partner you held on to them for as long as possible. The good ones were harder to come by than snow in July. Hairlines, waistlines and even wives would come and go over the course of a good partnership. The running joke was that a partner was better than a wife because even though neither one of them would fuck you, at least a partner would pick up the check every once in a while. Quincy and Phee just clicked. Phee often referred to Quincy as his "brotha from another motha." Quincy could feel that something was bothering his brotha. He thought it ironic that the only time he had ever lied to Phee was at Father Conner's. After they put this case behind them, Quincy would tell Phee what was really bothering him, just as he was certain that in time Phee would do the same.

17

P hee had gotten to Cipriani's five minutes early. Even though it was his father's custom to arrive ten minutes late no matter who he was meeting with, Phee never took a chance on letting his father arrive before him. Clay Freeman was not the type of man to be left waiting. Phee sat at the table and ordered two Arnold Palmers. As the server left to retrieve his drinks, he looked around at all of the movers and shakers, climbers and wannabes. The storied eatery was thick with egos and gamesmen. Per capita, there was arguably more power and money currently in this restaurant than any other on the East Coast. Phee stood out for a couple of reasons. Not only was he the only African American present, but he was dressed decidedly much more casually than those around him. A black leather jacket with a crew neck sweater beneath was in stark contrast to the $4,000 suits that surrounded him. It wasn't that Phee went unnoticed; he simply went unscrutinized. He had been frequenting these types of establishments since he was born. His father had instilled in Phee and his brother AJ that the proper exposure to power was the basis of the proper assumption of power. Clay believed that the historic socioeconomic chasms suffered by so-called minorities were one of the most crippling disadvantages for people of color. It was never reduced or over simplified to just a black/white thing. Phee's father saw the disparity as much more global. Phee and his brother were groomed for success in whatever goals they pursued because, like their white counterparts, they were taught it was their birthright. Underdressed or even uninvited, Phee was never taught to feel apologetic for his presence. He was taught, no matter where he found himself and under whatever circumstances, to always carry himself like he belonged.

At exactly 2:10 Phee looked out the window and saw his father's limo pull up. As the driver escorted Clay through the front doors, Phee watched the many handshakes and backslaps that greeted his hero. He watched with a certain pride as captains of industry and the city's elite acknowledged the former street hustler turned power broker. At sixty-five, Clay was still a commanding presence. Wavy salt and pepper hair, smooth skin and warm hazel eyes. Had he the interest, he could still make a formidable ladies man. As he approached the table, Phee stood and affectionately hugged his father. It had been two months since they'd actually seen each other and Phee found himself holding on a beat longer than normal. After separating, Clay stepped back and sized up his son.

"Still a gym rat?" he asked.

"I get it in when I can."

As they sat, the server came over with menus. She was young and attractive with a genuinely friendly demeanor. When she spoke, she directed most of her attention to Clay. Not that she was in any way rude to Phee, but she just inherently understood and respected the hierarchy of power at play.

"I'm glad you could make it," Phee said as he watched the server walk off.

"You kidding? I'm glad you called. Gotta put in an appearance every once in a while to remind this town that the old man is still kickin' the Devil's ass." Clay sat up and sipped the Arnold Palmer that his son had ordered for him.

By the time appetizers were brought, a few people had sporadically stopped by to pay their respects. Phee was used to the concept of sharing his father and managed to squeeze in meaningful conversation between the interruptions. As they were finishing up their desserts, Clay looked at his son seriously and said, "I got a letter the other week."

"A letter from whom?"

"Who do you think?"

Clay reached inside his suit jacket and slid a sealed envelope across the table to Phee, who looked at it for a second before picking it up and turning it over.

"You didn't open it."

"No," Clay responded.

"Whatever it is, I'll deal with it later," Phee said as he put the letter into the cargo pocket of his leather jacket. Phee was relieved when the server came and dropped off the check and inadvertently dissipated the tension that the letter had introduced. As she walked away, Phee quickly reached for the check and his wallet.

"I've gotta be heading back to the station. We've got something big going on. That was one of the reasons I called you. Do you know a brotha by the name of Bradford Higgins? Runs a small Protestant church in Brooklyn?"

"Yeah, I know him. He changes his religion like he changes his underwear. He goes where the money is. Protestants must be paying well these days. Before he became Pastor Higgins and moved to Brooklyn he was the founder of some New Age bullshit called the Faithful Flock of Newark. Did the Nation of Islam thing back in the early '80s too. Before that he was a petty hustler out of Bed-Stuy back in the day."

"What else can you tell me about him?" Phee pressed.

"What do you want to know?"

18

L iam thought it funny that in all this time he had never been to his brother's place of employment. For years he had convinced himself that he had neither the curiosity nor the desire to see first-hand the world that his baby brother lived in. But in all honesty the truth was a little more difficult for him to swallow. As much as he would like to think that they had chosen such polarized paths, lately he had accepted that this simply wasn't true. There was a sobering parallel to their chosen vocations. They each saw the worst in man on a daily basis.

Liam approached the desk sergeant and asked for Detective Cavanaugh. The sergeant gave him the once over, then called out to a passing uniformed cop and instructed him to bring Liam upstairs to the homicide unit. The building didn't feel like Liam had imagined it would. Like so many people, his only concept of a police station had come courtesy of the cop shows that he had seen over the years. The 5th precinct in lower Manhattan was certainly not like anything that he had seen on TV. It was worn and poorly lit. All the people, employees and visitors alike, were bona fide New Yorkers, textured in every conceivable way: smells, sounds, dress and attitude. In the short walk to homicide, he saw a wide range of New York characters on display. Everyone from the boring and easily forgettable to the outlandish and absurd. He saw handcuffed teenagers with tears in their eyes next to veteran criminals who sat unfazed and unfeeling. He saw boisterous cops trying to win favor with their brothers and sisters in blue at the expense of some drunken offender. He saw angry fathers and weeping mothers demanding justice for crimes that he could only begin to imagine. He saw prostitutes and preppies. Guilty perpetrators and innocent victims. He saw only a fraction of his brother's life and wondered how Quincy faced it every day.

As he was led into the conference room, Quincy crossed to him and hugged him before introducing him to Maclin and Phee. He had heard the name Phee several times before and was happy to finally meet his brother's partner. Liam felt a bit awkward that it had taken over four years and now a pressing murder case for the two most important people in Quincy's life to finally meet face-to-face. As the three strangers shook hands, Liam took in more of his surroundings. The room was musty and lacked proper ventilation. Not that the smell bothered him. Just the opposite, he appreciated the smell of effort and hard work. He noticed the papers and photos taped and tacked to every wall in the room and accurately surmised that this was somehow the command center for their investigation.

"I just wanted to thank you for taking time out of your day to come down here and give us a hand." Maclin said.

"No problem. You know if my brother had paid more attention in Bible study to the text than he did to the girls, you wouldn't need me," Liam said teasingly.

"You trying to create more work for me? What fun is being agnostic if you can't use it to your advantage?" Quincy laughed.

"You guys might not want to stand too close to him. That lightning bolt is coming any day now. So how can I be of help?" Liam asked.

Maclin briefed him on the case and then led him to the thirty-nine scriptures which were all neatly taped to the wall in the chronological order in which they were received.

"This might take a while," Liam warned.

"Take all of the time you need," Maclin responded.

The three cops sat back down at the table and resumed their work as Liam read each passage, carefully and repeatedly. He took his time and very deliberately analyzed the thirty-nine texts.

Quincy occasionally looked up and watched his brother. He had once or twice sat in on Liam's services, seen him officiate family weddings and funerals. He had even seen him speak publicly at community rallies and protests. Quincy loved his brother and was very proud of him. He regretted that in the last few years their busy lives had compromised how much they saw each other. And as much as he enjoyed seeing Liam, under these circumstances he felt an uneasiness and sadness. Quincy thought of his brother as the one constant positive in his life, the most consistent reference he had to goodness and purity. This was the main reason he had never introduced him to Phee. As much as he loved both men, he needed to keep what each of them represented to him as separate as possible. When Quincy looked around and saw all of the accumulated data and evidence on the most heinous case he had known, he regretted bringing his brother into his dirty world.

Liam stepped back and sighed. "I don't know if this means anything, but he's using three separate Bibles."

"What do you mean?" Maclin asked.

"Well, in '81 the first twelve references are from the NIV version. The twenty-four verses from '91 and 2001 are from the King James Version. The last three are translations from the Latin Vulgate version, which was the Bible's first translation from the original languages."

"To us layman and sinners, what does that mean?" Phee asked.

"Not much. There are just subtle differences in wording and phrasing. The meaning's all the same. The Vulgate was written from the prevailing language at the time, which was Latin. This version is a little more highly regarded by scholars and some theologians because they feel it is less likely that verse would be compromised in translation. But ironically that doesn't really apply to the verses left by your killer because all three translations are pretty much the same."

"If the Vulgate version is the most regarded, why did he just start using it now in the last three murders?" Maclin joined in.

"Well, he started off with the NIV version, which is the

simplest to understand. Then he switched to the King James and finally the Vulgate," Liam said.

"Okay, but you just said that even though he used the older, more accurate version, the verses that he referenced aren't really different in any of the Biblical translations," Phee stated.

"That's right, very minor differences," Liam responded.

"Then why go through the trouble of changing to three different Bibles over the years?" Phee asked.

"Maybe it's not about the subtle differences in the Bibles," Quincy said.

"So then what is it about?" Maclin asked.

"The differences in him. Isn't it safe to say that he is academically evolving?" Quincy offered.

"That's one way of looking at it," Liam said.

"What's another way?" Maclin questioned.

Liam looked at the three of them and said, "That he is spiritually evolving."

They all quietly looked at each other, none of them certain of the implications of Liam's comment.

"Would this evolution in any way affect his pattern of killing?" Maclin asked.

"Again, maybe subtle changes. The more specific his knowledge of scripture becomes, the more specific his execution. I'm just guessing because I don't know what his pattern was to begin with. Would you like for me to look at any photos of the killings to see if anything jumps out at me?"

"I don't think that's a good idea," Quincy jumped in.

"You talking as a cop or my overprotective brother right now?" Liam shot back.

"Both," Quincy said.

"I'm a big boy. I can handle it," Liam responded.

"Quincy might be right," Phee chimed in.

"You all asked me to come down here to offer my opinion and professional perspective. I'm here to do that," Liam stated.

Maclin appreciated the awkwardness of the situation, but objectively knew the value of Liam's presence. She had a killer that she had been trying to catch for ten years. Everything else was secondary.

"Well, if you really don't mind, it could be helpful," she said.

Liam looked at Quincy for some type of approval, which came in the form of a halfhearted nod. Quincy hated the fact that Maclin was right. As much as they all needed Liam's input, Quincy's instincts were to protect Liam from the images that would undoubtedly be forever burned into his memory.

They rotated the large dry-erase board that had been facing the wall. Dozens of gruesome photos of the thirty-nine victims were neatly taped to the board. An organized collage of the murders through the years. Liam unconsciously sucked in air and made the necessary effort to steady himself. His eyes glazed over as he stood completely mesmerized by the visual diary. As Quincy made a move in his brother's direction, Phee gently stopped him. Liam stood frozen, forcing himself to look at each and every one, mentally documenting every detail that he could. The room was quiet and uncomfortable as he studied the photos for at least fifteen minutes. When he was done he muttered, "The eyes."

Maclin stepped closer to him and asked him to repeat himself.

"The eyes are only open in the last three," he said quietly.

Quincy jumped in and said, "Yeah, one of the most recent bodies was positioned to face Biblical images on a ceiling and another was looking at images on a stained glass window. The third victim, with the arrows, wasn't killed in a church."

"Which direction was he facing?" Liam quickly asked.

"East," Phee told him.

"He was left facing the Holy Land. All of this is consistent with his evolution," Liam noted.

"What does that mean?" Maclin asked.

"The laws of the Old Testament were much more violent and unforgiving. Whatever the victims were looking at was an important final image before they died. Centuries ago when people debated the existence of hell, many priests believed that an eternal reminder of one's earthly sins or offenses was the ultimate retribution."

"So are we chasing some nut who thinks he's a centuries-old priest of some kind?" Phee asked sarcastically.

"I really don't know what you're chasing, Detective Freeman," Liam offered.

As the three cops debated and discussed the new information they had received, Liam stood quietly, still staring at the photos. After a few seconds, Quincy noticed his brother and the tears that began to fall. Liam made no movement or sound, he just stared at the pictures and, seemingly unaware, started to cry.

Quincy moved closer and put a hand on his brother's shoulder.

Maclin and Phee stepped back and busied themselves with work to give the two of them a little more space.

"Come on, let me take you home," Quincy said softly.

As he walked him to the door, Maclin and Phee both thanked Liam for his insight and assistance. Liam recommended a few literary references that could possibly be of help. Quincy said he would be back in a couple of hours and then led Liam out the door.

At 3:30, the drive uptown wasn't bad. Quincy's choice of routes only added to their good fortune. Cops, like cabbies, were hip to every shortcut or alternate route that the city had to offer. Liam stared out the window without speaking. In the first ten minutes of their drive, Quincy had hoped for an organic conversation to present itself. When it didn't come, he chose not to force it. From the time that they were small boys, they had enjoyed great conversations and amazing overall communication between them. But on this warm October day on their ride home, there was no evidence of it. No words, no laughter, no communication at all. Even though Quincy saw that his brother was hurting, there wasn't much he could do. When he dropped him off in front of the church, Quincy honored his brother's needs and gave him no recycled adages or philosophical one-liners. He quietly hugged him and watched him disappear behind the large alder doors.

19

Quincy hopped on the Henry Hudson and hoped that his streak of luck would continue all the way back downtown. By the time he made it to 14th Street, he had given into the feeling that he wasn't in the mood to immediately head back to work and to the claustrophobia of the second-floor conference room. He didn't mind pulling double and triple shifts; he just needed to pace himself. The long hours gave focus to his time and energy and was a means to keep certain memories at bay. Purpose granted him at least the illusion of normalcy. He hadn't slept in over thirty years. Not real sleep. Not the type of sleep that most people take for granted. He normally got by on two to three hours a night. Rarely more than that. As best he could remember, the last full night of sleep he had was June 4, 1979.

He grabbed a pastrami sandwich from a deli once he made it

back downtown. He decided to head to the park before the sun set. Before he headed back to work, he needed some downtime. He pretended that he needed the decompression. That he needed the fresh air. The simple fact was just that he wanted to see her.

Elena saw Quincy the minute he came into view. She found herself looking in the direction of the park's entrance, anticipating his arrival. She wanted to apologize to him for her behavior last night. She didn't mean to come off as defensive as she had. He had made her uncomfortable, but not in the ways that she had led him to believe.

The park was filled with people taking full advantage of the favorable weather. New Yorkers knew a good thing when they had it. The bench where she wanted to sit at was occupied by two teenagers who were much more interested in rising hormones than a setting sun. She looked in Quincy's direction and saw him glance at her as he sat on the last free bench. The walk toward him seemed longer than it actually was. A shyness that she hadn't known was accompanying and attaching itself to her like tiny remora. By the time she made it to his bench, she neither looked at nor spoke to him. She couldn't. Her apology would have to wait. She focused on the water and hoped that it would help settle her. He quietly ate a pastrami sandwich and without a word, offered her half as though they were old friends. Not quite certain what to do, she accepted and nibbled on the offering.

What scared her the most was how comfortably he welcomed her into his personal space. Without even formally acknowledging her, he made her feel at home and that there had been a history between them. Even though she tried not to, she found herself stealing glances at him. He sat south of her and was seemingly too engaged with his half of the sandwich and the view to notice her peeping in his direction. She took in what she could. His strong jaw line and dimpled chin. The different directions in which his hair naturally grew. She noticed for the first time a few strands of gray hovering just below his temple. The thing that she found herself gravitating toward the most were his hands. They were large and masculine and held Elena's attention. They were hardworking and old-fashioned. His hands told stories, both good and bad. They were strong enough to exude mercy and tenderness, but also great force.

Shortly after the sun disappeared, they found themselves alone. As she finished off her half of the sandwich, Elena noticed him smile, and then shortly afterward she heard his laughter. He deftly tossed her "the in" that they both needed.

"What's so funny?" she asked.

"I wish I had known yesterday that all it took to bribe you to smile was a pastrami sandwich."

"Technically, half a pastrami sandwich," she clarified.

"Even cheaper," he said.

"Actually, I wanted to apologize to you if I came off as rude in any way yesterday."

"No need to apologize. I didn't mean to make you uncomfortable."

They made small talk and very methodically eased into slightly more personal conversation. She asked him questions about being a cop and he in return asked her about her native Colombia and what she thought of New York. As he listened to her talk, he found the hint of her Spanish accent sexy. He could tell that she had spent concerted time and effort in trying to anglicize her speech patterns, but the more she relaxed, the more her natural cadence came out. She talked in great detail about being an artist, and he shared with her his secret love for architecture. Quincy was pleasantly surprised when she revealed that although soccer was her first love, she was also a huge baseball fan. As badly as he wanted to ask to take her to a Yankee's game, he didn't want to risk pushing for too much too soon. He told her a few jokes, some that were successful and some that weren't. Neither of them had laughed much lately and appreciated the sporadic releases within the conversations. There were the occasional lulls as well that became less and less awkward.

Elena twitched at the unexpected clap of distant thunder. Neither of them knew whether the storm was heading toward them or if it would pass. Quincy saw her half smile and simultaneously detected a hint of sadness as well.

"What's wrong?" Quincy asked.

"I was just thinking. When Joaquin was around five or six, he was terrified by the sound of thunder. One day when he was freaking out, I told him that thunder was just the sound of God laughing and that was His way of reminding us that He was always there, even in the rain."

"Did he buy it?"

"For a while. Until he figured out that it was just my way of helping him to deal with his fear."

"Smart kid."

"Yeah, he was. But one of the beautiful things about him was that even when he knew it wasn't exactly true, he still played along, and learned how to laugh at even the loudest storms. He got much better at it than I did. Joaquin used to say that we had to give God more reasons to laugh. He always made it his personal mission to try to make sure I was doing my part."

She grew silent for several minutes and Quincy respectfully granted her the emotional space that she needed.

A great blue heron foraged for food in the shallow banks of the water. It occupied a small area of the manmade patch of marsh that had recently been installed under a Bloomberg initiative. The tip of the large bird's right wing was bent at an unnatural angle and looked either broken or deformed. Each time it tried to take flight, it was defeated by gravity and its compromised wing. The failed attempts were equal parts comedic and sad. Quincy immediately called the bird Forrest Gump as Elena said a short prayer for the animal. Most of the migratory birds on the East Coast had already started their southern sojourn. Quincy wondered aloud if the bent wing had prevented the bird from migrating and thus sealed its tragic fate. She smiled and told him, "God decided his fate long before the broken wing."

"Then I guess we're talking about two different types of fate."

"I only know of one kind," she said.

"That bird breaking its wing had more to do with coincidence and being clumsy or careless than God or some master plan," he laughed.

"I'm just not a big believer in coincidences," she added.

"Look, I'm just saying, I don't think some bird with a bad wing that will more than likely die in a few days means anything beyond those facts," he retorted.

"We should just change the subject then, 'cause I don't know how to have a conversation on fate and the balance of nature and somehow conveniently leave God out."

"One thing being a cop has taught me is that we're more responsible for our 'fate' than we wanna give ourselves credit or blame for."

Quincy looked at his watch and realized that it was after seven. He stood and turned to her.

"I've gotta get back to work. Can I drop you off at home?"

"No, I'll be fine," she declined.

"Are you sure? What if I told you I had another pastrami sandwich in the car?"

He did what he could to make her laugh as they walked toward the opening of the park. The last thing he wanted was for some debate on God and fate to put a damper on the time he had finally spent with her. By the time they reached his car, he asked again if he could drive her home. She allowed him to convince her of what she had already decided to do. Elena accepted his offer as he held the car door open for her. She wished she lived a little farther from the park just to enjoy his company a little bit more. There wasn't much waiting for her at home besides a father with whom she barely spoke, and of course the constant reminders of Joaquin.

As they arrived at her father's home, Quincy got out and walked her to the front of the apartment building. Elena stood on the first step, which elevated her to his level. She wanted equal bearing on the things in which she was in control. In the midst of their awkward goodbye, he asked if he could see her again. As she agreed, they exchanged cell numbers, and each in their own way tried to protect their composure. He watched her closely as she stood on the step before him, shifting her weight back and forth.

He was trying to read her body language and decipher what it was saying to him. His focus kept returning to her lips, but he resisted doing what he had been wanting to do for the last two and a half hours. As he watched her walk up the stairs, he regretted his decision to not kiss her before she could even put her key in the lock.

20

Liam didn't eat that night. Sister Frances had prepared some smoked trout and roasted potatoes, which in the past had been a favorite of his. But tonight his plate went untouched. He couldn't get the images out of his head. Especially that of Father Conner. He had met the older priest years ago at a mixed denominational conference in the Poconos. When Liam found himself in Father Conner's neighborhood, he had on occasion stopped in to say hello. He wouldn't classify them as having been friends, but they were certainly friendly with one another. The sight of Father Conner skinned alive would forever be branded in his mind. Of all the gruesome images, Conner's was the one that made Liam feel as though he was right there next to the corpse. Father Conner's murder was much more personal to Liam.

Liam hadn't kept many personal secrets from his brother. A few things, but usually nothing of great substance. Obviously things discussed in the confessional were the exception. He had found himself in this gray area before, but not like this. He had wrestled with some of the horrible things people had told him in the privacy of a small dark booth. But of all the things that he heard over the years, nothing came close to the confession he heard last week from a fifty-something-year-old white male with thinning red hair.

Abraham Deggler had been living in New York now for four years. In those four years he had led a relatively mundane existence. He worked for Ardmon's, which was one of the largest church supply manufacturers in the country. They sold everything from pews, Bibles and robes to communion wafers and grape juice.

Deggler was a hard worker who had been with the company for over thirty years. In fact, he was the best field rep they had. Over the years they had moved him from city to city. He started working for the company in San Francisco when they first opened operations. Back then they were a small, family-owned business who had known Deggler from church since he was fifteen. He was twenty-three when he started working for the company. They originally hired him because it was Deggler who convinced the owners that their business could greatly benefit and expand with his knowledge and skill of the growing craze of personal computers. Once he set them up and showed them how to improve their bookkeeping, advertising, and expand their customer base, they immediately saw a 30 percent increase in revenue.

Deggler had been a terribly shy and awkward teen who blossomed into a full-blown antisocial young man. He was a beautiful child. Stunning in fact. His curly, chestnut hair and ocean blue eyes made him look like something out of a da Vinci painting. As a baby and small child, women were constantly fawning over him. He had always gotten lots of attention, unfortunately, both good and bad. He started life undersized. Although beautiful, he was skinny and weak. Once he reached puberty he started filling out, but by that time he had already been abused to a point beyond repair. His father was a Baptist preacher who was filled with fiery sermons and speeches and limitless imagination when it came to new ways of torturing young Deggler and his mother. Punishment and abuse were more of a sport to Deggler's father than anything. His sadism was cloaked in his twisted, so-called love for Jesus.

Deggler's father was his twelfth victim. The younger Deggler had needed to hone his skills and perfect his ways before sending his father home to his maker. With eleven trial runs, he was trying to determine which form of Biblical torture would be the most appropriate and fulfilling. His first kill was October 17, 1981, on his father's birthday. He started with the crucifixion of an evangelist who was feeling up little girls in the pool of baptism. The others that followed were thieves, hypocrites, pedophiles and schemers masquerading as men of God. His original plan was to culminate with his father's death, but two murders in, God spoke to him. God told Deggler the purpose of his birth and suffering. God told him that he was chosen and that he was highly favored. Deggler grew up reading in the Bible how God had commanded Abraham to kill his only son Isaac. Being as faithful to God as he was, Abraham set out to do God's bidding. Just before he was about to plunge the knife into his son, an angel intervened because Abraham had proven his loyalty to God.

Deggler was proud that, just like his namesake, he was willing to do whatever his Lord commanded him to do. The isolation of Deggler's childhood had left him with two passions: weightlifting and an obsession with all things electronic. By the time home computers became popular, Deggler had either learned or taught himself how to navigate cyberspace like a pro. His other passion, lifting weights, became a form of therapy to him. Once he started, he never stopped. His introduction to anabolic steroids allowed him to sculpt the type of body that he had only fantasized about as a young boy. By the time he was twenty-three, he stood at 6'4" and 237 pounds. His compulsion had nothing to do with vanity or narcissism. He was a chosen soldier of God, and as such, he needed a body that could facilitate God's power and bidding.

Deggler spent the better part of his life visiting churches and selling them whatever they needed. He was good at his job. It was the only time he felt comfortable around people. He was proud of the fact that he had personally sold over one million Bibles in the course of his career. He was equally proud of the fact that he alone had eradicated thirty-nine enemies of the church.

Deggler was methodical and meticulous. He studied his subjects for months and, in one instance, years before killing them. He used his expertise of electronics and computers. Once he had established a relationship with a church, he would offer his services to upgrade their security systems at a discount. When necessary, he would either plant his own hidden cameras or gain access to the existing ones via remote feeds. He saw the things that God knew. He saw the wickedness of the weak. He saw the true souls of men who purported to walk the path of the righteous.

And just as he had used surveillance to choose his victims, he had also used it to select his confessors. He believed confession was good for the soul. It was one of the reasons he converted to Catholicism several years ago. It wasn't so much that he saw the slaying of God's enemies as a sin; he was, after all, doing God's work. The confession was for the strange sexual feelings that accompanied him while executing God's work. Each killing aroused him. None greater than that of his own father. He had tried unsuccessfully for years to keep his personal demons at bay and be a more righteous soldier. He knew God was testing him, and he did everything in his power to prove his worthiness. Thirty years ago after the first wave of killings and his feelings of lust and depravity, he had gone so far as self-castration. He took his cue from the Book of Matthew and removed the offending member with an ancient Roman dagger not dissimilar to the type that Peter used to cut off an ear of a soldier the night Jesus was arrested. Deggler purified himself. After nearly bleeding to death and several operations, he took his survival as a sign from God that he would be forgiven his transgressions as long as he consistently repented.

Deggler had watched Liam Cavanaugh from St. Augustine's for months. The young priest from Washington Heights had a great reputation in the community and seemed a devoted servant of the Lord. The more Deggler watched him, the more convinced he was that this was the man to hear his confessions.

21

nybody dig up anything new on our latest vics?" Maclin asked
as she breezed into the conference room. Quincy and Phee
were still combing through the files of all the old victims as Stan
and Asif were making phone calls.

Phee looked up from his notes and responded to her.
"Detectives Flowers and Booth are still in the field, but I got
something on Higgins. Pastor Bradford Higgins's real name was
Alvin Hightower. Had a couple of charges of extortion and
pandering along with intent to sell, growing up in Newark. His
big 'come to Jesus' moment came in the early '80s, which is when
he started preaching. Bought up a few churches and rented them
back out in Brooklyn and the Bronx under a shell company called
Lark Enterprises. Over the years Lark's churches have been hit with
no less than fifty-three building and safety violations. The church

that his body was found in was closed down a year ago because of high levels of asbestos that was reported to him seven years ago. He didn't own anything under his name. Everything was hidden under his mother's maiden name. His net worth was three mil."

Maclin looked at the Bible reference under Higgins's photo. "Never heard of a church slumlord before. The scripture makes more sense now. 'Because of my house, which remains a ruin, while each of you is busy with his own house.'"

Maclin reexamined and reevaluated the photos of the victims and the scripture under each of their photos. She turned and looked at Phee and Quincy.

"Of the last three, Father Montrelle was the only one who wasn't killed in a church," Maclin stated.

"Yeah, but technically he was still killed on hallowed grounds. I ran a history of the building. It was a church that was converted into a hotel in the early 1900s," Quincy responded.

"Good work. Now we just need to put a name to his sin," Maclin added.

"The Brandstrum Arms was a big-time whorehouse back in the day. I don't know if that had anything to do with Montrelle being murdered there," Phee said.

"Well, the one thing that we do know is that there is a specific reason why his body was found there. Our killer doesn't do anything arbitrarily," Maclin countered.

"I'll get Booth to see if he can dig up anything else on Montrelle," Quincy said.

"Good. So based on the scripture and the fact that Father

Conner was skinned, am I the only one who's thinking that his offense was probably a sin of the flesh?" Maclin asked.

"Definitely would make sense," Phee agreed.

Quincy looked at both of them and nodded his agreement. He thought it wise that though he was the first to know, he was the last to agree.

"Okay, so the first thirty-six murders all had scripture from the book of Psalms. The last three are from three completely different books. Why?" Maclin asked.

"Maybe it really is as simple as what Quincy's brother said, about the spiritual evolution," Phee said.

"I still think it's more than that. Serial killers like him very rarely change their MO. For him to change anything after thirty years of success tells me there has to be a big enough reason for that to happen," Maclin countered.

They all went back and forth on every aspect of the case for hours. They discussed, debated and argued different points until midnight. Detectives Flowers and Booth had returned and jumped right into the fray. There were other parts of the job that cops loved more than sitting in a funky room for hours playing the "what if" game. But whether they liked it or not, they couldn't afford to miss any angle or possibility here because the clock was ticking and it was just a matter of time before they got the call on another dead body.

22

Reverend Elias Bell ran a very large Protestant church in Queens. He was born and raised in the Texas panhandle. He was preaching by the age of twelve. He had inherited the "gift" from his father, who had gotten it from his father before, and so on and so on. Reverend Bell was proud of his lineage and the long line of preachers whose footsteps he had followed in. Of the four generations that preceded him, Elias was considered the best. He was very learned and eloquent. He was a smart businessman who truly understood what people wanted and how to sell it to them. One of the first things he learned in a business course he took years ago was "know your product and its value." He flourished as he did because he instinctively knew that people were consistently willing to pay for hope. Selling Jesus was his thing, and not many people did it better than Reverend Bell. God was good, but even blessings and miracles came with a price tag. Reverend Bell got his members to buy into the tithing and prosperity gospel, hook, line and sinker. His 6,000-member church raked in twenty million plus annually. Some of the money taken in had made its way into an untraceable account in the Cayman Islands. There were the cars, jewelry and houses in six different states, and the mistresses that went along with them. It was after midnight and he was driving home to Long Island to his wife and six kids. The brand-new Maybach that he was driving at least made the trek more bearable. Just as he turned onto the LIE., he felt the jolt of some idiot rear-ending him. As he got out of the car, he noticed a tall, muscular man with red hair.

"What the hell is wrong with you? Are you blind? This is a $400,000 car, you asshole," Bell said irately.

Deggler smiled as he walked toward the man, knowing how much he was going to enjoy his next kill.

Maclin, Quincy and the crew were still going at it when the call came in around 1:15 a.m. The seven of them drove out to Queens to the large Christian Tabernacle Center. There in the parking lot they saw the remains of a man who had been tied to the back of a Maybach and dragged for who knows how long. Skin and muscle were missing on many parts of the corpse. His legs exposed bone and severed tendons. He had lost his jawbone along with his left hand. Four feet away from the dead man were his entrails and some other body part that Quincy couldn't quite identify. The beginning and end of the blood trail helped the team to establish a theory on Bell's torture. The parking lot was huge, with more than enough distance and isolation for this to have been a long, drawn-out process. The car had to have been traveling at a high speed and respectable distance to commit the type of carnage that they saw before them. Quincy looked at Maclin and Phee to see if he could detect in them anything similar as the toll this case was beginning to take on him. He thought it was his personal responsibility to better understand the killer. He was supposed to have been able to offer some insight and perspective that none of his colleagues had. Quincy was supposed to understand the type of rage and hatred that it took to do this to another human being because less than forty-eight hours ago he sat in Father Conner's office on the verge of giving in to his own murderous intent. Quincy hated the priest that molested him. He hated Father Conner, and more than likely he would have hated the victims he was investigating. But for all of his hatred of these men and even his deep-seated indifference to God, Quincy was thankful that he was not the type of animal who was capable of doing something like this.

"The disciple Mark was literally dragged and torn to pieces by the people of Alexandria," Quincy said to no one in particular. It was odd to him that he remembered that. Ironically, this case had done more to motivate him to read about religion than anything else in the past thirty years.

The three of them looked at the body and the blood trail that seemed endless.

Phee and Quincy thought they had seen the worst with Father Conner. They were wrong.

"Any witnesses?" Maclin asked.

"Uniform said that the security guard took off at nine," Phee responded.

"He knows their every move and when they're most vulnerable," Quincy added.

"This nightmare is just getting worse and worse," Maclin sighed.

None of them felt confident that they were any closer to stopping the killings than they were a day ago. There was something daunting about the weight and responsibility that the three of them felt over their roles and expectations. They were supposed to protect and assure the people of New York that they were safe. But looking at the remains of Reverend Bell, they feared that if the killer so decided, no one was safe. As the three canvassed the scene, Maclin said what they were all thinking.

"He's escalating," she said. "He's not even following his own time frame. There's a reason he's changing his profile as much as he is. In the past thirty years, he's never killed this many people this quickly. Not to mention all of his past victims were found inside of a church, and now this."

"Are we certain that we don't have a copycat on our hands?" Quincy asked.

"Hair sample says it's him," Maclin shot back.

"Could have been a plant," Phee added.

"You've been tracking him for ten years. What does your gut tell you?" Quincy asked her.

"Gut calls can be wrong. I prefer to rely on facts."

"Ok, so what do the facts tell you?"

"That his change of MO has us second-guessing ourselves. We stay the course, we'll catch him."

Quincy nodded at her as he looked at the several news crews that had already set up behind the police barricade and were jockeying for the best location to give their reports. "The vultures will eat well tonight."

Quincy was right. Exterior crime scenes always left the cops fighting for containment as best they could so that the case was in no way compromised by an overzealous reporter. The papers and broadcast stations were understandably going crazy with the events of the last two days. If murder was great for business, this was a gold mine. New York hadn't had a gory murder in several months, since an out of work schoolteacher savagely murdered his wife and twin toddlers because he could no longer take the effects of the recession. His plan was to commit suicide, but at the last moment he lost his nerve. It played out on the covers of all the newspapers for two days before it was replaced by coverage of a tipsy judge getting into a fender-bender. The clergy murders had legs though. If the press did their job there would soon be citywide paranoia. There would be politicizing and gossiping. There would certainly be splinters and spinoffs of the original stories. If handled correctly there would be enough to feed the machine for at least a week or two. It all depended on the final act.

Kravitz rarely visited crime scenes. He left that for the amateurs. Those who knew him were surprised to see the large man waddling toward the detectives and Agent Maclin. Phee was the first to see him approaching and tapped Quincy. Whatever reason that brought him here had to be important. After getting Maclin's attention, they decided to meet the big man halfway.

"Got something interesting for you," Kravitz said, sucking air.

"What's that?" Quincy asked.

"Well, I ran the hair samples a couple of times and came up with something."

"Is this the part where we do a drumroll, or do you just want to tell us?" Phee asked teasingly.

"I found traces of heavy metal poisoning, better known as HMP, in the roots of the strands of hair I tested. HMP is an alternative cancer treatment where you intentionally pollute the body with heavy metals, and as a result pollute the cancerous cells."

"He's got cancer?" Maclin asked.

"That would definitely be my guess."

"It would help explain why he's escalating," Quincy joined in.

"He's trying to finish what he started before he dies," Maclin added.

"That's a big help, Kravitz. Thanks. We all know how much you hate these scenes. Why didn't you just call it in?" Phee asked.

"My wife goes to this church. I had to see this one for myself," Kravitz responded.

The discovery that Kravitz made was a big one, but unfortunately at this point it didn't put them closer to specifically identifying or stopping the killer. It could be useful later when other information had been gathered, but for now the only thing it told them was that very soon there would be more killing.

23

They all stayed at the scene for another hour before calling it a night. Quincy dropped Maclin off at the hotel and got home around 3:00 a.m. He half watched an old episode of *Gilligan's Island* before falling asleep. He had several short dreams. Some were just abstract images with no linear storyline whatsoever. Fragments of the killings, with it being revealed that he was in fact the murderer. One short dream was even of Gilligan in Biblical times. However the dream he remembered most and with the greatest detail was of him and Elena. They were happy. This was the dream that awoke him. An hour and a half after first falling asleep, he was wide awake and ready to face the day that lay ahead.

At 6:30 he was in the park with tea and muffins. By 6:45 he saw her jog into view. The minute she saw him, she broke into a smile and made her way over to his bench where he had cranberry muffins and tea waiting for her.

"I figured you might have worked up an appetite."

"You still trying to bribe me with food?" Elena asked.

"I'm half-Italian. It's what we do."

"You sound like my boss. I'm hostessing at an Italian spot called Emelio's just off Wall Street. You should stop in for lunch sometime. Give me a chance to repay your bribery," she said as she nibbled on the muffin.

"Call me old-fashioned, but the first formal meal has to be on me."

"You're making my father out to be a liar."

"I'm not sure what you mean."

"He's always telling me that chivalry is dead in New York."

"Well then, you'll just have to tell him that I'm bringing it back."

"All by yourself? That must keep you pretty busy with the ladies of New York."

"Not at all. That's definitely not my style."

"So what is your style?"

Quincy couldn't help but laugh. "When I find out, I'll be sure and let you know. By the way, what's your favorite food? I need to know that if I'm going to take you out," Quincy said.

"That's a tall question. I eat everything."

"Okay, but what would be the perfect meal for me to take you out for?"

"You promise not to laugh?"

"I promise."

"Anchovy and pineapple pizza."

Quincy looked at her and burst out laughing.

"You said you wouldn't laugh," she said as she playfully hit him.

"I'm sorry, but I definitely didn't see that one coming."

They laughed as Quincy vowed to find her the best pineapple and anchovy pizza that New York had to offer. Other people came and left the park as the two of them tried to squeeze in as much conversation as they could in their limited time together. Since he had worked until 2:30 in the morning, Quincy wasn't expected back into the office until at least nine. Sitting in the park talking with Elena was the best way for him to refuel himself. He was surprised how easily he opened up to her. As much as he wanted to know things about her, he wanted her to know him. She told him things like how she lost her virginity the night of her high school graduation and also how her American mother was killed in a car accident shortly after she was born. He opened up to her and told her things that he hadn't shared with anyone else. For years there had been an unspoken agreement between Quincy and Liam that never allowed them to discuss what had happened to them as children. There were things that Quincy walked around with that he never had an opportunity to express. He didn't tell her everything, but certainly enough.

As he started questioning whether or not he had shared with her too much, too soon, he found himself attempting to shift the conversation to safer subject matter. He was surprised when Elena reached out and held his hand. It was then that he realized that she was quietly reassuring him that his exposure was both appreciated and protected. The simple gesture gave him things that no one else had ever accomplished. Her contact gave him courage and peace. She held his hand and listened to him with no judgment or assumption. As he eventually grew silent, Elena took control of the conversation and reciprocated his openness. She talked about everything from her relationship with her father to how much she missed her son. Throughout the course of the conversation she spoke freely of her son's suicide. There were times when her grief resurfaced and she grew quiet and fragile. He knew the things that she didn't know were the things that hurt her the most. It broke his heart that she felt like her son's suicide was somehow her fault. He couldn't help but think about the glaring differences between Elena and his mother. Elena blamed herself for things that she didn't know, whereas his own mother chose to ignore the things that she did know. Although there was a dilemma he faced, after careful contemplation Quincy decided that Elena needed to know at least some of the things that he had learned about Father Conner. He had to be extremely careful how he told her. He had to be certain to present it as his suspicion based on his conversation with Joaquin's friend, Alberto. But regardless as to how he presented it, he was certain that it would hurt her. He had no idea how she would handle the revelation of Conner's crimes against her son, but he decided that her not knowing was not only painful but ultimately much more dangerous. Now it was his turn to hold her hand and give support and assurances.

Once the truth was revealed, he saw in her anger, and then

pain, and then anger again, and so on and so forth. It was frustrating to him because when she questioned his certainty, he couldn't tell her that he had gotten Conner to confess a few hours before his demise. All Quincy could tell her was that as an abuse victim himself, his conversation with Alberto had left him with a gut feeling. Nothing that he could officially act on, but a feeling nonetheless. He explained to her the sensitivity of the investigation into Conner's murder and suggested that she speak with Alberto for herself. He felt that the boy might be more forthright with her. At first he wasn't sure if this information would somehow compromise what was growing between the two of them, but he was relieved not to feel like he was holding something of such importance back from her any longer.

Quincy was nervous because of the huge risk that he was taking and how it could have easily backfired with her being angry at him for not divulging his suspicions earlier. One of the many things that he had learned as a cop was that grief was at times illogical and unpredictable. As she allowed him to continue to hold her hand, he was happy that he hadn't in any way lost her. He was happy that she trusted him.

24

By the time Quincy got to the station, Phee was already there going through files of old cases.

"In the four and a half years that we've been partners, this is the first time I've ever gotten to work before you. You must have finally gotten some good sleep," Phee said.

Quincy just smiled and asked, "Maclin here yet?"

"She just called. Should be here in a few. So what do you think is the deal with her?" Phee asked.

"What do you mean?"

"She's like a robot. Don't get me wrong. I think she's damn good, but I also get the vibe that something's missing. I don't know if it's true, but one of my boys out of DC told me she had some kind of breakdown years ago."

"It's a tough job. She's been chasing this nut a whole lot longer than us. Who knows what that alone can do to a person," Quincy responded.

Quincy's phone vibrated with a text message. As he looked at it, he read: Thank you for your honesty. And btw, cranberry muffins are my favorite.

Quincy broke into involuntary laughter and a broad smile.

"What the hell is wrong with you?" Phee asked.

"Nothing."

"Then why are you smiling like a zoo baby at feeding time? Did you hit something last night?"

"What are you talking about?"

"Ass!!! Did you hit some ass last night?"

"The only thing that amazes me more than us being partners as long as we have is that I haven't 'accidentally' shot you yet."

As Quincy grabbed the small file on last night's victim and sat down to read, Maclin came in with a cup of coffee in her hand.

"Morning," she greeted them.

As they responded, she walked over and taped photos of Reverend Bell and Pastor Higgins next to Father Montrelle and Father Conner.

"Today we should focus on the info Kravitz gave us last night. I pulled up the thirty-two different treatment centers and facilities in the five boroughs that provide alternative medical care for cancer patients. Let's paper them all with the partial description we have. Hopefully he's going to one that's registered. It's not a lot, but it's more than I've had in the last ten years," Maclin said.

"We should start in Manhattan and work our way out while

we have the other detectives work their way back to us," Quincy added.

The seven of them split up the list and spent the first part of the day going to every registered facility. Because Maclin didn't know how to get around the city that well, she rode shotgun with Quincy. The three primaries checked in with the other team members every half hour to give updates in case they had picked up any additional information in their visits. Cops inherently made people defensive. It made no difference whether they were guilty of something or innocent as hell; the thought of talking to a cop was a turnoff to most. Phee was up in Spanish Harlem at the third spot on his list and making the same lack of progress that everyone else had been making when he had an idea. Since it was almost lunchtime, he waited outside in his car until the young Latino intern that he had seen earlier stocking boxes came out and headed up the block. Phee followed him to a tiny Dominican takeout spot. As the intern went to pay for his order, Phee put a twenty on the counter in front of him. Phee's Spanish was flawless and seemed to put the young man at ease as they walked outside.

"If I were trying to find people who offer the same level and quality of services that you all do but more underground, a place where they don't keep records on patients, where would I go? If you come up with some names and numbers for me, there's fifty in it for you," Phee said in Spanish.

The intern took Phee's card and nodded as he headed back to work.

Quincy and Maclin didn't have any success either. Since they were already down in Chinatown they decided to stop and grab a quick bite. Quincy ordered slow-roasted Peking duck soaked in oolong tea and a side of pineapple and shrimp-fried rice, while Maclin ordered the honey-glazed walnut shrimp with a house specialty citrus sauce. It wasn't until the server actually brought the food that they realized just how hungry they both were.

"So you grew up with brothers. How many?" Quincy asked.

"Three. How did you know?"

"Because you still guard your food."

Maclin looked down at the defensive position of her hand and started laughing.

"Do you ever stop being a cop?" she asked.

"Don't know if that's possible. Do you?"

"It's the only thing that I'm good at."

"So is the job your life?" he asked.

"What life?"

"I guess that answers my question."

"What about you. How long you been on the job?"

"Next year will be nineteen for me."

"So your brother's a priest, and you're a cop. How does that happen? That had to have made both of your parents proud."

"My father died when we were kids. As far as my mother goes, we're probably who we are more in spite of her than because of. But then again, I guess it's a parent's job to try to screw up their kids as much as possible."

"I take it you don't have kids."

"Not even close. You?"

"Came close once."

Quincy could see that in spite of her best efforts to hide it, he had hit a nerve. He smoothly changed the subject to less personal matters. They were laughing about Quincy's addiction to '70s sitcoms when Maclin accidentally spilled plum sauce on her jacket. In the process of her removing her jacket, the sleeves on her blouse rode up an inch or so, allowing Quincy to quickly see horizontal scars on both wrists. As they both pretended that he hadn't seen anything, Maclin lowered her sleeves and stood up.

"I'm going to the ladies' room. Would you have her bring the check? We should be heading back."

Quincy and Maclin made it back to the station by four. As they entered the front door and headed toward the stairs, Quincy spotted Elena sitting on a bench in the hall.

"I'll meet you upstairs," he told Maclin.

Elena rose as Quincy crossed to her.

"Are you okay?" he asked with real concern.

"I talked to Alberto," she said.

From the look on her face and the tears that started falling, Quincy knew immediately that Alberto had confirmed for her what Father Conner had done. Quincy escorted her upstairs a back way and quietly took her to an interview room where they could have privacy. The minute they were in the small room, Quincy grabbed and hugged her tightly. He allowed her to let go and release the burden of her confirmed information. She cried and cried, and when it seemed she would stop, she started again. They were in the room for ten minutes and neither one spoke.

She may not have been able to articulate exactly why she came, but Quincy understood that it wasn't for words. Fortunately she had fully regained her composure a few minutes before there was a knock at the door. As Quincy crossed and opened it, he discovered Phee standing outside.

"Maclin's asking for you," Phee said.

"I'll be right there," Quincy responded.

As Phee turned to leave, he got a glimpse of Elena and remembered her clearly from the time they met two months ago.

"I'll let you get back to work," she said. "I just needed…"

"You don't have to explain yourself to me. I'm just sorry that anything happened in the first place."

"Just do me a favor," she said half demanding, half pleading.

"Anything," he said.

"Just make sure people know who Father Conner really was."

"Absolutely."

25

Maclin and Phee were back in the conference room working when there was a knock on the door followed by a cop sticking his head in.

"Hey Phee, you got a visitor," the cop said.

When Phee exited the conference room, he saw the intern from earlier. They spoke briefly and as Phee discreetly slipped him cash, he handed Phee a piece of paper with two addresses and telephone numbers. Phee reentered the room with more energy and pep just as Quincy arrived.

"I might have something. Maybe, maybe not. I'm thinking, if he's managed to stay under the radar for thirty years, then that's somebody who thinks every move through. Even with the cancer thing. Maybe he's trying the alternative treatment to stay off the radar. But this guy's so paranoid that even if he's doing alternative medicine, he's not gonna go to a place that we can track. I got the names of two more places that wouldn't appear on our list."

"I definitely think it's an angle worth looking into," Maclin said.

"Quincy, you take the one in Chelsea; I'll take the one uptown," Phee said as he wrote out the address for Quincy.

Quincy turned to Maclin. "You riding with me?"

"No, I'll ride with Detective Freeman," she said as she avoided eye contact with Quincy.

Quincy nodded and then headed out the door.

As Phee went to grab his jacket off the back of the chair, he said to Maclin, "You can just call me Phee at this point. Everybody does."

"Yes, I know, but I've just never done well with nicknames on the job."

A bit later, Quincy sat in his car across the street from a townhouse on 22nd Street. He watched a frail woman being escorted from the building by a home care specialist. Quincy crossed the street and entered the bottom floor of the building behind a FedEx delivery man. He waited in a small holding room with four chairs and one elderly gentleman. As the FedEx man left, the receptionist called out to Quincy.

"May I help you?"

"I'm here to see Mrs. Sundrah."

"Do you have an appointment, Mr....?"

"Cavanaugh, and no I don't, but I really do need to see her. It's very important and I promise not to take up too much of her time."

"May I ask what this is in regard to?"

"It's personal. If you don't mind, I'd really feel more comfortable talking directly to Mrs. Sundrah."

"She's in with someone right now, but have a seat and I'll tell her you're here," the receptionist said.

Quincy sat across from the older man and thumbed through a few holistic health magazines. The old man had fallen asleep and Quincy noticed a small stream of drool making its way to his chest. The man looked to be in his eighties, possibly even older. It was hard to tell. However old he was, he didn't look like he had much time left to live. The old man made Quincy think of his own mortality. He wondered if he would live to be so old or if he would even want to. Maclin was right. The job was their life. He wondered when he had reached the back end of it, whether or not it would have been enough.

A door opened down the hall and a few moments later an elderly woman was escorted to the older man across from Quincy. If Quincy thought the man looked old, then the woman looked even older. He noticed a piece of gauze taped to her forearm where she either had blood drawn or an IV inserted earlier. As she gently shook the man and called his name, the man woke and immediately stood up. He held her hand and kissed her as though they had been separated much longer than they actually had. Quincy saw in both of them more energy and life when they came together than he had seen in them when they were separated. He appreciated the years and history that must have existed between them. Quincy saw in the old man's eyes someone who was lucky enough to have found the love of his life. The old man never let go of her hand as they slowly walked toward the exit.

"Mr. Cavanaugh, Mrs. Sundrah will see you now," the receptionist called out to Quincy.

Mrs. Sundrah was an East Indian woman in her midfifties with long flowing black hair with gray streaks in the center.

"My assistant said it was a personal matter?"

"I'm wondering whether or not you can help me. And don't worry, I'm not here to hassle you and what you have going on here," Quincy said as he flashed his badge.

"How exactly can I help you?" she asked.

"We are pursuing a murder suspect who we believe is receiving alternative treatment for cancer. A redheaded white male, in his midfifties."

"I don't have any patients who fit that description."

"You mind if I look at your appointment book?"

"Actually I would."

"Why?"

"Because my relationship with my patients is a sacred and private bond. One of the major tenets of holistic healing is trust, Mr. Cavanaugh."

"I'm asking only as a courtesy. You do know that I could shut this hocus-pocus stand down if I wanted to?" he said.

"That's ultimately your choice. But it won't change the fact that you asked me a question and I already answered you honestly. I only treat elderly women, Mr. Cavanaugh. The woman who just left here is ninety-three years old. She was diagnosed with cancer when she was seventy-four. Doctors had written her off a long time ago. It's funny what a little hocus-pocus can do when you believe that the body and spirit can heal itself."

"Doctors make mistakes on the body all the time. And as far as the spirit thing, I personally don't believe in all of that," Quincy said pointedly.

"That's the difference between you and the women who come here. They walk by faith and not by sight. We both seem to be clear on what you don't believe in. The only question is are you equally clear on what you actually do believe in? Have a good day Mr. Cavanaugh."

———

Phee was very familiar with the neighborhood. The irony was that considering how much crime took place in the area, cops were never welcome. No matter what went down, the unspoken rule was cops were the enemy. At Phee's suggestion, Maclin had let her hair down and did what she could to look more casual. They had each decided to play the part of a desperate couple searching for alternative cancer care that they could afford. Even though she had agreed to play the part, Maclin was a bit surprised when Phee held her hand affectionately as they sat in front of Horace Pine, the man who ran the facility. As she listened to Phee explain his "girlfriend's" diagnosis, she realized that it had been a very long time since a man had held her hand. Even under false pretenses. After talking for twenty minutes or so, Maclin asked if she could make a formal appointment as soon as possible to start treatments.

She looked at Phee as Pine checked his computer for the next available slot. As Horace gave them a tour of the four-roomed facility, Phee pretended to have left his cell phone in Pine's office. Unescorted, Phee quickly went to the computer and used his phone to take pictures of the names he scrolled through on the screen. Phee then rifled through an appointment book and snapped a few more pictures as well. As he heard Maclin and Pine returning, he pretended to be engaged on a phone call. After hanging up, he grabbed Maclin's hand and thanked Pine for accommodating them with an appointment for the following week. Phee knew that they were both still in character, but was caught a little off guard when Maclin held his hand all the way to the car.

26

By 6:00 p.m., they were all cross-referencing the names of male patients that they had gotten from the licensed facilities as well as the twenty names that Phee had stolen.

Phee had also discovered the name T. Smith that was scheduled in the appointment book for a treatment session after hours for the following day. The seven of them had to literally check the eighty-three names against every name on file connected to the victims. Quincy thought of ways to pace himself for the long, boring night that lay ahead of him and the rest of the team. Elena had flashed through his mind periodically since her visit to the station. He was quietly disappointed that he had not been able to meet her in the park at sunset to check on her. Quincy had never had any type of routine with a woman, but he was surprised at how easily he welcomed this pattern. He had decided earlier that he would call her on his dinner break, if they bothered to take one. If not, he'd find a way to at least hear her voice, even if only for a few minutes.

A cop knocked at the door and told Phee he had another visitor. Quincy thought it odd that for some reason the cop had a strange grin attached to his face as he talked to Phee.

As soon as Phee exited the conference room, he saw the brown-skinned tranny with the platinum blond wig from the other night. A few of the cops glanced at Phee and either quickly turned away or looked at him with a weird smirk. Had Phee been more prepared, he might have been able to play the tranny off as just another infor-mant. But the look of shock on his face indicated to anyone looking that clearly there was a personal relationship between the two. Phee roughly grabbed the tranny by the arm and led him to an interview room. As he opened the door, Phee violently tossed the man against the far wall and slammed the door shut behind them.

Phee was pure rage.

"What the fuck are you doing here?"

"I need to talk to you."

"No you don't. This is my job, you asshole!!!"

"I wouldn't be here if it wasn't important."

"I don't give a damn what you think is important. You had no right coming here."

"This has nothing to do with me and you. I want to report a murder. You are still a cop aren't you?"

"What the hell are you talking about? Who was murdered?"

"My friend Shay. She got in a Bentley last night with a john and no one has seen her since."

Phee tried to use the part of him that was a cop to bring himself back from the anger that was pulling and dominating him. There were no magical breathing exercises or time-outs that could bring him back. He had to rely on the one thing that demanded the most amount of logic in him and the least amount of emotion.

"Does Shay have a last name?" Phee asked.

"DeVane," the tranny answered.

"So I'm assuming this Shay DeVane is just like you," Phee said still with an edge.

"You mean a T-walker, yeah," he responded.

"So a tranny gets in a car with some john, you can't find him and you automatically start screaming murder. I can't believe you're bothering me with this shit."

"We look out for each other. She wouldn't just disappear without telling me. I got a quick call late last night with her hysterical and screaming that her john was trying to kill her. Then the phone went dead in the middle of the message."

"If you were all that concerned about him, why are you just now reporting it?" Phee asked.

"I'm not. I reported it at the 34th precinct, and they pretty much blew me off the way you're trying to do right now. Nobody cares about us, Phee. We don't matter."

"Write his...I mean her name down and I'll make some phone calls."

"Thank you."

"Don't ever come here again, okay. No matter what."

"Sure, Phee. I'm sorry I embarrass you."

"You do it to yourself much more than me."

The tranny crossed to the door and hesitated.

"I wrote Daddy a letter. Did he tell you about it?"

"No."

"My doctor said that I've stopped responding to my meds and that it's just a matter of time before my immune system starts shutting down. I just thought I should let you all know."

Phee's brother opened the door and left.

27

E lena left the park at 6:30, well after dark. Most times she ran for physical and/or mental stimulation. This evening she ran for emotional grounding. She was still a raw nerve. A bundle of kinetic energy that had the potential to manifest itself in darker ways. Even though Quincy had told her how busy he was with work, she had waited and hoped that he would somehow surprise her and show up. His presence seemed to be one of the few things that came close to comforting and calming her. She tried as best she could to distract herself with thoughts of the things that she enjoyed most. She thought of water, she thought of art, and she thought of Quincy. Even though her thoughts were only short reprieves, she focused as hard as she could to prolong their calming effects. Her thoughts of Quincy lasted the longest. Whatever temporary peace she thought she was finding was being interrupted every ten minutes or so by her father's incessant phone calls. Each time, Elena let it go to voice mail. She was determined to hang on to whatever sliver of peace she had convinced herself that she had found. This was actually the calmest that she had been since Alberto confirmed her son's abuse. She wondered if her father knew, and if he didn't, how did he miss the signs? She had anticipated the countless possibilities of hurt and anger that this new information might bring for the rest of her life. She was aware of the challenges that this presented to her faith. She even thought about the greater difficulty that lay ahead in the reparation of her relationship with her father. In time she would be prepared for it all. She only asked the universe that tonight she be allowed to feel nothing but peace and lightness. She needed to savor the few positive things in her life right now. She rejected her father's interruptions. She refused to relinquish the few things that could help her through all of this. All that she had tolerated, all that she had endured…she was at least deserving of these quiet moments. Her phone vibrated for the umpteenth time, and Elena turned it off as she walked around with no particular place in mind to go. She would have turned it off earlier but held out hope as long as she could that Quincy might call or text. Even though it was later than usual for her to be out after her run, she took her time going home, hoping that she could somehow shed some of the anger and pain that had been dragging her along. She was fully aware that nothing she did would miraculously erase any of her feelings or the dread of facing Romero.

From the moment that Romero had to make the fateful call two months ago to inform Elena of her son's death, he was terrified that he had lost her. By the time she arrived in New York and he was able to see her personally, the disconnect and detachment that he felt from her confirmed his fears. It hurt him deeply that his daughter's love for him had disappeared and been reduced to nothing more than her tolerance of him. He never confronted or reproached her because of one simple fact: He couldn't blame her. Romero's grandson had killed himself on his watch. Could he have found forgiveness had anything happened to his child while under the care of another?

When Romero convinced Elena to let Joaquin come to stay with him, he felt it was best for all of them. Romero was lonely, Elena was struggling with finances, school and single parenting, and Joaquin was beginning to show signs of preteen rebellion back in Colombia, more than likely because of the absence of a strong male influence. Since coming to live with him, Romero had diligently supervised his schoolwork, instituted more structure and discipline overall and even convinced him to be an altar boy for good measure. For some strange reason the young boy had become progressively withdrawn. In hindsight, Romero wished he had done things differently. Communicated with Joaquin differently, been less authoritarian. Anything. Whatever mistakes he made ended up costing him the life of his grandson and the love of his daughter.

Romero ate a quiet dinner alone and tried as best he could to watch a telenovela that he had seen many times before. His mind was racing as he kept having nagging thoughts of his daughter's safety. He was waiting in the living room when Elena walked through the front door.

"I've been going crazy worrying about you. Where were you?" Romero demanded.

Elena turned to face her distraught father. "I'm sorry. I was just walking around."

"It's after nine. You could have at least called."

"I said I was sorry. I didn't know I had to check in."

"Don't twist this around. You leave to go for a jog, and you don't come back until hours later and don't answer your phone. Of course I'm gonna be upset."

Romero continued his rant as Elena was becoming more and more irritated by his growing inquisition. All she wanted to do was escape to her room, take a shower and attempt to sleep. It wasn't indifference that left Elena without compassion for assuaging her father's concern and worry. It was something darker. On some level, she wanted him to be upset. Why should he have a moment's peace? His sense of overprotectiveness was both mistimed and misdirected.

"I don't understand why you couldn't at least answer your phone when I called you," Romero continued.

"Because I turned it off. Look, I'm tired and I'm not in the mood. I just wanna go to bed."

"Not in the mood? I've been sitting here worried out of my mind, and the best you can say is you're not in the mood?"

Elena felt it snap before she even spoke. She felt the muzzle fall away and the anger spilling out.

"Okay, what about this? If you had been a lot more worried about my son, maybe he would still be alive and the sight of you wouldn't make me as sick as it does right now."

Elena didn't wait for a response. She just turned and went to her room. She didn't see the horrible wound she inflicted. She didn't see the hope that she had robbed Romero of. Had she waited five seconds more, she might have heard the distinct sound of her father's heart breaking.

As Elena soaked in the tub, she played back the argument she had with Romero. Like all people, she had done things in the past that she wasn't particularly proud of, but she had never been intentionally cruel to someone. She was, to say the least, disappointed in herself. Simultaneously, there was also a degree of fear creeping in. Elena feared that once her anger was released, it had the power to consume her.

After her bath, she went to her room and tried painting, more as a means of distraction than expression. Around 11:30 she went to the kitchen for a glass of juice. As Elena's bare feet stepped on the kitchen tiles, she felt something cold and wet beneath her. She noticed the light of the refrigerator shining in the darkened room. As she turned on the lights she found herself standing in a puddle of milk. Stepping toward the refrigerator, Elena discovered Romero lying face down on the floor with a spilled carton of milk by his side. As Elena rushed to her father and turned him over, she saw that Romero's face was terribly contorted and locked to one side. His entire body twitched in an odd, tremulous rhythm. The front of Romero's sweatpants was wet with milk and urine. Elena discovered a trickle of blood just behind Romero's hairline and assumed the injury had occurred during her father's fall. She noticed that Romero's skin, although covered in a thin layer of sweat, was cold and clammy to the touch. Elena quickly grabbed the kitchen phone and dialed 911 as she feebly tried to comfort her father.

28

Quincy heard about Phee's brother's visit. He had decided to take a break so that he could call Elena, but his partner needed him. Phee had told Quincy about AJ the first year of their partnership. At that time the mere mention of his name caused Phee and both his parents great pain. Growing up, the two brothers were relatively close. Not as close as Quincy and Liam, but close enough. AJ may have been the firstborn but he never quite lived up to his father's expectations. He was always more sensitive and blatantly closer to his mother Dolicia. The more love and adulation that their father gave Phee, the more distant AJ reportedly became. Clay and Phee had major issues with his homosexuality and were even less prepared for the self-loathing and destructive tendencies that AJ started showing signs of. By sixteen he was estranged from his family, and for the next two decades embraced the most indulgent and decadent lifestyle he could manage. As far as Phee was concerned, AJ broke their mother's heart and sent her to an early grave.

Quincy pulled Phee aside and offered to take his workload, suggesting that he call it an early night. His mind wouldn't be fully on the job anyway. And if anyone had pulled his or her weight today, it was definitely Phee. Tomorrow they would discuss the late-night appointment of T. Smith, but for now it would have to wait. Quincy patted him on the shoulder, but didn't push for anything else because when Phee wanted to talk about his brother, he would. Quincy hated seeing his partner in so much pain. He felt that on some level Phee had always looked at him as a replacement for the brother he had "lost."

At 12:17 it was just down to Quincy and Maclin. She had been a bit standoffish toward him since they returned from lunch. They had successfully cross-referenced every name on the list and found no matches or parallels whatsoever. T. Smith was the only name not cleared. The plan was to return to the facility tomorrow evening. It wasn't much to go on, but it had to be checked out just the same. Quincy's phone rang and he saw Elena's name on the caller ID. He excused himself and stepped outside the conference room and heard an emotional Elena on the other end. Quincy was having problems understanding her through her crying and frantic ranting. The only words that clearly registered were "father" and "hospital."

29

Cryptogenic stroke, Dr. Fong explained to Elena, meant that it was a stroke of unknown origin. Because of the swelling in his brain, Romero was placed in a medically induced coma. Dr. Fong told Elena that this was done to put the brain in a state of hibernation to allow it a chance for recuperation. They needed to rest Romero's brain and reduce its need for blood, oxygen and glucose. He was direct and honest in describing Romero's condition. There were possibilities of him not surviving, and even if he did, it would take a few days to determine the long-term prognosis. Only time would tell if his paralysis was permanent or not. In trying to give her something positive to hold on to, he told her that because Romero had been in "generally good shape," he stood a realistic chance of fully recovering. Elena thought it interesting that whenever Dr. Fong referred to Romero, he made sure to do so by his name. It made Elena feel better that he humanized her father and didn't reduce him to anything generic or less personal. Elena was directed to the ICU., where she sat at the bedside of her unconscious father. She hadn't really prayed since before the death of her son. And even though it was the only thing that was in her power to do, she was still unable to.

It was just after 1:00 and there was an eerie calm throughout the ward. The whir of machines and the occasional message over the PA system were the only invasive sounds. The overall silence was a bit off-putting to Elena. She needed movement and energy. Those were things that represented progress and hope to her, or at least some semblance thereof. Even though there was nothing physical she could do to help her father, the relative silence left her feeling restless. In the quiet, she could smell the sickness and death over the ammonia and antiseptics. Worst of all, in the quiet, Elena's guilt and imagination got the better of her.

In the morning when the specialist came, they would be able to better assess the prognosis. Elena sat at her father's bedside until the nurses assured her that Romero was in good hands and that she should just come back tomorrow. Regardless of the status of their splintered relationship, the fear of losing her father terrified her.

She stepped outside into the October air and realized how boxed in she had been in the hospital. As she headed toward a nearby taxi, she heard the one voice that moved her like no other.

"How about a police escort?"

Elena turned and ran to Quincy and buried herself into him. She savored the things she appreciated about him. She was thankful for the strength of his hands, how his size enveloped her, the way he smelled and how he felt. Of all the things that she appreciated about him in that moment, none was greater than her thankfulness for him being there.

"I tried to get upstairs to you but they said visiting hours were closed. Even flashed my badge but it didn't work," he said.

Elena enjoyed the resonance of his deep voice against her body. She responded without looking at him.

"I'm just happy you're here," she said.

Quincy decided he would hold her as long as she needed holding. She kept her head firmly planted against his chest. She smelled him and submitted even more to his hold. She felt one of his large hands in the small of her back and shifted her weight to his support. She cried because she remembered how much she loved his hands. Quincy wasn't certain why his arrival had made her emotional, but just knowing that his mere presence was both a buoy and comfort to Elena was enough for him.

The extrication was a process. It was on her third attempt that she was finally able to separate from him. Quincy sensed that she was standing on sea legs, and kept his hand on her, gently steadying her. As they walked to his car, she updated him on her father's condition and how she had found him lying on the kitchen floor after an argument that she now regretted.

They arrived at her father's home quicker than he expected. As was becoming the habit, they had gotten lost in each other's company and conversation. He had thought at some point he would have some preparation, but the moment had snuck up on them prematurely and unannounced. He was torn between what he thought he should do versus what he wanted to do. He didn't want to come across as trying to take advantage of a tragic situation, but he also had no intention of leaving her alone.

Elena thought of telling him how lonely and uncomfortable she would feel in the house by herself. She thought of hiding under the guise of inviting him in for coffee that she wouldn't drink. She hoped that he would make an excuse to invite himself in. Most of all she hoped she would soon know what it felt like to have him inside of her.

Elena couldn't help but be nervous. She was treading water as she chatted about less significant things. Quincy grabbed her hand, midsentence, and led her to the front door. There was no longer any room for formality between them. As they entered the apartment, her sea legs returned. They only made it in as far as the mirror that hung over the demilune in the small foyer. As soon as the door closed behind them, her body was begging for his touch. Quincy stepped to her on cue and pushed back the hair from her face. He remained quiet as though words would have interrupted or compromised something between them. She had been wanting his lips for a while now. As she felt his breath upon her, she prepared herself for his kiss. Once they made contact she was immediately aware of the fullness and softness of Quincy's lips. Had it not been for his large hands holding her, her legs may have failed.

She watched him step back and take her in as though it were the first time he had ever seen her.

"Are you okay with this?" he asked.

"Absolutely."

"Take off your coat."

Elena kept her eyes on him as she removed her coat.

"Now your dress."

She felt a definite turn on to him telling her what to do. Elena felt her fingers grow thick and rigid in the process of unbuttoning her clothes. As she stood completely naked before him, she actually saw him shudder. Elena saw in his eyes great pleasure derived from her simplest acts. Quincy made her face the mirror as he stood behind her, his large hands firmly planted on her shoulders. He made her look at herself, because he needed her to see what he saw. He needed her to understand the source of his adulation.

As Quincy undressed in front of her she gladly assumed the role of the voyeur. He was at least ten years older than her, but he was still toned and athletic looking. His body was far from perfect, but beautiful to her nonetheless. There was always the odd intersection where the imagined and the realized either complemented or canceled each other out. The pressure of fantasy far outweighing reality. But there was also room for pleasant surprises. Quincy was much more gentle than Elena had ever imagined. Her body responded to his innate balance of strength and tenderness.

Elena's body frustrated Quincy. He'd never known anything to make him feel so insatiable. Just when he thought he was fully consuming her, she made him hungry for different parts. Her body was in competition with itself. Every time he tried to focus and enjoy one part of her, another part would call and demand his attention. Her breasts competed with her neck, while her inner thighs grew angry at the time he spent kissing her navel. Her body pulled him in different directions. Each stop he made granted him more gratification than the previous. There had always been a certain amount of emotional detachment that Quincy had associated with sex, but everything about Elena's touch and feel made him more present and connected to her.

Elena tried to match his every kiss, his every nibble, bite and suck. She was having trouble breathing, literally. Her short quick breaths soon had her hyperventilating. When Quincy's mouth wasn't covering hers, she made a point of taking in bigger gulps of air. But that meant if he wasn't on her lips then he was discovering some other overly sensitive part of her body. She traded one pleasurable torture for another. She gladly accepted that he was intent on canvassing her entire body with his lips and tongue. Quincy deftly expanded whatever she thought she knew of her erogenous zones. The back of her knees, her pelvic bone, feet, inner thigh, neck… even the little dip just below her biceps, all became his playing field. His attention to detail during foreplay made her open up to him even more and left her wanting to match, touch for touch, the pleasure he brought to her. With all the current tragedy in her life, she found exoneration and solace in Quincy's touch. She let him take her thoughts far away from her son's death and her father's hospitalization. The more he touched and pleased her, the more he allowed her to lose herself. As her knees wobbled and buckled, Quincy lifted her and carried her to the nearby sofa. She never took her eyes off him even as she guided him into her.

Quincy didn't know how long he had been inside of her. From

the very beginning of his initial penetration, his concept of time became progressively blurred. All that mattered to him was the now. He was a bit thrown by how well she seemed to know his body. She made him respond to touches and movement like no other woman had done before. As he both listened to and felt her body rhythm change, he matched her move for move. By the time both of them came, Quincy and Elena were certain of one thing: Regardless of how long it had taken, they both knew the very thing that they had been hoping and looking for had been finally found. The two of them basked in the peace of knowing they were home.

30

Quincy awoke just before 6:00 and found himself alone in Elena's bed. For the first time in what felt like forever, Quincy had really slept. As he sat up, he saw something on the nearby coffee table that caught his eye. There, propped against a stack of magazines, was a beautiful sketch of Quincy sleeping. The pencil print was detailed, and made him feel that Elena had channeled him more than merely captured his image. He was floored by her obvious talent. In the lower right-hand corner of the sketch, Elena had signed the words "Force Majeure." Quincy looked over to where he last remembered seeing his clothes and reached for them. As he got dressed and exited the front door and got in his car, there was no doubt in his mind where he would find her.

Just as the sun broke the horizon, Quincy approached and sat next to Elena on their favorite bench. As she placed her hand in his, she continued looking straight ahead at the water. Quincy noticed that her eyes were red and that she had obviously been crying. As hard as it was for him, he thought it was better to wait and let her volunteer information instead of trying to solicit it. After a while, she finally spoke.

"Do you remember what I was doing the first time you saw me here?"

"Of course I do. You were right over there and you were meditating," he said.

"I was thinking about my son and how after he died, nothing else mattered to me."

She wanted to tell Quincy that she had been trying unsuccessfully to pray. Every day was harder and all she could do was keep hoping and waiting for God to teach her what to say to lessen the pain. She wasn't meditating, she was begging God to send her a reason to keep living. No matter how she presented herself to others, deep down her faith was running out. She was slowly growing bitter that she might never know the whys or whens of fate. She tried and failed to convince herself to believe that faith was the unconditional acceptance of the answers God didn't give us more than the ones He did. She had cried earlier for a couple of reasons. She cried for her father and the possibility of losing him. She also cried because of God's deaf ear toward her.

Quincy held her hand and was quiet for a while.

"I know things haven't been great between you and your father, but let me ask you a question," Quincy said.

"What's that?" Elena asked.

"Do you love him?" he asked her.

"What kind of question is that?"

"A simple one," he said.

"At this point I don't know if anything about my relationship with my father qualifies as simple," she quietly responded.

"Either you love him or you don't," he said.

"My issues with my father have more to do with forgiveness than love."

"Is there really a difference between the two? You remind me of my brother. I'm definitely no expert on the whole God thing, but isn't forgiveness supposed to be what He's all about?"

"You don't have a child. I don't think you can ever really understand," she said.

"Maybe not but…"

"When you lose a child, there are no 'buts.' There's not a damn thing you can say to even begin to understand what that feels like."

"You're right, but I do understand what it's like to have the one person in the world that you depend on the most for protection to allow you to be hurt. Nothing that you or Alberto said indicates that your father knew what was happening. I know that regardless, you still feel that he let you and Joaquin down."

"Because he did," she shot back.

"And I'm not making light of that."

"Good, because some things aren't as easy to forgive," she responded.

Quincy quickly snapped back.

"Whoever said forgiving was supposed to be easy? At the end

of the day, it's all about choice. I had to choose to forgive my mother and at some point you're gonna have to choose to forgive your father and whoever else it is that you're really mad at."

Both of them had been a bit more forceful in their responses than they had intended to be. As she tried to listen to and hear him objectively, she realized that he was trying to get her to focus more on her self-preservation than the emotional preoccupation of past transgressions. Even though she wasn't fully prepared to accept all of his observations and opinions, she welcomed the fact that ultimately everything he said came from a place of love.

Minutes after he stopped speaking, Elena leaned on him and looked at the water. On the nearby bank they both saw the wounded crane that Quincy had named Forrest. It hadn't moved too far from the spot they had last seen it in. For the most part, it seemed to be making itself as comfortable as possible under the circumstances. It would periodically attempt to take flight, but each time, the compromised wing would pull it back down to earth. Quincy knew the bird wouldn't make it. He was surprised that it had lived as long as it did. In his opinion, it was just a matter of time. What Elena romanticized as hope and fate, Quincy simply saw as just another random inevitability.

31

Even though Quincy came into the building happy, by the time he made it up to the conference room there was a foreboding feeling that something bad was going to happen. Quincy discreetly pulled Phee aside and made sure he was fine after last night's visit from his brother. They both agreed that after this case, a boy's night out would definitely be in order.

Quincy, Maclin and Phee spent the better part of the morning uncovering the details of Reverend Bell's double life. Maclin had called DC and had them do an aggressive search on any money trails that could be connected to the dead preacher. Her contact was able to track down money ties to dummy corporations and a hidden account in the Cayman Islands. Quincy and Phee were able to track down the houses, cars and several mistresses. The thing that kept bothering Quincy was how the killer knew his way around the security of each location, as well as knowing when the victims were alone and most vulnerable. As they reviewed the clandestine nature of the victim's offenses, Quincy was now certain that the killer had to have had some type of thorough exposure to them in his selection process. The three of them drove to the respective churches of the victims and presented the partial description that they had of the killer. Even though uniformed cops had already asked if anyone fitting the suspect's description had been a member or visitor, the team still felt it was worth an even more detailed try. They inspected the security systems and interviewed anyone who had access to them. They even played a hunch and interviewed the various security monitoring companies and came up short.

Maclin tried to make any connection she could between the most recent cases and the thirty-six she had investigated for the last ten years. At Reverend Bell's church they finally caught a break. An administrator at the church vaguely remembered somebody fitting the description, having sold the church new Bibles almost a year ago. It didn't take them long after that to track down the name of the church supply distributor headquartered in San Francisco. Two minutes into the conversation they had a name. Abraham Deggler.

Back at the office they pulled up everything that they could on Deggler. In a cross-reference to the earlier murders, the name Everett Deggler came up as the identification of the twelfth victim. They reviewed the father's file and discovered that the murders had started on his birthday, and that he was the only victim to have suffered a combination of Biblical tortures. He was boiled, cruci-fied and beheaded.

The press ran the younger Deggler's photo nonstop. Hotlines were established in a very short time and calls started coming in immediately. Of course they knew that the first wave of calls would inevitably be everything from the nut jobs to the paranoid old woman who just saw the killer having tea with Lee Harvey Oswald. But eventually something concrete would come of it.

There were two potential downsides to going public with the killer's identification. One was that the publicity would drive him so far underground that he would disappear for who knows how long. The other was that his exposure would send him into a tailspin. He might decide to accelerate his spree and go out in a blaze of glory. Unfortunately there wasn't much to do now but wait. To channel their collective energy, the detectives and agent decided to still go back to the holistic facility uptown to discover who T. Smith was.

32

S hortly after Deggler butchered his father, God commanded him to slay and deliver a total of forty-eight souls of the "wicked righteous." He had come this far and gotten this close and, cancer or no cancer, he wouldn't leave this earth until he had obeyed his Lord. Deggler often wondered if it was a test of God or the steroids that had caused the cancer. He was diagnosed a year ago, but it wasn't until six months ago that his body had started failing. Chemotherapy and aggressive radiation wasn't an option for him. He couldn't risk the debilitating side effects compromising his mission. He had done extensive research on alternative cancer treatment and came across the concept of heavy metal poisoning. For his particular type of cancer, HMP was a long shot for long-term survival, but his only concern was that it kept him strong enough to complete his duty to God. Nothing else mattered. He could deal with the tumor in his head and the excruciating pain and suffering that went along with it. He could ultimately even deal with his inevitable demise. Dying was nothing for him to be afraid of because, unlike most people, he believed that God's greatest reward was in death and not in life. He believed this because the Bible told him so.

He chose the unlicensed facility on 117th Street after three weeks of searching for a place that would allow him to receive his treatments with no questions or records of his existence. He needed to be at a place where his anonymity was in the interests of both parties. After surveilling the owner of the facility, Deggler discovered that Horace Pine was also using his facility to sell large quantities of marijuana. He had found the right place. As long as he had something over the owner, his privacy would be protected.

The immediate effectiveness of his sessions lasted about a week. Unlike chemo, he felt rejuvenated and strong afterward, possibly because he was still cycling steroids. Tonight's final session would have to last until he was done. He just needed another week or so. Now that the cops had identified him, he was forced to speed things up even faster than the cancer had prompted him to. As much as he had followed the same ritual and patterns for thirty years, he now had no choice but to kill as many as he could, as fast as he could to finish the Lord's masterpiece.

33

Father Montrelle was a whoremonger. Father Conner was a pedophile. Pastor Higgins was a charlatan. Reverend Bell was a thief and adulterer. Quincy stood in front of Maclin, Phee and the four other detectives and detailed as much as he could about the nature of the victims' offenses. They each died in one way or another being reminded of their sins. Father Montrelle died in a whorehouse. The last thing Father Conner saw were the innocent cherubs that were painted on the dome of his office. Likewise, Higgins's final image was a reminder of his neglect and abuse of God's house. Reverend Bell was tied and dragged to death by the personification of his excesses. A night guard who worked a sleazy hotel that Montrelle frequented with his whores confirmed the priest's activities after seeing his photo on TV. Quincy told the team that he had gotten his info on Father Conner from the mother of one of his victims, which wasn't altogether a lie. They now clearly had Deggler's motivation, which made his overall MO that much clearer to them. The progress that Maclin and the detectives made had given her more info on Deggler than she ever had. Agent Willington's progress had cost him his life. If Maclin got things her way, Deggler wouldn't live to see the next week.

"I just got off the phone with DC. Deggler has one surviving older half brother living in Florida. He changed his name to Noah Holloway the year before their father died. TSA. said he flew from Miami to New York a week ago. Nobody has seen or heard from him since. And get a load of this. He became an ordained minister in '08," Maclin announced.

"Maybe that explains what my brother was talking about. Deggler's whole spiritual evolution thing," Quincy said.

"You mean that his brother is some kind of spiritual mentor to him?" Phee asked.

"Makes sense, doesn't it? He might not be physically helping him with the actual killings, but he could be teaching him about the Biblical semantics," Quincy said.

"I agree with Quincy. Can't be a coincidence that Deggler's brother comes to New York a couple of days before the killings start. At the very least, we should run his picture as a person of interest," Phee said.

"Definitely. I'll also ask the local feds in Florida to pull up more information on him," Maclin added as she pulled out her phone and made a call.

Quincy went back to work on one of the many files on his

desk. He wasn't looking for it, but he stumbled upon it nonetheless. As he checked the work histories of all the victims, he saw the name of his own abuser in Father Conner's file. Father Seamus Burns. Evidently it was Conner who oversaw the placement of young priests in the area where Quincy grew up. It was Conner who had assigned Burns his original post at Quincy's church and, subsequently, it was Conner who reassigned Burns to another church after internal whispers of his inappropriate behavior started surfacing. Quincy had tried the majority of his life to avoid speaking the name of his abuser. His surprise discovery caught him completely off guard. The case itself had already dug up the most painful memories for Quincy, but somehow just literally seeing the priest's name was like a punch to the gut. He was momentarily winded and vulnerable. As all victims do, he lived with the constant possibility that the slightest or most innocuous event could at a moment's notice floor him. He was in no position to be distracted or compromised. This case had come to represent so many tangible and intangible things to Quincy. He hadn't admitted it to himself but it was still true that on the most primal level, this case would either liberate him of his demons or destroy him in the process. His reaction to the current blow made him more insecure about the latter occurring. He looked at the clock, grabbed his coat and told Maclin that he was going to grab something to eat. Phee took the hint that he wasn't invited. Like any marriage, good partners read the unspoken language as well—if not better than—the spoken words.

Quincy went straight to the hospital to find Elena. It was the first time in his life that he had someone who lifted his spirits and improved his moods the way she did. Most women in his past had only managed to have a temporary effect on him. Physical, carnal, intellectual, and maybe even the rare instance of infatuation. But none ever filled the voids.

However distorted his concept of love may have been, he always felt that there had to be more than what the women in his life had thus far offered him. He believed there was more, and as a result, he had waited and hoped for the arrival of such. The irony was that the baggage of his childhood had rendered him aloof and removed to the type of love that could have helped him most. In addition to the actual abuse, his own mother's shortcomings had made him unfairly exacting of women, holding them to an impossible standard. Of the many demands he made of a woman's love, the first and foremost was that she elevate him. Elena was the only one who left him feeling that way. Whereas his mother's neglect had left him feeling small and inconsequential, Elena made him feel confident and important. To her he was both needed and necessary. Most of all, Elena made him feel unconditionally loved.

When he walked into her father's hospital room, he found her napping on a two-seater in the corner. He quietly sat beside her and watched her sleep. He could tell she was dreaming from the REM that occurred beneath her eyelids. Even closed, he easily remembered her eyes in great detail. He loved her face in general, every delicate feature and varied expression, but from day one, it was her eyes that undid him. As he watched her peacefully sleeping, he thought of the many things her arrival in his life had taught him.

Since meeting her, he accepted greater knowledge of himself. He accepted that she had taught him invaluable lessons about who he thought he was and who he actually was. She taught him possibilities of things he had long conceded. She showed him capabilities that were left dormant beneath the image of himself that he had incorrectly accepted. And although he had struggled with it most of his life, she made feeling easy to him. She made it natural, and even necessary, for him to do so. Of the various ways he felt dead inside, the arrival of this unexpected woman in his life presented a very new and different outlook on life.

Elena had fallen asleep in her father's room not from fatigue but because at times it was her best defense against an overactive mind. When she awoke, she had forgotten where she was. In the short time that she was asleep, she had dreamed of Quincy twice, maybe three times. Lately her dreams were brighter and richer in tone. As Elena opened her eyes, she found herself leaning on Quincy's shoulder. She smiled at him as she sat up straight.

"How long was I asleep?" she asked.

"I don't know. You were knocked out when I got here. I didn't wanna wake you. How's your father?"

"The swelling in the brain still hasn't gone down. They won't really know anything until that happens."

"I'm sorry to hear that. How are you holding up?"

"It's just weird. One minute a person is fine, and then the next they're…" She trailed off.

She had no idea how much he understood what she was trying to say. In his line of work, he saw too often how death and tragedy often came as the most painful of unexpected intrusions. As he pulled her closer, he played with her hands and made her smile. Even though he couldn't stay long, the moment he saw her smile he realized that alone was worth the trip. As he looked at her eyes, he had forgotten his initial reason for needing to leave his office and come see her.

Phee used his lunch break to do what he had been putting off. He drove up to the 3-4 and made his way upstairs to the homicide department. A lot of cops in the city either knew Phee or knew of him. He and Quincy had broken more than their fair share of high profile cases and had developed a decent legion of both fans and haters. In addition to the notoriety he had achieved as a cop, his earlier success in the NFL had garnered him a different level of respect automatically. Many New Yorkers followed him through his college playing days. He came to the force as a preexisting celebrity of sorts. The brass and the much older cops gave him "lotsa dap" simply because of who his father was. Their respect may have initially been handed to him, but over the years he had more than earned it for himself.

Phee talked to a detective by the name of Alex Gamba about his brother's missing friend. "Did you catch a case on a missing T-walker the other day? I think the name was Shay DeVane," Phee asked.

"Yeah. Freak came in here hysterical talking 'bout how he thought somebody had killed his friend."

"Did you look into it? I'm just asking because it might somehow be connected to the case I'm working," Phee lied.

It was a lie that served a dual purpose. First, it removed any appearance of him being personally interested or of him having a direct connection to the *freak* that made the complaint. Second, it allowed Phee the right to confront the detective without offending him. Questioning a fellow cop's thoroughness on one of their cases was ranked up there with spitting in their face or insulting their mother.

"There wasn't a whole lot to look into. We ran the name, found out he moved around from city to city. Had a couple of priors and an outstanding warrant here for solicitation. Looks like he just bounced to stay out of jail," Gamba told him.

"Was there some kind of phone call?" Phee pressed.

"Supposedly. No way to really confirm what was or wasn't said. As far as I'm concerned, the two freaks could have had a lovers' spat. One bolted; the other's trying to track it down. Happens all the time with them."

Phee had rarely put a name to his brother's lifestyle because he had very rarely discussed AJ with anyone. As he talked to Detective Gamba, he became uncomfortably aware of the references his fellow cop bandied about because he realized he had similarly denigrated the likes of his brother. He was most aware of the detective referring to another human being as "it."

————

Maclin sat in a small, half-empty restaurant a block from the station. She sat at a table with a setting for three. Before she left the station she asked a uniform to recommend the best Greek spot in the neighborhood. The irony was that ultimately it made no difference how good the food was or wasn't, because she never cared much for Greek cuisine. Over the years she had tried it several different times in several different cities, but as hard as she tried, she never quite acquired a taste for it. But once a year on this date, no matter where she was, she performed the same ritual that she had started nine years ago. As Maclin sat in the Greek restaurant at a table set for three, she chased small cubes of fresh feta cheese and tart black olives with a robust Bordeaux.

Today was the ten-year anniversary of Agent Willington's murder. She had started this routine the first year after his death. Considering how much he loved Greek food, she thought it only befitting to memorialize him this way. His favorite dishes were paidakia (grilled lamb chops with lemon and oregano). Or moussaka (minced meat with sautéed eggplant and tomato, topped with béchamel sauce). And of course his weakness was baklava (phyllo pastry layers filled with nuts and drenched in syrup). Maclin liked the baklava, and periodically the yogurt and honey, but not much else. But it made no difference because this wasn't about what she liked or disliked. It was about honoring Willington in a way that he would have laughed at and appreciated her doing. As the waiter brought the food for three, he looked at her as oddly as he had done when she first placed her order. He was certain that he heard her talking to herself as he stood nearby and watched her toast her invisible lunch companions. As she drank the wine, Maclin laughed openly as if she were entertaining others. She drank to the memory of the only man she ever loved. And she drank to the child that would have been nine years old now. After a moment or so, she nibbled on the baklava and looked at her watch. She had to get back to the office and the mountain of work that awaited her. As she looked out the window at the darkening skies, she thought about the morning's forecast and how the weatherman was right for a change. A storm was definitely coming.

34

Deggler's brother Noah hated New York. To him the big city was nothing but a Godforsaken, updated version of Sodom and Gomorrah. He understood why his brother had chosen to come here. The wicked ran rampant and sin was ever present. Though Noah and Deggler had shared the same abusive father, Noah was the fortunate one. He and his mother had escaped the toxic marriage three years before his father found another wife with even less self-esteem. Growing up, Noah knew things about Deggler that no one else did. He had both lived and witnessed the personal hell that his younger brother had endured. For the better part of his life, Noah had often fantasized about saving his little brother in some dramatic fashion. His inability to ever bring those fantasies to fruition had long left him with a deep-seated sense of guilt and failure. Regardless of the crimes that Deggler had committed, Noah needed to prove to him that he was not an animal and that there was someone in the world who loved him unconditionally. Someone who would help him and be there for him.

As Noah rounded the corner with a few groceries from the tiny bodega, he saw three cop cars parked in front of his hotel. As Quincy, Phee and Maclin pulled up and jumped out of the car and headed into the hotel lobby, Noah lowered his baseball cap, crossed the street and headed in the opposite direction.

The hotel manager had called the cops after recognizing Noah's picture on a morning news program as a person of interest. Noah's hotel room was small but clean. The team found a couple of Bibles and several newspaper clippings of not just the most recent murders, but the first thirty-six killings as well. They were all neatly posted in three photo albums that Noah had hidden under his mattress. There was a red-lined map of the New York crime scenes and the churches that the victims worked at.

"Were your people able to dig up any more information on him?" Quincy asked as he thumbed through one of the photo albums.

"Everything they have on him indicates that he is a model citizen. People at his church can't say enough good things about him. Aside from his relationship with Deggler, there's nothing in his past or present to indicate that he would be tied to something like this," Maclin responded.

"Yeah well, I think all of these photo albums might suggest otherwise," Phee stated.

"So what now?" Quincy asked.

"I think if we find one, we find the other. Deggler's brother is no longer just a person of interest," Maclin said as they headed toward the exit.

Just as they crossed to the car they each felt the first drops of rain under the darkening skies. The hard rains were coming, and with them a type of storm New York hadn't seen in a while.

35

The first major storm of the season came into the city quickly and with ferocity. It had started down south and worked its way up to New Jersey, New York and Connecticut. Heavy rain and gale force winds. The rain pelted relentlessly on the car that Quincy, Maclin and Phee sat in on 117th Street. Maclin sat in the driver's seat while Phee rode shotgun and Quincy sat in the back. They had arrived at 7:20 in anticipation of T. Smith's 8 o'clock appointment. During the drive uptown, Quincy had managed to send off a couple of texts to check on Elena and her father's status. Despite how busy he was, he wanted her to know that she was still on his mind. Quincy hated not being there in person for Elena. He hated that she had to face this alone. He hated most the reason why he couldn't be there.

The rain seemed to come down even harder than it had just

a few minutes ago. Quincy glanced at the dashboard clock which read 7:33 p.m. Looking across the street, he saw the silhouette of a large man calmly walking down the street in the downpour. He tapped Phee's shoulder and pointed in the man's direction. They had parked at a hydrant about thirty yards from the facility. They didn't want to draw attention to themselves by double-parking closer. On the opposite side of the street, the figure continued walking in their direction. Quincy and Phee both checked the clips of their guns. As the man reached the walkway of the building, he slowed for a beat but then continued, walking past it. Quincy wasn't sure whether or not it was their suspect who had somehow gotten spooked or if it was just another crazy New Yorker walking in the rain. The two cops exited the car and crossed the street after him. Just as they got within thirty feet of the man, he suddenly bolted down the street. Quincy immediately identified themselves as cops as he and Phee took off in pursuit. Maclin threw the car in reverse and sped down the one-way street backward. Quincy couldn't keep up with Phee. Fortunately Phee's body hadn't gotten the memo that he was no longer in the NFL. Phee ran fast. Quincy ran smart. Phee chased the suspect down 117th Street while Quincy took a nearby alley in an effort to cut them off.

Abraham Deggler moved very well for his size. His adrenaline compensated for the need of treatment that he had been feeling lately. As he heard the footsteps behind him getting closer, he ducked into an Irish pub and headed straight back toward the kitchen. When Phee entered shortly afterward, Deggler bullrushed him from his blind side, causing his gun to slide underneath the nearby refrigerator. As Deggler moved toward the exit, Phee tackled him just before he reached the back door. He had taken down many men before, but few this big.

Deggler turned over and kicked Phee as nervous workers ran to the front of the bar. Phee held his own for the first few minutes of the fight, but it eventually became apparent that he was no match for his oversized opponent. Deggler lifted Phee up and body slammed him into the refrigerator, dislocating the cop's left shoulder. As Phee yelled out in pain, Deggler punched him twice and then threw him through a glass partition. Deggler exited the alley fifty yards behind Quincy and ran in the opposite direction. Quincy fired a warning shot and then took off after him.

Deggler pulled out his own gun, half turned and fired three shots back at Quincy. Quincy returned fire as he gave chase for a few blocks before losing a visual on Deggler in the pouring rain. After catching a glimpse of a figure crossing Broadway, Quincy turned and quickly headed toward the intersection. Once he saw the figure was in fact Deggler, he raised his gun but was clipped by an oncoming car. As Quincy was knocked to the ground and disoriented, Deggler stopped and turned back in Quincy's direction. Quincy looked up to see Deggler crossing the street, heading toward him with his gun raised. Quincy's own gun had fallen too far from him to recover it in time.

Deggler cocked back the trigger just before hearing a car accelerating toward him. He turned just in time to see Maclin plowing into him with the front of her car. As the big man was thrown eight feet, an oncoming truck swerved to miss him and broadsided

Maclin in the process, knocking her unconscious. Quincy scrambled to his gun and crossed to the spot that Deggler had gone down but discovered instead that the killer had disappeared.

36

As Quincy entered Maclin's hospital room, he saw her talking with two fellow feds. The primary man was tall, serious and a bit too metrosexual for Quincy's taste. Quincy could tell from the energy in the room that he had walked in at an inopportune time. Maclin was clearly upset but tried her best to hide it from Quincy.

"How do you feel?" Quincy asked.

"Like I was hit by a Mack truck. Which is funny because, come to think of it, I was hit by a Mack truck. Detective Cavanaugh, these are Special Agents Michaelson and Nguyen."

One of Quincy's pet peeves was a man with a weak handshake. Michaelson lost him at hello.

"So I was just telling Agent Maclin that Agent Nguyen here from our New York office will be overseeing the investigation from this point on. You'll be reporting to him," the man said.

"I'm sure Agent Nguyen here is a competent agent and all-around wonderful human being, but reassigning the point person at this stage does nothing but compromise the investigation. Why would we replace Maclin when the doctor said she was free to check out in the morning?" Quincy responded.

"It's not Agent Maclin's physical state that I'm most concerned with at this time," Michaelson said.

"What is that supposed to mean Terry?" Maclin chimed in.

"You know exactly what it means. You came to New York pretending to be on vacation. You had no permission or authority from the Bureau to pursue this investigation. We've told you this for years; you're too subjective. Your personal involvement is clouding your judgment," Michaelson snapped back.

"There wouldn't be a Bureau investigation if it wasn't for my judgment. I was the one who called to tell you that he was here in New York," Maclin said angrily.

"Look, I don't know the protocol here, but I do know that two weeks ago Agent Maclin called our department and said that based on analysis and profile, she felt she had credible evidence that a serial killer would target victims in New York. Our department reviewed her claims and after assessing the validity of those claims we asked if she would be so kind as to come to New York and help us as best she could. She arrived here two days before the first killing and has been the primary reason for identifying the suspect and nearly apprehending him."

"You don't..." Michaelson attempted to interrupt.

"Let me finish," Quincy cut him off. "Before you and I get

into a cock-dropping contest, and I tell you that I will go to Bloomberg and the press and tell them that the Bureau ignored credible evidence from one of their own agents, I'm gonna try just asking you man-to-man to let her do her job so that I can continue to do mine."

Michaelson stared at Quincy for several seconds, and then turned with Agent Nguyen in tow and headed toward the door.

"If you don't bring him down in two days, I'll make sure both of you are off this investigation," Michaelson threw over his shoulder as he exited.

Besides her brothers and Willington, Maclin had never had anyone stand up for her with such conviction. The men that she worked with were either threatened by or in constant competition with her. Michaelson was a classic study of both. Even though he was above her in title, he could tell she never respected him much. Maclin had a way of nonverbally letting men know which of them she thought were frauds. Her intelligence and skill set had a way of exposing the incompetents that had managed to successively fail upward. If Maclin was in fact the person responsible for stopping Deggler, it would only be a matter of time before Michaelson was reporting to her.

Maclin was appreciative and impressed with how Quincy handled Michaelson because, if the situation had somehow been reversed, she would have gladly done the same for him or Detective Freeman.

"You're an impressive liar Detective Cavanaugh," she said smiling.

"I'm Irish and Italian. It's a talent that comes as a birthright."

"How did you know I was here two days before the first murder?"

"The Amtrak tag was dated on your bag, which I saw when I helped you at the hotel."

"Always in detective mode, huh? I wish I had contacted you in advance, but when you've been doubted and dismissed as much as I have over the last ten years, you start assuming that you're in every fight by yourself."

"New York is tough, but at least around here we watch each other's back. So how did you know that he would surface in New York?"

"He's done San Francisco, Chicago and Boston. New York was just the next logical choice for a big city of decadence."

"Not bad. By the way, thanks for the save earlier."

"I wasn't about to let you break up the band that easily. Not when we're just beginning to find our rhythm. How's Detective Freeman?" she asked.

"Phee's good. He's waiting downstairs. He doesn't do the hospital thing. Freaks him out. I told him you were fine."

Although he never lingered, Maclin knew that Quincy had glanced, however imperceptibly, at her now bare arms and saw the scars on her wrist much more clearly. The night's events had left her feeling that she no longer needed to cover up or be defensive in his presence. As she looked down at her own arms, she made a decision.

"Listen Quincy, there's something I need to tell you."

"No you don't. You're a good agent and I'm glad to be working with you. In my book, that's really all that matters."

Maclin had been in love once. Just once. It was with her former partner and fellow agent Edgar Willington, who had taken her under his wing and become a mentor to her. The two of them were working the Martyr's Murders case ten years ago in Boston the day she went to the doctor and found out she was pregnant. That same morning, Willington had gone to check on a possible lead in the case. His body was found later that night in an alley off Boylston Street. He had been beaten to death.

Maclin miscarried a week later after trying to take her own life. Throughout the whole ordeal Maclin never once cried. Not at the news of Willington's death or the ensuing list of tragic events that followed. She had never verbalized it or even put a name to it, but something in Maclin definitely died the day that Willington was taken from her. Although the Bureau never classified it as such, she knew in her heart that it was the Martyr Maker.

———————————

By the time Quincy made it to Elena's, he was exhausted. He had surprised her with a nice bottle of pinot noir. They drank and talked until 2:00 in the morning. He made a conscious choice to talk about everything but work. He selfishly needed separation of his two worlds. The uglier the case got, the more he felt the need to protect whatever existed between them from his job. The irony and hypocrisy of his decision was that it was the horrors of his world that had introduced them in the first place. Elena thought it was fate. He knew better.

When he made love to her, it was different from the night before. He did so with the knowledge that he had almost died earlier. It certainly wasn't the first time Quincy had faced possible death, but it was the first time he felt that aside from Liam and Phee, his death would have had a great impact on someone else. He had never considered that the act of falling in love brought with it responsibilities. Earlier Phee had told Quincy about the conversation between him and his brother. The thing that had stood out to Quincy most was when Phee said that AJ felt he didn't matter. Maybe to a lesser degree, and for different reasons, Quincy had experienced similar feelings throughout a large part of his life. The emotional residue from his childhood had prevented him from establishing any meaningful bonds with people other than his brother and partner. He'd had plenty of opportunity but very little success. Up until this point, the women in his life had functioned more as maintenance and recreation than any type of real necessity. They got him through. Through the loneliness, the boredom, the sleeplessness.

Elena had him reexamining things. She left him feeling lifted. Unlike what Phee's brother AJ had felt, Elena left Quincy feeling like he mattered.

37

Phee actually drove to Connecticut in the pouring rain. His shoulder was still sore as hell, but he had learned to function with much worse. The weather was bad enough; fortunately there wasn't much traffic. He got to his father's house shortly after midnight and decided that he would have to leave by six to make it back to work an hour later. His father was still up reading when he arrived. Phee chose not to discuss his brother's visit, and Clay pretended not to know that something was bothering his son. As they sat in Clay's office and drank 200-year-old scotch, they both lied to each other, more by what they didn't say than what they did.

38

Maclin left the hospital at 6:00 in the morning. She didn't officially check out, she just left. Her body was sore all over, but there was nothing that was going to keep her from this case. They were definitely close. She had no idea at the time just how close Willington had gotten. She just needed Deggler to remain committed to what he had started. Now that they had gotten close, there was a big risk of him disappearing. It left her feeling guilty but she needed him to be the psychopath that showed no fear or comprehension of danger. She needed him to be single-minded and impervious to the fact that she and the cops were getting closer. She needed his feelings of invincibility to buy her more time. She was fully aware of the risks. If he stayed in New York, there would be more killings. As conflicted as it left her feeling, she was ready to sell her soul to get him to stay.

Quincy picked her up at the hospital and, as he had done before, dropped her at her hotel so that she could shower and change. They were at the station by seven along with Phee. Each of the three had their own physical reminder of their encounter with Deggler. There was a fax waiting for them from Deggler's company listing every church that he had sold supplies to over his last four years in New York. They divided up the list and quickly confirmed that the three victims' churches had ordered supplies from Deggler. As Phee perused his list, he came across something that clearly disturbed him.

"Quincy, there's something you need to see," he said.

Quincy took the sheet of paper and felt his heart drop as he saw the name of his brother's church on the list.

"We ordered a few robes and books six months ago. My secretary was the only one to deal with him the one time he came here, so maybe you should be talking to her instead," Liam told his brother.

Quincy had come here alone. He needed to talk to Liam as much as a brother as he did as a cop. He needed him to feel free to tell him anything. Anything. Quincy also needed to be able to tell Liam things that, as a cop, he shouldn't. Liam knew all that they were up against. Even beyond his visit to the precinct earlier, he had his own reasons to follow the case as closely as possible. He had either known personally or known of each of the victims. Naturally there had been several phone calls and emails from those in his circle who passionately offered their own theories and speculation.

The Church community as a whole was terrified. Nothing fueled chatter and gossip like proximity. Most crimes were at least two to three degrees removed from the average Joe. The news was always about "someone else." Not only had this struck close to home, but it had done so with such viciousness and depravity that it had left even the most devout nervous and afraid.

"You said that there were over forty churches on your list. Doesn't mean he's targeting me specifically," Liam said.

"And it doesn't mean he's not," Quincy warned.

"Why don't you ask me what you came here to ask me, Quincy?"

"We're pretty certain that he's profiled every Church leader on the list. More than likely he has hacked into your computer and is even using your own security system to spy on you. He learns things about his victims that nobody else knows. Based on how he's targeting his victims, do I have any extra reason to be concerned about you?" Quincy asked uncomfortably.

"Are you asking me if I've sinned in the last six months? Of course I have. We all sin every day."

"That's not what I meant, I just…"

"I can't believe you come here questioning me like this."

"I know this is weird, Liam, but I'm just trying to protect you and everyone else from this maniac."

"I'm not just everyone else. I'm your brother!!! What are you asking me? Whether or not I've committed some egregious act that would make your killer add me to his list? The answer is no. Okay?"

"Sorry, but I had to ask," Quincy said apologetically.

Liam softened after seeing how uncomfortable Quincy was.

"Look, I'm…I've got a lot going on here at the church, not to mention everybody around me completely freaking out with all these killings. I know you're just doing your job. If there is one thing that this case is teaching everybody, it's that no matter how well you think you know somebody, you really don't."

Quincy knew his brother was right. Only a couple of days ago he had sat across from one of the victims and seriously contemplated cold-blooded murder himself. Who was he to question Liam or anyone else for that matter on the subject of moral corruptibility? No matter how much he had tried to avoid any comparison, Quincy knew that, fundamentally speaking, he and Deggler shared the same primal DNA. Quincy tried his best not to show his fear.

"Even though you don't have anything to worry about, I still need you to be careful. Make sure as much as possible that somebody is always with you," Quincy said.

He was scared for Liam and everyone else on the list. Even though there was no way to offer 24-hour protection to them all, the thought of just waiting around for Deggler to strike again was horrible. But the dark irony of it all was that as long as Deggler stayed in New York, it was just a matter of time before they caught him.

39

Friendly nurses alternated checking Romero's charts and monitors. Elena actually perked up when one would enter the room because it gave her sporadic moments of engagement. When left alone with her father, all she could do was wait. All she could do was be there. She studied Romero in great detail. The gray hair that had fought and defeated what used to be his shiny, black locks. Elena studied the shape and bone structure of her father's face. She grabbed and rubbed Romero's hands. She thought it funny that such rugged hands had held her gently as a baby. It was these hands that had lifted and balanced her on his lap. As Elena massaged her father's palms, she thought of the many reasons she had to be thankful for these impossibly large hands. Elena started seeing different details in her father.

She felt her cell phone buzzing in her jacket pocket. As she removed the phone and looked at it, she saw that she had a text message waiting for her. She smiled warmly as she read the message.

Just checking on you and your father.

She texted back. The nurses said there weren't any changes. Doctor should be stopping by any minute now to give me updates.

She and Quincy sent messages back and forth, and Elena found her spirits lifted. Even though he wasn't there with her, he managed to make her smile and reminded her to breathe. And though he didn't offer any details about his day, she texted him to do the same.

The minute Dr. Fong walked into the room, Elena knew immediately from the way he greeted her that the news wasn't good. She remembered her breathing as she rose, and both hoped for and feared his candor. He looked her directly in the eye and told her things she didn't want to hear.

"I have to be honest with you. I was hoping that some, if not all of his swelling would have gone down by now," he said.

"So nothing has changed?" Elena asked.

"Unfortunately, no."

"So where does that leave us?"

"The first forty-eight hours are crucial in cases like these. If there's no change by tomorrow night, we could be looking at a host of complications."

Elena opened her mouth to speak, but no sound came out. One of Dr. Fong's many talents was his ability to accurately gauge a person's level of endurance. Because of his directness, a handful of patients over the years had questioned and criticized his bedside manner. It was usually those that needed the truth to be pliant and agreeable. He believed in letting family and loved ones know the honest scope of what they were facing. Unlike most of his colleagues, he believed in the emotional intelligence of people. Most doctors dismissed the notion as oxymoronic gibberish. But when he stood before people like Elena, if they took the time to breathe, he was confident they could handle the truth and make more informed choices.

Dr. Fong did his best to clearly lay out the potential consequences of the persisting swelling. Intracranial bleeding, blindness and/or muteness, an even more devastating stroke, permanent paralysis…the list went on, climaxing in "possible death." If the swelling did not go down on its own, they would have to explore ways of assisting the process. That of course entailed things like partial skull removal and aggressive brain surgery, which could present equally dangerous reactions. Dr. Fong sat with Elena and answered all the questions she could think of. They talked about everything from miracles to worst-case scenarios. Elena in no way deluded herself; everything was riding on what happened between now and tomorrow night. After Dr. Fong left, Elena sat there taking in all that he had presented. She held her father's hand and hoped somehow that Romero had heard the doctor. That he would do his part and fight for his life. Elena held his hand to let him know that this was no time for weakness and fear. More than anything that had preceded this day, the next twenty-four hours would be Romero's defining moments.

40

Brenda Timmons had a weakness for Phee. Every time she saw him, she remembered how he had been the only man who "could take her there." He knew her body like no other. Not only did Phee know her spots, but he was even able to teach her about a few more that she had never considered. They had been fuck buddies back in the early '90s until she broke the unspoken rule of falling in love, deluding herself that she hadn't. Phee could have actually handled the former, but he saw the latter violation as something much more threatening. Of all things that he valued, clarity was at the top of his list. They had somehow survived the '90s with a strong friendship intact. She was an M.I.T. grad who had forgotten more about computer science than the tech-geeks on the police force had ever learned. No one on the force had yet been able to track the computer hacks back to the source. After

Phee had finished visiting the names of churches on his list, he asked Brenda to meet him at the station. The first thing she did when she got there was to talk to the technicians who had already started working on Father Conner's hard drive. She needed to know what approaches they had already tried so that she wouldn't waste any precious time. The three hard drives that belonged to Montrelle, Higgins and Reverend Bell had already been rushed back to DC to see what the feds could come up with. Phee had convinced Maclin to let his friend Brenda have access to at least one computer. Maclin definitely trusted Phee and Quincy's gut call on things, so she allowed Conner's computer to stay at the station with them. The techs were none too pleased to have an outsider second-guessing their work and doing the job that they took pride in doing. Phee made it clear that he had no interest in or empathy for wounded egos or the perception of toes being stepped on. The need to stop Deggler was bigger than everything else.

With Brenda it was never really a question of if she could break a code or crack a hack; it was just a matter of when. The minute she went to work on Conner's hard drive, she saw that she was in for a challenge. Working on computers as long as she had, Brenda had a repertoire of tricks and strategies that usually got her the results she wanted, but now she saw a few things that she had never encountered. A couple of hours into it and the most she had come up with were 20,000 rerouted email addresses that listed China as the point of origin. The hacker had used a sophisticated default program that she had never seen. No matter which avenue she went down or how close she thought she was getting, she eventually was led back to the same place she had started at. The team had pulled transcripts from some night courses Deggler had taken back in the early '80s. The professor who had taught the computer class wrote in Deggler's records that Deggler was the most skilled computer programmer he had ever had the honor of teaching. Phee gave Brenda a copy of the transcript because he wanted her to know what she was up against. If she was at all fazed, she didn't show Phee. She didn't care how good Deggler was. Brenda was determined to prove to him, and everyone else, that she was better.

Quincy, Maclin and Phee reconvened in the conference room and updated each other on their individual status and progress. Unfortunately, they were much longer on status than they were on progress. They had at least forty potential targets but no tangible way of determining which victim would be next. Quincy wanted to confiscate every computer that belonged to anyone on the list, but that was just the frustration talking because there was no way in hell any judge would even consider granting that warrant. Maclin was still sore from the accident, her movement a little slower than before. She had been working on seeing if Deggler had followed any geographical pattern in selecting his victims. When that didn't pan out, she looked at the list and saw something that excited her.

"Oh shit!!!" Maclin stood up and yelled suddenly.

"What is it?" Quincy asked.

"We've been looking at this thing all wrong. We're trying to make sense of old patterns, when we should be focusing more on the new ones. Forget geography, or age, or any other patterns we normally focus on," she said.

Maclin grabbed a marker off the table and crossed to the dry-erase board.

"Then what should we be looking at?" Phee asked.

Maclin wrote on the board as she blurted it out—"denominational patterns!"

"I don't follow," Phee said.

"You remember what Quincy's brother told us about Deggler's spiritual evolution? Deggler's always had the murder part down, but now he's honing the religious implications and aspects of the killings. There's nothing arbitrary in the messages and lessons he's trying to teach. Just the opposite. Since his growth and evolution, it's the first time in thirty years that he's killed two leaders from the same denomination back to back. And just so happens, they're Catholic. The oldest form of Christianity in this country. One of the books Liam recommended reading is called *The Chronology of Religion in America*."

Maclin crossed back to the table and picked up one of the books and opened it. She was getting more and more animated as she laid out her theory.

"Okay, so originally there were seven major forms of Christianity. Orthodox or Coptic, as it was called, hasn't really been practiced in this country for at least 150 years. And it doesn't appear on any of our lists. So now let's look at the remaining six. First there's Catholicism, then Protestantism and its four largest denominations: Lutheran, Presbyterian, Methodist and Baptist faiths. Every other form of Christianity is a byproduct of one of these six. Montrelle and Conner, victims one and two, were

Catholic. Higgins and Bell, victims number three and four, were both Protestant. Deggler's been emulating the torture of the twelve disciples, that part we already know. Now we have six forms of Christianity with two vics per denomination. That makes twelve. My money says that the next victim is gonna be Lutheran."

Her theory was consistent in pattern and made more sense than anything else they had come up with. They certainly couldn't afford not to examine and explore what Maclin had just laid out. On the list of forty-two that showed which churches Deggler had sold supplies to, six were Lutheran. Quincy called the nearest precincts and had them dispatch patrol cars to the possible targets.

Phee and Maclin immediately went to work on the phones calling the Lutheran leaders to make sure they were safe. Fortunately it was close to midnight and they were able to reach all of them at home. All except a Lutheran preacher by the name of Morgan Summers.

41

Quincy and Maclin drove to Summers's house in Park Slope while Phee stayed behind to check on Brenda's progress on the hard drive. Summers's wife was very close to what Quincy had expected her to be: a big breasted, heavily botoxed trophy wife past her prime but still fighting for her glory days. Even at midnight and dressed in a robe and nightgown, she still wore plenty of makeup and her hair was perfectly coiffed. Like her, the brownstone was a bit overdone. Both she and her home could have benefited greatly from the "less is more" approach. As Quincy and Maclin interviewed her, the three children sat quietly in a corner, the two younger ones crying as the oldest child comforted them. Throughout the interview, Clarice Summers kept trying to reach her husband on his cell. Maclin looked at Quincy knowing that Clarice's efforts were in vain. She and Quincy both had much less optimism about Summers's welfare and safety than his wife did.

Clarice told the pair that her husband had left the house around eleven saying that a new member of the church was in the hospital and had requested him to come. Of course when they called the hospital, no such patient had been admitted and no one fitting Summers's description had been there.

Maclin did the bulk of the questioning, but ironically it was Quincy who was able to get Mrs. Summers to open up more. Women often felt more threatened by female cops than men. They sometimes felt that the female cops were much more critical and judgmental of them, so they were more guarded in what they divulged. After she told Quincy that Morgan had been in his office on the computer before he left, Quincy gave Maclin a subtle look and nod, which she took as a cue.

"If you don't mind, ma'am, I'm going to go check on your kids," Maclin said as she moved off to give Quincy and Mrs. Summers more privacy.

"Mrs. Summers, do you have the password to your husband's emails?" Quincy asked.

"No, I never asked for it, and he never gave it to me," she responded.

"I understand that, ma'am, but my question is do you have the password, nonetheless?"

"I'm not sure what you're implying detective, but…"

"Mrs. Summers, I'm not implying anything. I'm asking directly if you can access your husband's account so that you can help us to possibly save his life?"

Quincy saw the conflict in her face and knew that she had the information he needed.

"There's something you need to understand about my husband, Detective Cavanaugh. He's a very complicated man. People take from him all the time. Sometimes he feels he needs to be the one doing the taking," she said.

"I understand that, ma'am. I'm not looking to judge or embarrass him. My only concern is stopping the man who I believe has abducted your husband."

Clarice led Quincy to the office and signed on to her husband's email account. She turned her back to Quincy and the computer, knowing what he would find. Quincy pulled up Morgan Summers's online history and focused on the emails and site visits of that night. He found the chat room and wrote down the information of a suggested rendezvous. As Quincy rushed out, Clarice continued to face the corner and refused to look at or otherwise acknowledge him.

Quincy and Maclin made it to the bar by 12:15 and found the engine of Summers's Mercedes still warm, even in the rain. His cell phone was turned off as it lay on the floor on the passenger side. They found drops of blood on the driver's seat. In that moment, they both simultaneously reached the same conclusion. And that was, if Summers hadn't already been killed, he was soon to face a painful and horrible death. One that could have possibly been avoided if only they had shown up fifteen minutes earlier.

42

Thousands and thousands of Bible pages and small wooden crosses completely covered every square inch of wall in Deggler's apartment. On the ceiling, written in bold red, there was even the English translation of the *Ninety-Nine Names of Allah*. References to God in all languages were integrated in various ways throughout the entire space. Most rooms began with the Book of Genesis and ended with the Book of Revelation. Each page was meticulously and chronologically pasted to a surface. Passages were highlighted in different colors by subject matter and specific verse. There was little to no furniture. Just the bare essentials. The closest thing to an exception was the row of twenty-one video monitors on a long table in what was assumed to be the living room. There were three computers and other electronics in the same room. Aside from these components, every other item in the apartment was of some religious significance. Deggler's apartment was a place of worship, not comfort or indulgence.

Deggler had work to do. He couldn't afford to be careless or distracted in any way because it was just a matter of time before either the cops caught him or the fire in his head killed or at least incapacitated him. The accident had left him battered and bruised, but he managed to use the pain as a form of both physical and mental stimulation. He stood naked in front of the full-length mirror in his bathroom and tended to his wounds. He had shaved his head completely bald, along with the rest of his body. His smooth, hairless skin exposed a four-inch, keloidal scar which occupied the area where his penis had once been. His back was a mass of old scars and cuts from years of self-flogging. Deggler had the first line of every passage in the Book of Revelation minutely tattooed to every inch of his body except his hands, neck and face.

Around 8 o'clock, he lowered himself into a bathtub filled with ice. Somehow he found the freezing water therapeutic and relaxing. The pain in his head left him cringing for peace and stability. He chose to do the one pleasurable thing that he could that helped distract him from his pain. He reached over and opened the little black box that he kept on the edge of the tub. Deggler was a cutter from the time he was nine. His current tool of choice was a stainless steel straight razor with an acid etched handle. He cut himself on average once a month to make sure that he had time to heal properly. His preference was three cuts across his chest, stomach or thighs. The thin sharp blade felt good against his skin and seeing his own blood was a powerful purging for him. As his blood clouded his bath water, Deggler closed his eyes and became more at peace. He was no longer angry with himself for almost killing the cop the night before. He had forgiven them, because like him, they were only doing the job assigned to them. The big difference was that he answered to a higher authority. He forgave them for hunting him like a feral beast because they were unable to comprehend that he was on a mission from God. He had known early on that there would be things that he couldn't control. Unexpected circumstances would occur from time to time. He just had to make sure he controlled the things that he could, especially his temper, which was often compromised by bouts of "'roid rage" caused by his many years of steroid abuse.

Deggler was a soldier at war, and he had accepted a long time ago that all wars had their share of innocent casualties.

After his bath, he read the Bible for an hour or so and then looked at the list of potential victims for his next kill. Deggler selected a Lutheran. More specifically Morgan Summers, a hate monger and hypocrite who was one of New York's most outspoken opponents of homosexuality while secretly indulging in countless gay trysts himself. About a month ago, Deggler had bugged Summers's office and hacked into his computer. Deggler made online contact with the preacher in a gay chat room. Summers only slept with either married men or powerful men like himself who had too much to lose if their true sexual proclivity was brought to light. Deggler had told Summers that he was a married father of three who was from a devout Christian family. He chose "three children" because Summers was in fact married with three children of his own. After a month of cyberforeplay, Deggler convinced Summers to meet him tonight at midnight at a quiet bar in the East Village.

As he stood across the street from the bar waiting for Summers, Deggler prayed in the rain. The searing pain in his head returned, reminding him that he was running out of time. He had popped several Vicodin pills earlier, but they seemed to be having little to no effect. It was only when he saw Summers's silver Mercedes pull up that the pain began to subside. He crossed the street in the rain and intercepted Summers before he made it into the bar.

When Summers regained consciousness, he found himself naked and tied upside down to two beams of wood in the position of the cross. The large, cavernous space of the abandoned church was completely quiet save for the sound of rain falling on the roof. Summers was completely disoriented, with a throbbing headache and the feeling of dried blood on his left cheek.

He called out a few times, but heard nothing in response other than his own voice echoing off the stone walls and back in his direction. After what felt like a half hour, Summers heard movement five feet to his right. Deggler's bare legs came into view first, then the rest of him, totally nude. Summers immediately noticed the man's missing penis and the hideous scar of his self-mutilation. His face looked vaguely familiar, but under the circumstances Summers couldn't place him.

Deggler carried a carpenter's mallet and railroad spikes in his hands. As Summers begged and pleaded, Deggler struck a spike in one of the frightened man's outstretched wrists. Despite the agonizing yells of Summers, Deggler calmly and without a word crossed to the other side and did the same to the other wrist. After he finished nailing the feet to the cross, he disappeared for another fifteen minutes. The physical and psychological torture was unbearable. Summers passed out once or twice, but was awakened by the sound of Deggler's voice.

"Do you know the weight of your soul?" Deggler asked.

From Summers's upside-down position, he saw a strange object in the large man's hands. It was a medieval weapon consisting of both an axe-like blade and a steel spike on the end of a long pole. The last thing Morgan Summers saw was the halberd swinging in his direction.

43

When Quincy and Maclin got back to the station after 1:00 a.m., it was more or less to wait for the dreaded call. At least Phee had some decent news.

"Brenda says that she can crack his coding, but she's gonna need another day," Phee said as he greeted them.

"And there's no way to speed that up?" Maclin pressed.

"Look, she's doing a lot better than the assholes back in DC," Phee snapped back.

Maclin knew he was right. She was also aware of how the frustrations of the case were beginning to make them all irritable and anxious.

"Ok, well, whatever she can do. Just tell her we appreciate it," Maclin replied.

Phee had responded with much more edge than he had

intended to. He was protective of his friends, but didn't mean to come off so defensive. Particularly not with Maclin. In the short time they had been together, he was surprised at how different she was from every other fed he'd worked with or met. He was pleasantly surprised by how well she fit in with him and Quincy. In tense cases like this, cops rarely apologized to other cops for anything. Besides the tough skin that came with the uniform, everyone accepted exactly what the job brought with it. Apologies were physical, never verbal. They were gestures, looks or nods at the end of a case. When the time was right, he would apologize, but right now they had much bigger things to deal with.

At 1:37 a.m., the call came in that they had all been expecting. Summers had been found. The abandoned church was in Alphabet City, which was less than two miles from the bar where Summers was abducted. As expected, the killing was violent and gruesome. Summers's body was nailed to a cross upside down and he had been both decapitated and castrated. The head was in a corner, ten feet away facing the severed penis.

As Quincy arrived at the scene with Phee and Maclin, it was the first time in his career that he felt he was just going through the motions. He kept to himself and had no interaction or routine with Phee. Quincy was quiet and withdrawn. At this point it was more academic than anything. They already knew the killer's identity, motive and profile. The only useful clue would have been one that revealed his whereabouts, but Deggler was much too smart to give them what they needed most. The case had started affecting him in a strange way. Each murder was desensitizing him more and more.

Of all of the cases that he had worked, of all of the dead bodies that he had stood over, none had left him feeling the things he was feeling now. There was always a range of emotions that went along with his line of work, but Quincy found himself feeling something toward the victims that he could have never anticipated. Apathy.

The slain men were all frauds, hypocrites and at the very least (moral) criminals who abused the trust of the very people who needed them most. Deggler was clearly a sick individual, but one of the things that scared Quincy most was that he understood part of the sickness. Psychology 101: Deggler had to have been severely abused as a child. And somehow the concept of God played a part in it. Quincy kept hearing in his head Clarice Summers describe her husband as "complicated." Somehow that was supposed to justify all the betrayals and wrongdoings. He hated the excuses that people made for the Conners and Summers of the world. Quincy wondered how many times people made excuses for his abuser. Culpability ran a lot deeper than some were willing to admit.

Every fantasy that Quincy ever had about the demise of his abuser was violent and excessive. It made no difference that the priest who had molested him and Liam had died several years ago in a horrible fire. Quincy still felt that the priest had gotten away with it all. Who knows how many victims he had actually left in his wake. He had never been held accountable for any of his crimes. From the time that Quincy heard about the priest's death and how he died, Quincy's only regret was that he wasn't the one who had started the fire.

Deggler acted out Quincy's fantasies, the same fantasies that he couldn't share with anyone. Not even with Phee, and not even with the one person who had lived the nightmare with him and bore the same injuries and scars. Quincy had always suspected that Liam had become a priest for the same reason he became a cop—self-reclamation. He thought of the bits and pieces, the chunks, the collective sum of things taken from them. It became more and more clear to Quincy that part of Deggler's killings were an attempt by him to take back what had been stolen. As insane as Deggler was, he was probably the one person who would understand Quincy and his demons the most.

Fortunately they only walked the scene for forty-five minutes. Without having to verbalize it, all three were on the same page about them already having the information and clues that the scene would normally offer them. More than likely Elena would be waiting up for Quincy, but he was in no shape to see her just yet. He couldn't bring to her the darkness that he was feeling. She had quickly become one of the few positives in his life; he would do what was necessary to protect that. He asked Phee to drop Maclin at her hotel and then got in his car and headed uptown. On the way, he punched in the word "confession" on his phone and pressed send.

44

Quincy sat in the confessional much more ill at ease than the last time. This time he wasn't here as a prank or joke at Liam's expense. He came to the church at this hour much more for his brother's help than God's. The only reason Quincy chose the confessional was because his feelings had left him too uncomfortable to face his brother directly. He needed the intermediacy. Liam sat quietly on the other side, waiting for his little brother to decide when he was ready to talk about whatever it was that he needed to talk about. Liam knew the root of Quincy's troubles was in one way or another usually connected to their childhood. More often than not, he felt the same way about himself. Liam listened to the fidgeting on the other side and waited patiently for Quincy to initiate conversation.

"How come we never talk about it?" Quincy finally asked.

After a beat or so, Liam responded to what his brother was referring to.

"Because I don't think either one of us could handle what it might do to you if we did."

"But..."

"I've always protected you, right?"

"Yeah."

"And you've always trusted me, right?"

"Yeah."

"Then trust me on this. I've had some people tell me their darkest secrets only to have them become consumed and eventually destroyed after the fact. I know how your mind works better than anybody. You start rehashing what happened and it'll eat you alive."

"How do you know it hasn't already?"

"Because you're still fighting. Even if that means coming to see me in the middle of the night in a place you claim not to believe in. I know it's a battle sometimes, but you'll always be fine, because there's inherent goodness in you. We don't choose our souls, Quincy; they choose us. Trust me, a good soul chose you."

"I'm not the priest. You are."

"Priest is just a title. Deep down you've got more goodness in you than anyone I've ever known. Myself included."

"I think you underestimate yourself."

"No, I don't. I'm just honest about who you and I both are."

"I'm nothing but a cop. You're a friggin' priest."

"Yeah, well, you're as much responsible for that as anyone."

"What do you mean?"

"Remember when we were kids and they sent me away?"

"Of course I do."

"Every day that I was in juvie, I prayed to God that He would watch over you and protect you while I was gone."

"That's funny considering that you needed more protecting than me."

"I made a deal with God the first night I got there, that if He kept you safe while I was away, then I'd do whatever it was that He wanted me to do for the rest of my life."

"Oh great, so now you're blaming me for being a 42-year-old virgin," Quincy said teasingly.

Liam couldn't help but laugh.

"You really are an idiot, you know that don't you?"

"Yup, but fortunately I'm your idiot."

The quiet night was filled with the brothers' laughter and mutual teasing. From the time they were kids, Liam had an amazing ability of finding ways to calm and reassure Quincy in the darker hours of his life. And even with the things that they disagreed on, like souls and God, and the New York Mets, Liam was able to validate their relevance, even if only temporarily.

45

After talking to his brother for a little while longer, Quincy felt better than he had when he arrived. By the time he left, it was after 3:00 in the morning. He was downstairs in front of Elena's apartment when he called her. He could tell that she had been asleep, even though she pretended that she hadn't. Quincy felt guilty about how selfish he was in coming this late with all that she was going through. But once Elena welcomed him, that feeling immediately subsided. She made him feel that there was mutual need and purpose in him being there. She cooked him a late-night snack and, as he wolfed it down, she understood something that her father had told her a long time ago. Food made from love often brought more gratification to the cook than the recipient. While he finished eating, she drew them both a bath. Diehard New Yorker that he was, he wasn't much of a bath-man, but somehow she knew exactly what he needed more than he did. If it was Liam who had lifted him out of his temporary darkness, then it was Elena in the tub next to him that temporarily rebooted him. After they had gotten out of the tub and laid in her bed, Quincy held her and played with her still damp hair. As he spooned her and gently ran his finger down the full length of her arm, he thought back to his earlier conversation with Liam.

"Let me ask you a question. I know where you stand on the God thing, but do you believe in souls?" he asked.

"I don't see how you can believe in one without the other," she said.

"Do you think they choose us or do we choose them?"

"Never quite thought of it that way. I'll have to get back to you on that one. Why do you ask?"

"Just something somebody said to me earlier."

"Do you believe in souls?" she asked him.

"Maybe by a different name and concept."

"What is that supposed to mean?" she asked.

"I believe everybody has a core, no matter who we think we are or try our hardest to be, and that core predetermines our outcome."

"And what about choices?"

"They're just speed bumps ultimately," he laughed.

Elena playfully elbowed him in his side.

"You don't fool me, Detective Quincy Cavanaugh. You're not nearly as cynical as you would have people believe," she said teasingly.

"And how do you know that?" he asked.

"Because God told me. Right after He told me about the extensive pornography collection that you had under your bed between the ages of twelve and sixteen."

Quincy laughed as he kissed her on the back of her neck.

"At least He got half of it right."

46

E ven though Deggler still had seven of the wicked left to kill, he had to assume the worst. His photo running nonstop on the news and the fact that the cops were waiting for him at the treatment center meant that they were definitely getting closer. He hadn't even been able to go back to his place and gather his things. It was much too dangerous. Every step that he took from this point on had to be clear and well thought out. If he was going to outsmart the cops, Deggler first needed to put out the fire in his head.

The pain had come back with a vengeance. He had been hiding in the church since 4:00 a.m., making sure the cops were nowhere near. The middle of the week was always the quietest times at St. Augustine's. From the utility closet up near the balcony seating, he had the best vantage to see all the comings and goings. Aside from the actual killings, the only other times the pain in his head seemed to subside were the two times he had confession with the young priest. Father Cavanaugh had a very soothing effect on him. Deggler had things in his head that he needed to let out. Maybe had he met the priest earlier he wouldn't have developed the cancer. God was often a difficult master to serve. Not all could pass His tests. And those like Deggler, who could, often paid for it in other ways. His service to God had been unimpeachable and steadfast. But his commitment and devotion had led to a life of loneliness and isolation. There was some consolation in the fact that the vast majority of Biblical heroes were ridiculed and shunned. Knowing how Jesus and his disciples were documented outcasts, Deggler had always aspired to be nothing less. Martyrdom was a blessing, reserved for a precious few. The sacrifices and demands were never intended to be understood by the majority. Deggler believed one of the reasons he had been chosen was because he was far above the usual banalities of most men. He also believed that it took a man with a righteous heart to even begin to comprehend God's chosen.

Deggler had found such a righteous man in Father Liam Cavanaugh. When Deggler first went to him, he was in the midst of another painful episode. It was shortly before he killed Pastor Higgins. His skull had literally felt as if it were cracking. As Father Cavanaugh patiently listened to him, he felt the pain slowly disappearing. He knew immediately that this was a sign from God. At first he only confessed to the priest the sexual weaknesses that plagued him in his service to God. As confessions go, he kept it pretty much standard fare at first. Little by little he began to open up. The more he did the less pain he felt. He knew the priest's vow of confidence and had no doubt whatsoever that Father Cavanaugh would honor it at all costs. He grew bolder and more explicit with the priest, sharing his calling.

Deggler had returned today because this was more than likely his last time seeing Father Cavanaugh. If he had any chance whatsoever of finishing his mission, he needed things from the priest. He needed him to take the pain away as well as cleanse his soul and make him ready to meet his Holy Father. He took the risk because this would be his final confession. Deggler had already accepted that he would die soon, either at the hands of the cops or from the conflagration in his head.

As Liam sat in the confessional and slid the divider open, he heard the voice that he recognized immediately.

"Forgive me, Father, for I have sinned...."

47

Brenda had a major breakthrough on tracing the source of the hack. She had stayed up all night, throwing everything she had ever learned against the complicated coding. At about 8:00 in the morning, when she could barely keep her eyes open, she tracked a viral stream back to an account that had originated in the states.

Maclin ran the info through DC that pinpointed the router to an exact address in the South Bronx. When the address came back, Phee smiled at Maclin with an unspoken "I told you so" look. That look alone was icing on the cake for Brenda.

SWAT was the first in. They moved strategically as a single unit, with each appendage performing an individual task. What had taken an hour to coordinate and prep for was succinctly executed in two minutes. They moved in complete silence until the point of attack. Splintering wood and broken glass echoed through the back alley of the dilapidated row houses. The SWAT commander radioed outside to Maclin that, unfortunately, Deggler was nowhere to be found. By the time Quincy, Maclin and Phee entered the basement apartment, there was no doubt whatsoever that this was Deggler's home. The cramped space was damn near uninhabitable. It was dank and fetid with leaking pipes and rat droppings. A small windowless space that was claustrophobic and dark. The three of them looked at the walls and ceilings, which were plastered with Bible pages and thousands of tiny wooden crosses. A jar of empty capsules lay on a table nearby.

A uniformed cop escorted the landlord in to talk with Maclin and the detectives.

"I never seen him once," the squat, balding landlord told them.

"How's that?" Maclin asked.

"When I listed the place three months ago, he called, said he was familiar with the building and neighborhood. Left an envelope of cash for four months' rent in my mailbox and had me leave a key above the door. Said he worked late but wanted to move in right away. In the few months that he was here, he was quiet as hell, never had no problems with him. Had no idea the nut job had done this to the place. He really the one killin' all them priests?"

Neither of the three responded to his question. After asking the annoying man to leave, they walked the space and discovered the monitors, computers and even some medieval weaponry. In the last few days, they had seen the violence and aftermath of Deggler's disturbed mind. Now they were standing up close and personal in the epicenter of his madness.

It was Quincy who found the list. Tacked to a corkboard above one of the computer monitors were twelve names, five of which were those of the already deceased victims. Just as Maclin had theorized, the names were listed by denomination. Two Catholics, two Protestants, two Lutherans, two Presbyterians, two Methodists and two Baptists. At the top of the list, two words were written in bold print: THE BEFALLEN.

48

Back at the station, it was Maclin who asked Phee to convince Brenda to stay on and help them with the new computers they had retrieved.

"Besides, we all know that she's faster and better than the assholes in DC," she said smiling.

"Careful Agent Maclin, rumors might start flying that you actually have a sense of humor," Phee said playfully.

Maclin laughed and walked off as Phee pulled out his cell and called Brenda. He owed her big, but after the events of the last few days, he would be open to all forms of negotiations.

Quincy had placed security details on the remaining seven men listed. Ironically, he had been met with some resistance from two of the men on the list. Once the papers started speculating that the victims had been killed as a form of punishment for spiritual transgressions, the acceptance of security became a quiet admission of guilt. There were those that were willing to jeopardize their lives in an effort to maintain the illusion of their untarnished service to God.

Deggler carefully drove by the homes of three men from his list and saw the police cars stationed outside. Fortunately his confession with Father Cavanaugh had momentarily stopped the pain. What he needed now was to be able to think as clearly as possible. All of these years, he had always been smarter than the cops. Even now he wouldn't panic or allow himself to feel defeated. Deggler just needed a little time and a little strategy. What he needed most was a game changer.

49

When she was a child, Elena had enjoyed a very special relationship with her father. Even though she was young, he respected her for the woman he knew she could grow up to be. He never condescended to her or treated her as though life was something much too complicated and sophisticated for her to comprehend. From the time Elena was nine, she noticed a shift in her father's attitude toward her. He held her more account-able for her actions. Up until that point, Romero had been a bit of a disciplinarian. Like his father before him, he believed that sparing the rod spoiled the childand he never hesitated to spank her when he felt Elena deserved it. But shortly after her ninth birthday, she noticed that the spankings were replaced by appeals to her conscience. Hearing her father say that "he was disappointed in her" or "expected more out of her" cut her more deeply than any blow he had ever directed her way. When Elena was nine years old, Romero treated her as what she was: a young woman in training. And it was because of this that she had worshipped him.

She had spent many days of her childhood and adolescence with Romero in his favorite park overlooking the beautiful water. She loved her father's wit and wisdom. He was her rock for all things big and small. Their conversations fluctuated between whatever was going on in Elena's life at the time to topical issues affecting the world. They discussed poetry, art and their shared love of soccer and baseball. He tried to teach her how to cook, but she never took to it the way she did when he taught her how to fix cars. He shared with her his perception of the things about women that both fascinated and frustrated men since the beginning of time. He used to jokingly tell her that, "Women were very simple creatures. It was just everything they said and did that was complicated as hell."

They spent those afternoons in the park laughing and eating the chicken and ham sandwiches he made for them. When she turned twelve, they talked openly about sex and the sexes. Romero didn't want his daughter to have any misconceptions or schoolyard idiocy about her own sexuality. In the absence of a mother, her father did a rather impressive balancing act. Romero married an American-born Latina named Marisol when Elena was thirteen. Marisol was an amazing stepmother and she and Elena clicked and connected from the moment they met, up until her death from a seizure when Elena was twenty-two. Although it had taken him several years to find her, Marisol was clearly the romantic love of

Romero's life. Elena loved how her parents looked at each other. They made her realize the tragic mistake she would have made in marrying her son's father. Like Romero had done, if necessary, she would wait the better part of her life to find the person that looked at her similarly. Her parents had spoiled her. They made her realize that she could never just settle. She thought of Quincy and realized how much she loved the way he looked at her.

50

Brenda was briefing the team on some of her initial findings on Deggler's computer. He had smartly rigged his account so that if he were ever hacked, it would trigger a series of crippling viruses to the intruder's system. Once again Brenda was impressed with Deggler's skill and ingenuity. The pressure was still on her because the team was hoping that his computer might provide still pertinent information or maybe even a clue to his whereabouts. Brenda's ego and professional pride would not allow her to be outdone, no matter who it was.

"He basically has two Trojan viruses set up to infect any intruders. It's a boomerang defense designed to damage our critical system files and the operating system."

"Any way around it?" Quincy asked.

"There's a way around everything; it's just gonna cost the one thing you don't have a lot of—time," Brenda responded.

"How much time are we looking at?" Maclin asked.

"Hard to say. First thing I'm trying is a phantom program. In laymen's terms, I'm trying to get into his system without it knowing that I'm there. I get lucky with that, I can be in in two hours. If not, I'll try something else. No idea how long that would take. By the way, I intercepted an incoming email before it was protected in his system. I hacked the sender's account so Deggler wouldn't shut us down," Brenda said.

"What did it say?" Maclin asked.

"Not much, just, 'We need to talk,'" Brenda answered.

"Any way to find out who or where it came from?" Phee asked.

"The address originated in Florida somewhere," Brenda answered.

"Deggler's brother," Quincy said.

"Any way to track that account?" Phee jumped in.

"His last three logins were from two different satellite feeds," Brenda added.

"Just means he was moving around," Quincy said.

"Or he's splitting his feed so it makes it harder for us to track him," Maclin said pointedly.

"Could be. I'm not sure at this point. Just thought you should know. If I'm able to get in through the phantom program, I'll be able to tell you more," Brenda said.

"Okay, well do your thing and hit us as soon as you have something. Oh yeah, and Brenda, Eze," Phee said as he exited with Quincy and Maclin.

Brenda and Phee were the only two to know his meaning. She knew he was negotiating with her, even though it wasn't necessary because there was no doubt that she was doing everything that she could as fast as she could. But still she was clear in what he was offering. Eze was a small medieval village near Monte Carlo that Brenda had wanted to visit ever since the early '90s when she read about it in college. Phee was the only man who she shared that fantasy with because he was the only man who she had fantasized about making love to in the quaint little village in the South of France. She smiled at Phee as she turned and went back to work.

As Phee caught up with Quincy and Maclin and made their way back to the conference room, they were intercepted by a uniformed cop who approached them with urgency.

"Somebody fitting Deggler's description just shot a priest up in the Cloisters."

51

'm just saying, none of it makes sense. This shooting goes against everything that he's been doing for the last thirty years," Quincy said as they parked the car and walked in the direction of the crime scene. Quincy had basically driven from the bottom of the island to the top in twenty minutes. The Cloisters was a medieval park located in Washington Heights. Because there was no road or real path available, they had to park about fifty yards away next to three waiting cruisers and a paramedic's rig and walk up an incline to the crime scene. A wounded priest was being attended to by two paramedics and a cop. The other cops were searching the periphery of the scene, looking for gun shells and any clues that they thought Deggler may have left behind. Quincy and Maclin approached the wounded priest to interview him as Phee did a general walk of the scene. The priest was in his fifties, short and pale with black hair.

He had been shot in the right hip and was lying on the ground on his left side while being attended to.

"I walk the park every day, never saw him before. He made small talk, then walked past me. Next thing I hear a loud noise and feel a sharp pain in my hip," the priest told them.

"When you said he made small talk, what exactly did he say?" Maclin pressed.

"At first he talked about the weather and how beautiful the park was after the rains, and then asked me something about a Bible verse."

"Which verse," Quincy asked.

"Matthew 2:13."

"And what exactly is that?" Maclin asked.

"It's essentially about how King Herod killed the infants in Bethlehem, and how the Holy Family escaped by going to Egypt."

As Quincy and Maclin absorbed what the priest told them, Maclin was approached by one of the cops they had passed earlier.

"Excuse me Agent Maclin, there's an Agent Michaelson on the radio for you," he said.

"Why didn't he just call me on my phone?" Maclin asked rhetorically.

"He probably did. This is one of the worst dead zones in the city," Quincy responded.

Maclin confirmed Quincy's statement when she looked at her cell and didn't even have one bar.

"I'll be right back," she said.

Maclin followed the cop back down the hill in the direction of the parked cars.

Phee made his way back over to Quincy.

"Anything?" Quincy asked.

"No. You were right. Nothing about this scene adds up," Phee told him.

"Ok, so let's run it. What do we know?" Quincy asked.

"In thirty years, he may have honed, but he's never broken profile. Never left a vic alive. Never done anything as boring as just shooting a vic. And it completely goes against the denominational pattern that he's been following lately," Phee said.

"He's been way too precise and consistent to get this sloppy now. Just doesn't make sense," Quincy replied as he crossed back to the priest and began questioning him again.

"Are you sure he didn't say anything else to you? Or do anything that you might have forgotten? It might be something that sounds or seems insignificant to you, but it might be helpful to us," Quincy said, almost pleading.

"No, I'm certain that's all he talked to me about. The weather, the park and the verse. Although it's not specifically referenced in the Bible as such, Matthew 2:13 is often referred to as The Slaughter of the Innocents. I don't know if that helps you in anyway," the Priest added.

"No church, no ritual and a vic that's not even on his list. He chose this place and the priest for a reason," Phee said.

"Yeah, but not in the way that he normally does. He wanted us here for a reason. Oh shit!!!"

"What?" Phee asked urgently.

"The priest was never the intended victim. Slaughter of the Innocents."

Phee realized where his partner's thinking was headed.

"Where the hell is Maclin?" Phee demanded.

By the time he asked the question, Quincy was already on the move. The two cops ran as fast as they could down the hill back toward the cars. Quincy was momentarily relieved when he saw the cop that had escorted Maclin back to the cars sitting in the driver's seat of one of the parked vehicles. As he and Phee got within five feet of the cop, however, they saw the long crimson ring around the dead cop's throat. Along with one of the missing cruisers, Agent Maclin was nowhere to be found.

52

Although Elena had stayed up all night talking and making love to Quincy until 6:00 in the morning, she found herself restless. After he left for work at 7:30, her plan was to sleep in for a couple of hours and then go to the hospital by eleven. The early morning rain had eliminated the possibility of a morning run. Even though she was tired and needed sleep, the empty apartment made her feel anxious and jittery. As exhausted as she felt, lounging around was not an option. She cleaned the kitchen to both channel her restlessness and reestablish some semblance of order since Romero's hospitalization. As she cleaned the three-bedroom apartment, she was careful to avoid her son's room. She was in no way, shape or form ready for the emotional minefield that awaited her on the other side of his door. The combination of thoughts of her father and son were at times overwhelming. After she finished the kitchen, she strategically directed herself toward her father's room. Cleaning his room took on a therapeutic purpose. It was no longer a matter of light dusting and straightening things up. She needed an all-consuming project to throw herself into. Elena threw in one of her father's CDs and went to work. As Hector Lavoe played in the background, she changed the bedding, polished the wood and vacuumed the carpet. Even though Romero had always been an orderly person, Elena still found ways to make the bedroom look better. It had been a long time since she had done anything personal for her father, but now she was motivated for several reasons.

After finishing the bedroom and bathroom, Elena moved to Romero's closet. Having lived in small apartments over the last several years, she had mastered the art of arranging cramped closets for optimal usage. She grouped Romero's clothes together by color and length. Slacks, shirts and shoes were placed on the right side, while coats, suits and blazers were put to the left. She removed sweaters from hangers and neatly folded them and placed them in drawers from the large bureau just outside the closet. As she opened the bottom drawer, she discovered four large, cardboard shoeboxes. As she moved one of the boxes to the side, the top fell off, revealing countless letters packed within. The large box contained two separate rows of letters stacked two piles high. There was chronology to both rows. Each box was labeled and dated, spanning the time from the year Elena was born up until her seventh birthday. She wrestled with the fact that she was invading her father's privacy when she pulled out one of the envelopes from the first box. She was surprised to find that all of the envelopes were unopened and marked return to sender. There were easily a few hundred letters. Her father's name occupied the upper left corner of each letter as the sender. Each letter was addressed to: Christina Slotnick.

Elena sat and made herself comfortable on the floor. She went back and forth in her mind with the thought of going further, and wondered if the content of the letters would, in any way, further compromise the current fragile image she had of her father. She appreciated the great risk in opening the letters. Whatever the content, it would be with her forever. Knowledge once gained was nonrefundable. She found the discovery of the boxes of letters bizarre, yet it was precisely that which had piqued her curiosity. Even though she sat there for fifteen minutes or so doing nothing, the decision had already been made. As she thumbed through the letters, she found what seemed to be the first of the long series. It was dated June 20, 1982, the year of her birth.

Dear Christina,

I wanted to let you know that Elena and I made it back safely to Colombia. The first two hours of the flight was the toughest part for her. Let's just say, she made her presence felt. Should she decide that she wants to be neither an artist nor a dancer, I think (and several unfortunate passengers would agree) that she might have a future in the opera. The funny thing is, no matter how challenging she may be, every time I look at her, I swear, I fall more and more in love with her. I think she's the most amazing baby. Even at just twelve weeks old, she looks at people and things so inquisitively. She's already curious about things, and I'm not exaggerating, but when she engages, she seems to do so with incredible wonder and understanding.

I won't lie to you Christina. The thought of me raising her without you scares me to death. I know that you made it clear that you weren't ready to be a mother, and to tell you the truth I certainly never saw myself raising a child at twenty-three years old and definitely not on my own. But every time I look at her, I thank God for interrupting my plans. The only thing I'm asking of you is to keep an open heart. I'm willing to do whatever is necessary to have you be a part of Elena's life. You and your family made it abundantly clear that the future I used to dream of with you was no longer possible. As difficult as that was, I've accepted your wishes and the things that I don't control. The only thing that I ask of you is that you reconsider participating in our daughter's life, in whatever capacity that you feel most comfortable with. Please Christina, this no longer has anything to do with you and me. Your daughter needs you in her life. Just say the word and I'll come back to New York and find a job and we'll work out whatever arrangement that works best for you and Elena. We've truly been blessed with an angel, and though I know things won't be perfect, I know if we work together we can create a situation that allows Elena to have all the love she desperately needs and deserves.

I wish you nothing but love and happiness, and await your response.

Sincerely,

Romero

Elena sat for a while, going through the boxes of envelopes. She read no less than thirty letters. Each letter was dated a week apart, and from the first one sent to the last, spanned the first seven years of Elena's life. The first few letters were all similar in tone, persistent attempts to convince Christina to take part in Elena's life. Elena could tell from the letters when Romero had abandoned hope of Christina ever becoming a parent to her. It was when the letters eventually turned to nothing more than updates and fill-ins. First dance recital, first sleep over, first fight. Photos accompanied the letters written just after holidays and birthdays. He told Christina of both the minor and major events and occurrences in Elena's life. Elena found it odd to read a summation of the first part of her life. The detailed accounts of things she never knew or had long forgotten. By the time she skipped to and opened the last letter, she had begun to view her life with a totally different perspective. The letter was dated the day of her seventh birthday. She noticed a slight tremble in her hand as she began to read.

Dear Christina,

Today our daughter turned seven. We had a big party in the park that I used to tell you about so much. It's amazing how much she loves the water and appreciates nature. I've seen her sit still for long stretches at a time and watch the ocean as if she alone knew its secrets.

I've written you letters every week for the last seven years in attempts to share with you what I thought were the most important moments of our daughter's life. I realize now how wrong I was. All of the moments were of equal importance. Everything from her crying loudly on the plane when we first left New York to her sleeping peacefully her first night home. From every scrape to every smile, they were all important moments that you made the decision not to be a part of. For the last seven years, I've done nothing but hoped and prayed that one day you would decide that loving your daughter was a blessing and not an inconvenience.

Two years ago, I read a review of a dance recital that you had in Lincoln Center. The critic said that you danced with a fierceness and passion that your peers rarely comprehended. I remember the review specifically because I immediately thought how well that described how Elena lives her life. Even at 7, she's fearless and passionate about the things that move her. I used to be afraid of the potential repercussions of your absence in her life. I worried if there would be any imbalances or emotional ramifications as she got older by not being raised by a mother. But she's taught me things. She's taught me more about courage and confidence than I could ever make you understand. They say by nature that children are malleable and adapt to their environment much more easily than adults. Maybe because she never got a chance to know you, or never had to forget you, she's adapted to the role of a motherless child seemingly quite easily. This morning was the first time that I ever really talked about you to her. This morning was the first time that I ever lied to her. Because I've accepted that at this point, even if you decided that you did finally want to be in her life, it would probably cause more pain and confusion than anything else.

I elected to tell her that her mother passed away in a car accident two weeks after she was born. I didn't do this out of any kind of vindictiveness or malice. I did it because the alternative of telling her that her mother could never find a place for her own daughter in her life seemed to be the cruelest of the options. I didn't want her to spend a minute of her life hoping that one day she would be worthy of your love. I did it to give her a closure that she never even knew she needed. You made the choice to stay out of her life this long. I now only ask you to stay true to your choice and never contact Elena. As difficult as it has been, I have accepted and lived with your choice. Now I'm imploring you to live with mine. She doesn't deserve to be hurt.

I wish you well in all that you do, and all that you pursue.

Romero

Elena sat still as the letter trembled in her hand. She didn't know when it had started. The numbness and paralysis. She didn't know when all feeling had left her body. She didn't know when she had forgotten how to breathe. She didn't know when the waterfall began. All she knew was that she had a mother who never claimed her.

53

H ow the hell do you lose a federal agent?" Michaelson barked
at Quincy and Phee.

The agent and four of his subordinates along with Quincy
and Phee's captain stood at the scene of the cop's murder and
Maclin's abduction. Bernie and Alvarez, two of the detectives
who were assisting the team, were now present. The number of
uniformed cops and detectives had tripled since they first arrived
to investigate the priest's shooting. If the original murders weren't
bad enough, now the cops had lost one of their own and possibly a federal agent to boot. Nothing banded cops together like a
fallen fellow officer. Especially one killed in the line of duty. Cops
operated on the basis that each day presented the possibility of
their own demise. The very nature of their function and success
was predicated on keeping that knowledge at bay. When a fellow

officer was downed, the reminder of their own mortality was a somber dose of reality.

"Everything about the shooting of the priest was a setup. The location, the bad phone reception, everything," Quincy snapped back.

"In my fifteen years on the job, I've never seen such incompetence," Michaelson fired.

"That's because the view is a lot different behind the safety of a desk," Phee said defensively.

"Glad you feel that way, because that's where I want the two of you for the rest of this investigation. Turn over everything that you have to my agents. We'll take it from here," Michaelson said.

"The hell you will," Quincy said, looking at his captain for support.

"Don't look at him. I'm the one in charge here. This is a federal case that we allowed you to work on because Maclin thought you could be an asset. The minute you turned into a liability, the two of you became of very little use to me."

"Who the hell do you think you're talking to? The three of us made more progress on this case in three days than you and your boy scouts made in thirty years," Phee shot back, becoming progressively heated.

Not only could Quincy not believe what Michaelson was saying, but he didn't even have the luxury of getting pissed off about it because of the dangers of his partner's temper. Before things got worse, it was up to him to step in as the peacekeeper.

"Look, we need to all bring it down a bit and find a way to work together," Quincy said as calmly as possible.

"And I feel the best way for us to do that is for the two of you to bring my agents up to speed with your intel and take more of a supporting position. This is not personal. Saving this investigation is my number one priority," Michaelson said.

"Funny, because I would think saving Agent Maclin's life would be your number one priority," Quincy retorted.

"Maybe if you and your partner had been more attentive and better at your jobs, we wouldn't be having this conversation right now."

"Fuck you, you asshole," Phee spit out at him.

"Fuck me? You mouth off to me one more time and I'll have you back in a uniform busting Trannies on a Friday night. At least that way you'll be able to keep a closer eye on your brother," Michaelson threw back at Phee.

Quincy was the only one to see it coming, and there was nothing he could do to stop it. Before Michaelson had fully gotten the word "brother" out of his mouth, Phee was on him. Phee had successfully delivered two well-placed punches before anyone except Quincy understood what was going on. As Michaelson's agents moved toward Phee, Quincy, Bernie and Alvarez and all of the New York cops instinctively moved to Phee's defense. New York cops had many creeds and unspoken rules that they lived by. High on their list was the mantra: Fuck with one. Fuck with all. The feds were outnumbered and outmuscled. It was Phee's captain who ordered the officers to stand down while Michaelson's men picked him up off the ground.

"For the record, that was personal," Phee said pointedly.

Michaelson was beyond saving face at this point, but the agent tried to at least minimize the damage by nonchalantly brushing himself off and calmly speaking as though nothing happened.

"Here's the deal: You turn in your gun and badge right now, I don't have you arrested for assaulting a federal agent," Michaelson proposed.

After he calmed down a little, Phee looked at his captain and saw from the look on his face there weren't a lot of options available to him. He never took his eyes off Michaelson as he removed his gun and badge and handed them to his captain. As Phee turned and walked away, Quincy stepped up to Michaelson.

"You're in luck today. We're running a two for one sale," he said as he also handed his captain his gun and badge before walking off to join his partner.

54

An hour later, after Elena emerged from Romero's bedroom, she quickly got dressed and caught a cab to the hospital. As she made her way to her father's room, she consciously avoided the eye contact from the passing nurses. She knew how her mind worked. Elena didn't want to misinterpret anything in their gaze. She didn't want the news of her father's progress to come to her in pieces. If it was bad, she would want to get it directly from Dr. Fong all at once. As she reached Romero's room, she made herself comfortable and settled in for her indeterminate watch. Looking at her father from head to toe, she thought about her fascination with hands. More than any other feature, they represented what life had both given and molded. She thought it appropriate that prints and palms identified us and in some beliefs even predeter-mined our fate. They told us of our past, present and future if we knew how to read their stories. As she held her father's hands, she looked for their story. She knew of the letters they had written, the paintings they had painted and the love and protection they had given her. But still she looked for them to tell her things she didn't already know. Romero's hands felt peaceful. Like his mind, they were at recess from troubled times. Elena wished she could do the same. She wished she could turn off her brain and take a break from herself. Anger, bitterness and pain were heavy objects to lift and carry over the last two months on a daily basis. They had become her default program in regard to her father. She hated that it was what she automatically resorted to. Seeing how innocent he looked now, she felt guilty for constantly blaming him. The stillness was actually very becoming to Romero. It allowed Elena to see an attractiveness in her father that she had all but forgotten. She wished she could take certain things back, that she could change things. Even though he couldn't hear her, she offered up the best apology she knew in that moment.

Before leaving the house, Elena had stuffed a couple of the unread letters in her bag. She thought that at some point she would be able to read them, if for nothing else but to pass time. As she waited for Dr. Fong to come visit her, she began to read. The letters were more or less the same in tone as the ones she had read earlier. She reasoned that they were easier to finish now because she was more mentally prepared. After she finished reading one of the letters, she reached into her purse and pulled out a pen and some paper and started writing. She had written quite a bit by the time Dr. Fong entered. He brought her up to speed on her father's condition and said that there had been additional swelling in his brain. He immediately launched into their list of challenges and options. He made no attempt at concealing his great concern about Romero's current condition.

"We could try decreasing his medication to what's called a level of conscious sedation. One potential advantage of that approach would be stimulation of the cognitive center of the brain. I really want to be clear here though. Taking your father off medication could kill him," he said.

"And if we continue doing what we've been doing, he could die as well, right?" Elena asked.

Dr. Fong looked at Elena and didn't pull any punches.

"At this point, and I don't mean to sound crass in any way, but we could be looking at a damned if you do, damned if you don't situation."

"Take him off the drugs," Elena said calmly and confidently.

"Are you sure?"

"Yes, I'm sure."

Dr. Fong had Elena sign a couple of release forms and then immediately started the process of reducing Romero's medication.

Since a major goal was to stimulate the cognitive part of his brain, Elena had spent the afternoon trying various ways to penetrate her father's conscious barrier. She read to her father, she sang to him and even held one-sided conversations with him. She found herself more animated than usual, somehow thinking that would help. Dr. Fong and some of the nurses came into the room every fifteen minutes or so to monitor Romero. After Dr. Fong left, Elena asked the nurse for a few moments of privacy with her father. As the nurse headed out, Elena sat at her father's bedside and stared intently at the person who had watched over her for her entire life. When she had asked the nurse to leave, it wasn't as if she had some particular game plan or specific reason other than a daughter needing to be alone with her ailing father.

In her anger she had already lost time with him. She fought the depressing thoughts and possibilities that it might very well be time that they would never have again. The thought of losing her father scared her for various reasons. Some obvious, some subtle, but most of them selfish. In her childhood, she had depended on him. In her adulthood, she had grown independent of him. In her grief, she had become emotionally alienated from him. As was often the case, the threat of loss brought a greater appreciation of even the simplest of things. She thought of random things that now, under the circumstances, took on greater significance. Moments and memories were now magnified. The ballet classes where Romero was the only man present. The countless peanut butter and jelly sandwiches that he made with the same detail and care that he put into a gourmet meal for her. The bedtime stories, the daughter-daddy teas, the preteen conversations about boys and sex. The tears wiped, the laughs shared, the pride shown and the dreams nurtured.

Of the snippets and flashbacks, there was one incident that had always stood out to Elena. She remembered the time when she was eleven years old and going on a class trip. Romero had reminded her repeatedly that morning to make sure she didn't forget the lunch that he had prepared for her. He had smoked some pork the night before and gotten up a little early to make a few extra sandwiches for those of her friends who were constantly begging her to trade food. Her popularity had grown in part by being known as the girl with the best lunches in school. Despite his several reminders, Elena still left the house forgetting her lunch. By the time she and the other kids were exiting the bus at the museum, Romero was out front waiting for them. It was a simple moment. Undramatic and small in scope compared to many of the other things he had done as a father, and yet as he stood there waiting for her with the bags of lunches she had forgotten, Romero became a hero to his little girl. She had thought about the incident from time to time over the years, but never bothered to put words or definition to it. She hadn't decided as a child that the experience would stand out and reverberate for years to come. The significance of that moment had chosen her, not the other way around. The only other man's presence that had affected her in a similar way was when Quincy showed up for her at the hospital.

"I've been wanting to tell you that I met someone. He's an amazing man and one of the most beautiful people I've ever encountered. I mean his heart. His mind. The things that you taught me were most important. I know you'll like him, even though in some ways the two of you are complete opposites. But the more I come to understand him, the more similarities I see between the two of you."

As Elena continued to talk to her father about Quincy and any other subjects she could think of, she began to have more and more difficulty keeping her energy upbeat and optimistic. Even though she was trying to be casual and proactive on the surface, underneath she was battling the difficult thoughts of her father's mortality. No matter how much she tried to evade it or pretend that it wasn't real, there were unexpected moments when she found herself unable to escape the truth. When the truth struck, it became increasingly more difficult for Elena to hold it together. She did her best to fight back the fear and guilt. Elena was teetering on the thin line of holding it together versus a full-blown meltdown. The four walls of the small room started closing in on her. The only other time she had ever felt this alone and afraid was when her son died. Elena was doing all that she could to keep her emotions at bay when she finally got up and exited the room. Just as she made it to the hallway, she heard the distant clap of thunder, even though it was only lightly raining outside. Elena was desperate and looking for even the simplest gesture from God. Whether He came loudly or slipped in unannounced with no fanfare, that would still be enough. She knew that a white lie told to her child to ease his fears was a poor excuse for a miracle, but she couldn't help but hope that maybe God was laughing to let her know that He was still there.

55

Quincy and Phee both needed to believe that Maclin was still alive. They had to believe that if Deggler wanted her dead then there would have been two corpses left behind. Operating off that hope, badge or no badge, neither one of them had any intention whatsoever of leaving Maclin's life in the hands of Michaelson and the Bureau. Even if only as an honorary member, she had become one of them, and New York cops took care of their own. How long she stayed alive was another conversation that they weren't ready to have just yet.

Twenty minutes after they left the Cloisters Park, Quincy got a text from Detective Alvarez telling them to meet him in Harlem on the West Side Highway and 125th Street. The last word of the text was Urgent. Alvarez got there ten minutes after Quincy and Phee. The minute he got out of his car, both

Quincy and Phee knew the news wasn't good. The expectation of bad news and the actual delivery of it was always a terrible playing field for the imagination. Both Quincy and Phee had in the past lost a partner in service. They had both experienced the hole and hopelessness that came with the news. Quincy subconsciously took a step back as though that might somehow buffer or delay what was coming.

"Deggler made contact. Maclin's alive, but not for long," Alvarez informed them.

The partners exhaled a collective sigh of relief.

"Either we turn over the remaining seven preachers on his list or he kills Maclin. He said after he kills her, he'll then kill six other innocents every hour on the hour if we don't do what he wants. He gave us until 5 o'clock today," Alvarez continued.

"That gives us just under four hours," Quincy said as he looked at his watch.

"How did he make contact?" Phee asked.

"Maclin's phone was left in the cruiser," Alvarez answered.

"What's Agent Michaelson's game plan?" Quincy added.

"If he's got one, he hasn't bothered to share it with us yet," Alvarez told them.

"All right. I need you to stay close to the captain. Since you were fourth point person on our team and since the three of us are out of the picture, they'll be looking at you to fill them in on every angle we were working. You gotta be the one to keep us in the loop," Quincy told him.

"No problem," Alvarez responded.

"We're Maclin's best chance, you know that don't you?" Phee added.

"I know. That's why I came to you," Alvarez said as he walked toward his car.

After Alvarez drove off, Phee made two phone calls. The first was to Brenda because she alone was their best shot at tracking Deggler. Phee filled her in on the recent events and urged her to do whatever she had to do to speed up her progress. The second phone call Phee made was to his father. Clay was the one person who could get them the things they would need to stop Deggler.

56

D eggler thought that, overall, Maclin hadn't changed much. The differences that he noticed were to be expected. She was older and a few pounds heavier, and absent the bright smile that she wore in the picture he had taken from Willington's wallet. But all in all she looked pretty much the same as she did when she hunted him ten years ago. He tied the still unconscious agent to a steel girder in the basement of an abandoned church. She started to come to as he gently wiped the blood from her busted lower lip. It took Maclin a second to realize where she was and how she had gotten there. While she was under, she had dreamed of Willington. Short, sporadic dreams. She just remembered they were both eating Greek food. As she fully regained her bearings, she became more aware of the throbbing headache and ringing in her ears. As she remembered the circumstances surrounding her abduction, she had a flash image of the young uniformed cop and the endless blood streaming from his throat. This was the last thing she remembered before Deggler knocked her unconscious. She knew better than anyone else the violence and sickness that Deggler was capable of. Not a day had gone by in the last ten years that she hadn't thought of killing him. Being this close to him only reinforced how deep her hatred of him ran. Her hatred was what used to get her out of bed in the thick of her depression. Just as her grief had taken away her reasons for living, hate had given her purpose and motivation. It pushed her and made her excel. It was her hatred that had somehow delivered her to this moment in time.

Deggler had nothing personal against her. She was just a means to an end. Maclin was a bit surprised at Deggler's interaction with her. He washed her face and made sure that the heavy plastic zip tie he used to restrain her was as comfortable as possible under the circumstances. Every movement that the large man made in regard to her was methodical and borderline ritualistic. He was, for lack of a better description, gentle toward her and courteous. She noticed that he rarely looked directly at her. He treated her more as some type of valued object than an actual person. This close to him, she was surprised at the things she saw in him. His blue eyes were still youthful and gave no hint of the horrors they had witnessed. She found herself wondering things about Deggler. Namely what were the specific circumstances and mistreatment that had created the person he had become. Although Deggler hardly looked at her, she couldn't take her eyes off him. There was an interesting case of polarity at play. Deggler was objectifying Maclin so that at the right time, even though she was an innocent, he would kill her with no problem or hesitation. Maclin didn't mind humanizing Deggler because, when given the chance, she would still kill him without so much as a second thought.

The only weapons that Deggler had salvaged were the ones that he had kept in his van. He brought everything in from his vehicle and established the church basement as his new command center. He flipped open a laptop and immediately went to work.

57

Quincy and Phee met with Clay in a garage on 110th Street. Clay was with a scary looking man that did odd jobs for him. The man's name was Azuma Dabekko, but was known to most as The African. No one knew his exact age, but whatever it was, he looked more worn than his reality. The African was as black as half-past midnight in the bleakest of winters. An uninterrupted scar ran the distance from the corner of his mouth to the bottom of his right earlobe. Quincy noticed that the man was missing two fingers on his left hand. Although The African had been under Clay's employment for the majority of Phee's life, Clay had always made sure that his son had limited exposure to his personal "fixer." The African was a man who had a rather impressive resume of bad things he'd done in his life. Under more normal circumstances he was the type of man Quincy and Phee would have been investigating instead of colluding with. These were anything but normal circumstances, however, and The African and his services were exactly what they needed. Clay gave a slight nod to The African, who then popped his trunk and removed two suitcases. As he opened them, the two cops were impressed with the array of weapons that he presented. Every item was brand new and glistened under the overhead fluorescent lights. Phee, who was much more of a gun aficionado than Quincy, couldn't help but let out a whistle at the collection.

"How clean?" Quincy asked.

"Spotless. A manager at the factory where they're made pulls them off the line before they even get stamped. I'm only here and telling you this because of your partner's father. He wants you to know that there's no way any of this can ever be traced back to either one of you," The African said.

Phee glanced in his father's direction but avoided his eyes at the same time. His conflict wasn't just that he needed his father's help. It was the part of his father that he needed that bothered him. Even though Clay had been honest about his criminal past, Phee had still felt somewhat insulated and shielded by the passage of time.

Phee was in no way naive and knew that the power his father wielded took blood to obtain and occasionally even more blood to maintain. Metaphoric and or literal.

Phee had asked his father to help him obtain illegal weapons so that he and Quincy could save Maclin. He hated the fact that they were limited in both time and choices, but if they were going to stop Deggler, they would more than likely have to put him down.

If it did in fact come to that, they needed guns that couldn't be traced back to them.

Phee had never seen himself coming to his father under these circumstances. Clay had always been respectful of Phee being a cop. He was careful to never put him in a compromising situation. The day that Phee graduated from the academy was the last day that he and Clay talked in detail about Clay's more murky dealings and affiliations. Ironically, now it was Phee who was pulling his father into a criminal act. When Phee was finally able to look his father in the eye, he was a bit surprised by the look on Clay's face. There was neither judgment nor endorsement. Something that his father told him years ago suddenly came rushing back. When Phee turned eighteen, Clay had told him how he had killed his abusive stepfather when he wasn't much more than a kid. It wasn't anything that he bragged about or apologized for. He simply told his eighteen-year-old son that, "A man ain't a man if he's not willing to do whatever he has to to protect his family."

Phee hadn't gotten around yet to starting a family of his own. The force, Quincy, Brenda and even the adopted Maclin were the closest thing to family that he had created. As Phee looked at his father, both men's understanding of each other was a little more clear.

Phee picked out a silver-plated Sig Sauer and two matte black Glock 27s for good measure. Quincy selected a .45 and a 9mm. He wanted reliable power after his first encounter with Deggler. Unlike the other night when Deggler was hit by the truck and escaped, Quincy wanted to be certain that if he put him down, he would stay down. After Quincy and Phee left the garage, they drove downtown to meet Brenda. Although neither of them said it, no matter what happened, their careers were over. Phee wouldn't fight the consequences of punching Michaelson and Quincy wouldn't ask for his badge back. They collectively had over thirty years on the force, and they were both beginning to feel the burnout. The plan for Phee had always been that after his days on the force ended, he would take over some of his father's interests. For his part, Quincy just needed a clean break from the life he had accepted more than lived. He would never be the same after this case, good or bad. Too many things had surfaced within him. Things that would either free him or destroy him. And then there was the issue of Elena and what falling in love with her had cost him. She took away his sense of imperviousness, indifference and fearlessness. In his mind, these were some of the most important things that made him effective and successful as a cop. Both men, for very different reasons, had been thinking about getting out while they were still standing. Cops were like athletes: Once they started thinking about quitting, they had already quit. If necessary, they would take a good hard look at their decision and scrutinize what was already pretty clear to them. But for now, their only priority was saving Maclin and stopping Deggler.

58

Brenda had a beautiful loft in Soho. White-painted floors and walls accentuated with matching white furniture. Quincy's first thought when he walked in was that it was designed and furnished like a tasteful video shoot. The more he looked around the loft, the more he confirmed something that he had suspected shortly after meeting Brenda: she had, at the very least, a slight case of OCD. He had noticed back at the station how protective and orderly she was with her workstation. As often as possible, Quincy tested his instincts on people by assessing them in the first two minutes of meeting them. The habit kept him on his toes in regard to what he thought he knew of human nature. It took no special insight into human behavior to know that Brenda was in love with Phee. Quincy found the interaction between the two of them interesting. Both trying to maintain an air of professionalism and platonic friendship when the chemistry between them was so obvious. Over the years, Quincy had met several of Phee's conquests. Various races, sizes, backgrounds and professions. There certainly had never been a shortage of women in his partner's life, and at first he assumed Brenda was just another woman who fell under the heading of "general population" in Phee's eyes. But Quincy noticed, now that they were out of the station, that there was something different in Phee's demeanor toward her. Unlike any other woman that Quincy had met through his partner, it was the first time he had ever seen Phee so present and attentive to not only what Brenda said, but every movement she made. Quincy saw how Brenda looked at Phee. He thought it was very similar to the way Elena looked at him.

Phee had given Brenda an out. When he called her at the station and told her about the incident with Michaelson, he let her know in no uncertain terms that he was now pursuing the case as a cop who had either been suspended or terminated. He clearly warned her that everything that he did from this point on would be illegal and, if caught, highly punishable. He needed her to know the risk involved in continuing to help him. Earlier her participation had been sanctioned by Maclin, but now with Michaelson running things, her clearance would certainly be revoked. He would need her to do things that would put her at serious risk, like stealing files, hacking into the department's system and who knows what else. As he was carefully laying out the potential consequences of helping him, Brenda had quietly interrupted him by saying, "You need me, you got me. It's that simple."

Brenda had always been the reliable friend who Phee affection-ately referred to as his "ride or die chick."

Phee had always appreciated his friendship with Brenda because, unlike the way he felt for most people, he had a lot of admiration and respect for who she fundamentally was. Even in college, she was above and beyond the limited thinking of her peers. They were both freshman the first time that Phee asked her out. She didn't follow sports, so she had no idea that Phee was already a bit of a campus legend. She only knew him as a fellow student in her economics class. She didn't know that he was the son of a multimillionaire. To her, he was just another freshman trying to make ends meet. After turning him down three times, she finally accepted his fourth invitation to dinner on the one condition that they go Dutch. "Where I come from, we struggle together," she told him. Phee was impressed that she had never once deviated from that selfless mentality.

Phee had dated interracially, internationally and indiscrimi-nately. He dated doctors, lawyers, models and blue-collar women. Different races, religions and body types. Fortunately he had never been the type of man that was easily blinded by or too preoccupied with overly beautiful women. It had been his experience more often than not that stunning women disappointingly mistook their arrival for the event. He had found for the most part that they showed up with the expectation that their looks alone were the price of admission and very little else was ever expected of them. Brenda had always been the consistent exception. She was a perfect mix of beauty, brains and ethics.

For reasons both clear and unclear, this case had him reevaluating things. He was ready to make certain changes, professionally, personally, even romantically. This case had him not only questioning the value of life but also the value of living. He had kept Brenda at bay for years under the pretext of friendship, but the truth was that he was scared. He was scared of failing her, failing himself and even failing the example of love that his parents had left him. His father used to tease him as a teenager and young man. "Once you've seen love done right, you'll never forget what it looks like." Phee's "hit it and quit it" attitude had protected him from the work and exposure required to maintain anything of depth. It left him pretending to be something that he wasn't. Fulfilled.

He had seen enough hypocrisy and self-loathing in this case alone to last him a lifetime. He saw the toll of men being untrue to themselves and their core beliefs. He never went in much for the whole "Jesus Hallelujah" thing. Institutionalized religion had historically left him with more questions than answers. But despite any formal religious affiliation, he did consider himself spiritual and believed in the existence of a higher force. He just never felt a need to put a name to it. He thought whatever was responsible for us being here demanded more out of us in exchange for the privilege. Phee was no longer content with what he saw as his own self-denial. By no means was he as guilty as the recent victims he investigated, but he was guilty nonetheless. What if, in his own sick and twisted way, Deggler had it right? Maybe the man who lied to himself and lied to his god should be held accountable by the most brutal of standards.

Over the years, Brenda had often wondered if Phee would ever arrive. Even though she had accepted her role in his life as one of his closest friends, she never abandoned the possibility of the two of them ending up together. She had waited all these years for Phee not by choice but rather by circumstance. The few relationships that she had since college had left her comparing the men one way or another to him. Most men that she encountered were missing the things that she admired about Phee. She and her beautiful, successful but single girlfriends didn't know when it had started, but New York City had stopped producing real men. There was of course no shortage of the impostors and frauds. Men who sent their representatives way ahead of their realities. She and her girls had met them all. The Married. The Player. The Unstable. The Eternally Wounded. The Sexually Ambivalent. And of course Mr. Just Not Worth It. The things that she saw in Phee gave her hope that at the very least, there were other men out there like him. From the time that they were both freshman, she always felt that Phee had incredible potential, but she never depended on what he might or might not be. She took him for who he was in the moment. The beauty of being his friend all these years had afforded her the vantage point of seeing who he really was and not who he may have felt obligated to be. She saw Phee as a throwback to the type of man her father was, the type of man she admired. Phee had honor, integrity and long-forgotten practices of chivalry. Even at eighteen, he was properly schooled on which side of the sidewalk to walk on when in the company of a woman. He opened doors and pulled out chairs. She loved his versatility. He was an athlete and academic who appreciated the arts. In her opinion, he had a healthy enough balance of "macho-swag" to make him interesting but not annoying. One of the things that she loved about him most was that no matter the circumstances or stakes, Phee was a man who always tried to do what was right. There was nothing in the world she wouldn't do for him because of the simple fact she knew he was the one person who would do anything for her.

By the time Phee and Quincy had gotten to her place, Brenda had not only gone to work on her computer but had set up two laptops for the partners.

"I set these up for you to be able to follow me. I transferred everything that I worked on at the station, just like you told me to," Brenda said.

"Look Brenda, I know you and Phee go way back and I appreciate everything that you've done for us so far, but I really need you to understand what kind of trouble you can get into by continuing to help us. We're breaking some serious laws here," Quincy said.

"First of all, they'd have to catch us, which is not going to happen. And second of all, if my life was in danger, I'd like to think that someone would be willing to break some rules to save it. I appreciate the concern, but I'm already in."

"Ok, so you're positive there's no way for the feds to trace us?" Phee asked.

"You of all people should know not to underestimate the ability of a motivated woman."

"Sorry," Phee responded.

"Okay, so which do you want first, the good news or the great news?" Brenda asked.

"Let's start with the great news. We could definitely use it," Quincy responded.

"Everything on the hard drive was programmed to self-delete if an unrecognized source attempted to retrieve info from it."

"So how is that great news?" Quincy asked.

"Because in order for him to set up that type of defense, he had to establish a corresponding data code for remote retrieval if he lost everything. I'm using the same remote code to get in without him knowing I'm there. I just put in a GPS feed to find out at least the location of his last sign-on. Give me ten more minutes and I'll be able to tell you where he is and what he had for breakfast," she told them.

Quincy and Phee enjoyed as best they could Brenda's cockiness and attempt at levity. But foremost in all of their minds was the immediate danger that Maclin's life was in.

59

Pastor Boyle hated the way they looked at him. The only thing he hated more was when they treated him as if he didn't exist. As he sat in the back of the cruiser, he saw how his police escort kept stealing glances at him in the rearview mirror. The two cops had essentially ignored Boyle from the time they picked him up at the safe house. There were times that they talked among themselves as though Boyle was nonexistent. The ride was long and awkward for him, making Boyle feel more like a prisoner than a protected citizen or respected pastor. It was evident that somehow they had heard. As he looked out the rear window, Pastor Boyle thought how tragic it was that a man could spend his entire life accomplishing great things only to have them aborted by brief moments of weakness. He had fed the hungry, tended to the ill, clothed the homeless and saved countless souls. But he would be remembered most for his predilection for young girls.

He had fought the temptation for the majority of his life, but there were times when the little girls' innocence and beauty had rendered him helpless to his own desires. He had never gone as far as touching them, but he had grown adept at developing a strong enough imagination to fuel his masturbatory fantasies in the privacy of his office or home. Then there was also the extensive collection of child pornography that he indulged in on a daily basis. In his mind, his sin was not as bad as the things he had heard about the other targets. No matter what anyone said or thought, he was certain that God had forgiven him because only God knew his true heart. He waited for the day that he would break the cycle he had found himself in since he was a young man. He sinned. He prayed. He was forgiven. He sinned. He prayed. He was forgiven. He sinned. He prayed. He was...

Cops and cons still called them "short eyes." A derogatory '70s nickname for pedophiles. Both sides of the law hated child abusers with equal fervor. Even to the most hardened of men, there were few things lower than the animal who preyed on small children for sexual gratification. When the seven remaining targets were placed in protective custody, the whispers and accusations began to fly. Once word spread that the killer was targeting fallen men of the cloth, various charges and claims against them started rolling in. Deggler had inadvertently empowered victims and enablers to come forward and indict the church leaders. The clergymen's crimes were slowly coming to light. Long after Deggler was dead and gone, the horrors of what he had exposed would linger for who knows how long.

The cop car trailed Agents' Nguyen and Jacobson, the two feds in front of them. They resented being the ones who actually had to transport Pastor Boyle even if it was to his dialysis appointment. If the rumors were true about him, then they felt that his life certainly wasn't worth the trouble of prolonging. As they pulled up to the private medical facility, Nguyen and Jacobson jumped out of the lead car and walked back to the cruiser.

"We'll take him up. Make sure you secure the front and back," Agent Nguyen said.

As the two agents and Boyle rode up the elevator, no one spoke. After stopping on the fourth floor, they walked the long corridor to the dialysis ward. They brought him directly to the treatment room, checked it out first, and then waited outside the door as he entered. After getting him settled into his treatment, the agents knew that it would take anywhere from three to five hours for his dialysis session. As he paced the corridor, Nguyen resented the fact that he was now relegated to an escort detail when only days earlier Michaelson had teased him with the possibility of being point man over the entire investigation after Maclin was hospitalized. Nguyen had nothing but respect and admiration for Maclin, but these types of cases had the power to greatly change an agent's status and entire career. Now that Maclin had been kidnapped, Nguyen thought it was a waste of his time and talents having to babysit Pastor Boyle and his failing kidneys.

"Wait here. I'm gonna hit the head," Nguyen said to Jacobson.

Nguyen may have been Vietnamese, but he had always had a problem handling Vietnamese food. It wasn't that he didn't like it; just the opposite. Much to his Swedish wife's dismay, his mother's cooking was his weakness. He overindulged himself once a week at his family's gathering. His mother's bánh cams were his Kryptonite. They were deep-fried rice sesame balls filled with sweetened mung bean paste. His problem was that he could never stop at one. Even in the middle of his gluttony, he feared the price he would pay the next morning, but still that never seemed to deter him in the least. As much as he loved the food, there was something about it that just didn't agree with his system. He had needed to use the bathroom for the last hour or so, but he had to put everything on hold when Agent Michaelson personally assigned him to escort Pastor Boyle to and from the treatment center. He had heard the growing rumors about Boyle and the issues the cops had with the pastor, but he was never one to condemn a person without irrefutable evidence of their offenses. As his stomach grumbled and churned, Nguyen remembered that his most pressing issue with Pastor Boyle was that he had kept him from a much needed bowel movement.

When Nguyen walked into the bathroom, he noticed three urinals and two stalls. The farthest stall was occupied, so he entered the one closest to him. Ten minutes later he felt like a new man. It wasn't until he reached for the toilet paper that he realized that there was none. He knocked on the dividing wall of the next stall.

"Excuse me buddy. I'm out of toilet paper on this side. Can you slide me some under?"

Nguyen looked under the divider and saw the naked calves of the man next to him.

"Excuse me. Hello?" Nguyen called out again.

Nguyen quickly rose and exited and pushed open the unlocked door of the occupied stall. There he found a man dressed only in his T-shirt, underwear, socks and shoes propped up on the toilet with an obviously broken neck. Nguyen grabbed both his gun and walkie-talkie and raced toward the exit.

"He's in the building. Deggler is in the building!!!"

Nyugen ran faster than he ever had back to Boyle's treatment room. As he reached the anteroom, there was no sign of Agent Jacobson. Nguyen burst through the door of the treatment room to discover Boyle's body hanging and disemboweled.

"This is Agent Nguyen, lock the building down. Repeat, lock the building down. Deggler is here!!!"

60

Deggler was gone. But by the time he had left, the body count was up to four. In addition to the staff member in the stall and Boyle, the feds found Agent Jacobson stuffed in a janitor's closet with a broken neck and one of the cops out back in a dumpster with the same C.O.D.

Neither Nguyen nor Officer Todd, the surviving cop, were able to offer any useful information or concrete details of what had happened. Todd was in a state of shock, with periodic outbursts of rage. His slain partner was four days from retirement and one of the most popular cops on the squad. Several fellow officers comforted Todd one moment and restrained him the next. In one day, this was the second of New York's Finest to have been killed by Deggler. There wasn't a cop at the scene who, if given the opportunity, would hesitate to kill Deggler on the spot and piss on his still warm corpse. Michaelson and the feds wanted to arrest him, but the boys in blue wanted to crucify him. Nguyen was in mourning over the lives lost and the career destroyed. He was certain that he would never professionally recover. As progressive as the FBI liked to think of themselves as being, the female and minority agents still quietly viewed them as a good ol' boys network. Agents made mistakes all of the time, but unfortunately, some were held to a different standard than others. Now Nguyen would be forever viewed as the Asian agent that had been given an assignment and failed it miserably. The most important case of his young career, and he had been both literally and figuratively caught with his pants down. All of the ladder climbing and progress he had made would be overshadowed and undone by a few too many of his mother's deep-fried rice sesame balls.

By the time Michaelson arrived at the scene, cops and agents were everywhere. He stared hard and long at Agent Nguyen as he was debriefed. Michaelson was livid and made no attempt whatsoever at tempering or downplaying his fury. Nguyen was the unfortunate target of his boss's outrage. Fellow agents and cops alike felt somewhat sorry for Nguyen. Although they would never admit it openly, they all knew that they could have made the same mistake he had. They all lived with the daily fear that one wrong decision on their part could cost not only their lives but others as well.

Detective Alvarez walked to his car and called Quincy to update him on Deggler's latest killings. Michaelson was in mid-tirade when the agent was interrupted by his cell phone.

"Agent Michaelson," he barked as he answered his phone.

"If you turn over the remaining six, Agent Maclin won't have to die. If you don't, she'll be the next but not the last innocent to be killed," Deggler's voice said on the phone.

Michaelson immediately covered the mouthpiece of his phone and urgently whispered to Nguyen, who was standing closest to him.

"Have Richards track the cell towers for incoming on this line."

Nguyen quickly pulled out his cell and dialed as Michaelson uncovered his phone and spoke to the caller.

"You know I can't do that," Michaelson said.

"Can't or won't?"

"Same thing," Michaelson responded.

"Then you're ready to accept the consequences? You're willing to intentionally allow Agent Maclin to suffer, and I assure you she will. I'm giving you an opportunity here, Agent Michaelson. She already told me about the safe houses that you have them tucked away in out in Queens and Brooklyn. And the other two in the Bronx. If I were the senseless animal that you think I am, I would have already killed more of your agents to get to the men on my list. If you don't turn them over, this won't end well for anyone, especially not you and your colleagues. They can all burn with the wicked as far as I'm concerned."

"Look, you've already won. You've ruined the lives of the men that you wanted to. People know now. Things about them are beginning to come out. Let us take it from here," Michaelson pleaded.

"If you think that's what this was all about, then you have no idea how wrong you are."

"Then tell me, what is it about?" Michaelson asked.

"Maclin dies in one hour, then I come for the others."

As the phone went dead Michaelson quickly turned to Agent Nguyen.

"Richards said somehow the signal was split. It registered on seven different towers. No way to pinpoint it," Nguyen said.

Michaelson cursed out loud and then frantically dialed a number on his cell.

"This is Michaelson. Take the targets out of the safe houses. I don't care. Do it. Bring them out to Linden and put them in The Black Hole. Complete lockdown. No one in, no one out."

———

Deggler tried as best he could to plan for every possible outcome. He was a man of many contingency plans. He planned for failure more than he planned for success. He found cops simple and predictable. It was the reason he was able to successfully evade them for the last thirty years. The thing they did best was under-estimate him and reduce him to their limited imaginations. He knew when he took Maclin that ultimately her life would be of limited value to him. The cops would never barter or trade her for the life of one of his intended victims. Her usefulness came in the form of distraction. His abduction of her was simply to buy time and perfect his sleight of hand maneuvers. The fact that Michaelson believed him about Maclin telling him where the safe houses were was worth her abduction alone. It never occurred to the agent that Deggler had gotten the information from hacking into their system and getting the locations of the safe houses operated by the FBI throughout New York. Saying that the info came from Maclin had the desired effect. It made his threat more authentic and brought more urgency to Michaelson's reaction. Deggler's bluff paid off. Soon, very soon, he would have the remaining six all in one place, courtesy of Agent Michaelson. Even though time would not allow him to kill them the way he had originally planned, he had already been given another strategy that would be pleasing to his Lord. But before he killed them, there was one more thing that Deggler knew he had to do. Now that she was no longer of any use, the time had come for him to kill Agent Maclin.

61

The minute Deggler returned, Maclin knew something bad had happened. He moved her from the tiny boiler room where he had left her tied and gagged. After bringing her back to the basement's main area, he completely disrobed before her and flogged himself for fifteen minutes straight. She lost count at thirty lashes. After Deggler exhausted himself he knelt naked before her. There was nothing sexual about his nudity. He did it more as a confirmation of his punishment than any type of erotic exhibitionism. He stretched both of his arms to his sides and slowly turned for her so that she could see the welts and blood on his body. He seemed to take great pride in showing her the extent of his self-inflicted wounds. She had no idea why, but for some reason, he needed a witness other than God for his act of penance. As he knelt exhausted, she took in the strange details of his body.

His Biblical tatts, his missing penis and overly muscular frame. He put his face close enough to hers that she could smell his warm, stale breath. As he moved an inch closer, she felt the stubble of his unshaven cheeks. Deggler was incredibly gentle in all movement toward her. He took her still-bound hands and used them to slowly caress his face. As much as he repulsed her, Maclin couldn't help but notice how much he savored the simple contact. As he made a slight adjustment to the zip tie around her wrists, he ran a finger across the horizontal scars of Maclin's suicide attempt. Deggler kissed the back of her wrists before showing her similar scars on his own wrists from his teenage years. He offered her water from a bottle that he drank from. As she nodded her acceptance, he removed her gag and put the bottle to her lips. Maclin never took her eyes off him as she gulped the water. She refused to break the stare or give even the slightest indication of backing down in any way. Maclin didn't fear Deggler for the simple fact that she saw her current situation as having only two possible outcomes. Either he would kill her (which in some ways he had already done), or she would find a way to kill him. The simple equation allowed her to focus on what was most important to her, trying in some way to gain an upper hand on Deggler. She could tell it bothered him that he couldn't smell fear on her. Everything she did was now strategy and psychological warfare. Willington had taught her to trust her training over her instincts. He told her to never discount her instincts, but if the two were ever in conflict with each other, then to go with her training. As she continued to stare at Deggler, she understood more of what Willington meant. Instincts were usually based on and accompanied by emotion. Training and technique was objective and consistent. She was different from Quincy and Phee in that regard. They were guts and instincts first. Willington had taught her to be much more academic.

Deggler left Maclin's gag off in hopes that she might talk. It had been some time since he had heard the sound of a woman's voice speaking directly to him in anything resembling a real conversation. He wanted to hear her in one way or another give validation to what he had to do.

"I know you're only doing your job, Agent Maclin, but do you really feel that the wicked are worth protecting? Worth dying for?" Deggler asked.

Maclin looked at him and refused to speak. She refused to give him the interaction and attention that he was hungry for. If she had responded, she would have been doing so on his terms. Her silence wasn't a protest; it was an offensive strike. She defied him so that she could level the playing field. It was obvious that Deggler was extremely intelligent. Intelligence craved stimulation. The thing Deggler craved most of all was the opportunity to confirm the validity of his calling. She had every intention of engaging him, but the timing would be of her choosing, not his. Maclin defined the rules of engagement in terms of inches and seconds.

When she continued to stare at him and didn't respond, Deggler sat quietly for a few minutes. The next time he spoke, there was a downgraded shift in his energy. His voice was dull and his words were rhetorical. There was less effort in his speech, as if he were being more introspective.

"Your blood and the blood of the others killed today are on your hands, not mine."

Maclin again refused to respond, but was clearer on what he was looking for as he continued speaking.

"I had a dog named Troy when I was a kid. I wasn't allowed to have friends, just Troy. He was probably the only thing in this world that I truly loved. My father always threatened to take him away whenever I did something that didn't please him. One day, when he was beating me, Troy bit him. My father grabbed a two by four and beat my dog within an inch of his life. Three weeks later, after Troy recovered, he bit my father again while he was beating me. And again my father almost killed him. That night I carried Troy to the park and drowned him in the pond because no matter what it would have cost him, Troy would have always done the one thing he knew, because that was his nature."

"Just as it's your nature to kill?" Maclin finally spoke.

"My nature is to serve God and His will, Agent Maclin."

"It's funny how people always blame their own tragic flaws on God's will. You're not even original."

"Fortunately, faithfulness trumps originality."

"Sounds to me like you're confusing fidelity with narcissism."

"I'm doing God's will."

"Not if it's at the cost of ignoring His mercy. Let me get this straight. You're killing the very sinners that God is supposed to be all about forgiving?"

"Do you consider yourself to be a religious woman?"

"Not by the standards of a madman."

"I've dedicated my life to following the will of God and you've dedicated yours to following the will of man. So which one of us is really crazy?" Deggler asked.

"If you look at it that way, maybe both, but only one of us is horribly deluded," Maclin retorted.

"There is nothing delusional about my faith and commitment!!!" Deggler said emphatically.

Now that she had him acting more emotionally, Maclin decided to push a little harder.

"You can try to convince yourself of whatever you feel you need to, but if you really believed the bullshit you're saying you wouldn't need the absolution that you're trying to get from me now," Maclin responded.

Deggler tried to suppress and mask his anger by smiling at Maclin, but it was evident that she had touched a nerve and possibly scored a point. She would take them one at a time and stockpile her minor victories until she might be presented with an opportunity where she could use them as potential currency. The key thing was to stay ahead of Deggler and try to anticipate his next move. Deggler studied her for a beat before he spoke again.

"Unlike you, I don't have to convince myself of my beliefs."

"Isn't that what all of this has been about? You trying to convince yourself that you're better than your father? That you're more righteous than him?"

She saw a subtle change in Deggler's eyes. Maclin was walking a very fine line. Her goal wasn't to make him out of control, but just to rattle him and get him a little off-kilter. Sometimes that was the only hope to get smart criminals like Deggler to make mistakes or become sloppy.

"My father and I are two very different men. Just like the others, he used his beliefs to betray God. I use mine to serve Him," Deggler said.

"Is that what you have to tell yourself each morning before you get started?"

"People like you and I who believe in their purpose are never short on motivation. Aside from semantics, we're not that different. Given the opportunity, would you hesitate to kill me for what you believe?"

"Not at all. The world doesn't deserve your kind of evil."

Deggler looked at Maclin oddly, and then burst into laughter.

"The idealism thing doesn't really suit you, Agent Maclin. It wasn't idealism that made you pursue me for the past ten years. It was good old-fashioned revenge. His name was Agent Willington, wasn't it?" he asked her.

Maclin just stared, refusing to respond. The sound of Willington's name coming from Deggler's mouth caught her completely off guard. She fought the surge of anger that was rising in her. Flashes of Willington's battered and bruised body in the morgue came rushing back. Images and thoughts that she hadn't had in several years were now clouding her mind and judgment. All the while that she was trying to get into Deggler's head, he had countered her with the perfect unexpected jab. If she wasn't careful, Deggler would weaken her by making her subjective. Unseen by Deggler, Maclin dug her fingernails into her palm until she drew blood. She used the pain to distract herself from losing it. She fought for composure.

"Yes. Willington."

She attempted to confirm his name as though it had no value or importance to her. But when Deggler reached over to the nearby pile of clothes and pulled out an old photo of a younger, smiling Maclin and Willington, she could offer no defense or strategy. As she looked at the old photo, everything grounded and supportive left her. Maclin shut down. Her brain, lungs and training one by one let her down. They didn't function in the manner that she needed them to. It seemed that everything required extra effort, energy and thought. Deggler's voice continued ad nauseam.

"I never forget a face. The other night when you tried to run me down, the minute I saw you I knew who you were. I've carried this photo for the last ten years because, when I first saw it, it was the closest thing to true happiness that I had ever seen. He was definitely not someone I wanted to kill, but I didn't have a choice. I actually think that I could have even liked him under different circumstances. There was something noble about him. And at the same time, that was the same thing that made him dangerous for me. I knew he would have done whatever he needed to stop me. Just as I know the same about you, Agent Maclin. It's your nature. I don't take any of it personally. Just as I hope the same of you. If you don't mind, I'd like to pray for your soul."

As he closed his eyes and quietly murmured a prayer, Maclin felt something that she hadn't in years. Fear. Deep, heavy fear. The knowledge that she had run out of time and options. Deggler had won. He had gotten whatever it was that he needed from her and now no longer had any use for her at all. As he prayed for her, it was no longer a question of whether he would kill her, it was now just a matter of how.

He rose and quickly got dressed, then re-gagged her and led her back to the tiny boiler room. After locking her inside, he grabbed a propane tank and long rubber hose from a nearby corner. He placed the hose in a crack just above the door jamb and attached the other end to the tank. Maclin couldn't stop him from killing her. She had only succeeded in getting him to do so without violence. Her strategy had backfired on her miserably. Deggler avoided her eyes when he spoke.

"It'll be easier on you if you don't fight it. Just let the Lord take you. The last thoughts a person has before they die should be whether or not they know the weight of their soul," he glanced at her one last time before turning and locking her in the small room. With her feet and hands bound, there was no way for her to reach the hose hanging eight feet above her. She threw her body into the metal door repeatedly but to no avail. As the small space began to fill with gas, she tried as best she could to fight the dizziness and her loss of equilibrium. There was something more than the fear or sadness that overtook her as she lay exhausted on the floor gasping for air. There was the overwhelming regret that she came close but ultimately failed in accomplishing the only thing that mattered to her in the last ten years of her life.

62

Quincy and Phee barreled down Second Avenue, barely avoiding several near collisions. Two blocks from the address that Brenda gave them, they ran into thick congestion caused by an accident involving a van and a hansom cab. Quincy cut the wheel and hit the sidewalk and went around the accident. Before the car had come to a full stop, Phee impatiently jumped out and sprinted in the church's direction. Quincy did his best to keep up. As they approached the church, they both hopped the construction fence that surrounded the front. Phee pulled out his Sig Sauer and checked his clip as Quincy did the same with his 9mm. Quincy took the front while Phee made his way around to the back. Quincy entered through a broken window on the first floor. He moved deliberately and as quickly as possible. He wasn't concerned that his heavy footsteps announced his arrival. If Deggler was in the building, they wanted him to know that help had come and that he had been found. Phee found loosened planks covering the entrance to the basement and made his way in. As he checked all of the rooms of the basement he heard Quincy on the floor above him doing the same. Phee noticed the propane tank and the hose that was rigged to the hole at the top of the door. The closer Phee got to the boiler room, the more prevalent the smell of gas was in the air. As he quickly turned off the propane tank and unlatched the metal door and carefully opened it, he was hit with a potent gust of gas. He discovered Maclin's lifeless body curled on the floor in the corner of the room. Phee immediately yelled out for Quincy as he picked up Maclin and carried her outside.

As Phee frantically started mouth to mouth, Quincy immediately jumped in and alternated with chest compressions. The partners desperately worked on Maclin even as she remained unresponsive to their efforts. They refused to give up. They refused to lose her twice in the same day. As Quincy watched Phee attempt to blow life into Maclin's lungs, he said the closest thing he had in years to a prayer. "Please Lord, don't let her die." When Phee took a break from the breaths, Quincy went back to work on the chest compressions. Neither of them had any idea how long she had been down, but they had been working on her longer than what was considered the comeback zone. Neither of the men looked at each other. Neither one wanted to give or receive anything resembling doubt or failure. Against all logic and every indication of her death, Quincy and Phee continued to work to save Maclin. As Phee was breathing into her, Maclin suddenly and violently gasped for air. He literally smelled the acrid scent of trapped gas leaving her lungs. She was completely disoriented as Quincy turned her onto her side when she began vomiting. She panted and gasped heavily as her body demanded oxygen. Both men held her in the best position for maximum intake. It took her a few minutes to regulate her breathing and regain control of her body. She was still dizzy but fully aware of the eventual return of her cognitive skills. Maclin's head was pounding and her stomach was queasy, but she had never felt more alive. There was an involuntary silence that passed between them. Quincy thought about the partner that he had lost several years ago in a shootout. He remembered holding him as he took his last breath. There was nothing that compared to the feeling of helplessly watching a loved one die. Seeing Maclin come back was the best feeling he had ever had. She offered the partners the best smile she could muster.

"Thank you, Quincy. Thanks, Phee," she said.

"Now you really got me worried. That's the first time you ever called me Phee."

"Now that we've swapped spit, I feel it's the least I can do."

63

Dear Papi,

I met my mother today. I found her nestled in the bottom of your dresser drawer. And even though she wasn't able to tell me the type of things or offer me the kind of advice and counsel that most mothers normally do, she told me the most important things that I needed to know. I know it sounds funny, but when I was a child and you told me she had died, I used to fantasize about her return. I thought if I learned to pray the right way, somehow God would let her come back to us and we would be a family. Looking back, I now know that the first time I ever got mad at God was when He never sent her back. Sometimes the things we ask for are the very things we can't see. The mother that I met today could never measure up to the father that you've been. She could never be the unselfish and unconditional love that you've been. Like most people, I've spent a significant part of my life holding on to traditional or preconceived notions of how things should be. Mothers are mothers and fathers are fathers. But you've been every and anything but traditional or predictable. I know the core belief by which you define love is built on the things that aren't to be questioned or doubted. Unfortunately for both of us, you allowed me to take your love for granted. I knew it was something that was always there for me and on my own terms. And until I read your letters to my mother, I never stopped to think about the sacrifices you made and the toll demanded of you. When I was growing up, you used to love to ask me whether or not I thought "our character defined the choices we make, or did the choices we make define our character?" Maybe they're both the same thing, ultimately, but I also think that for some people like you, there really are no choices. Doing what is considered right and honorable is no more of a choice for them as breathing is for the rest of us. My mother made a choice and you made a commitment. To raise me. To love me. To put me before your dreams and needs. I was the type of mother that I was to Joaquin because of the type of father you were to me. When he died, I died. The only thing I had left was the hurt and anger. And it was all directed at you. It was the only feeling I had left. In a weird way, it became the thing that allowed me to feel the closest to being alive. A friend of mine suggested that it wasn't just you that I was angry with. Maybe he was right. Maybe you were just the easier choice. It's funny that when I was a kid and God didn't send my mother back to me, I *was so clear on my anger toward Him. But as an adult I lost the courage to be honest with myself and all others involved. Maybe directing my anger at you gave me something I needed most—a finite and tangible target.*

I remember when I was eight and our dog Picasso died. Every day for the next month, you and I caught a bus and went downtown and walked around looking at all of the tall buildings and skyscrapers. Every day you pointed out a different one to me. It took me a long time to understand exactly what you were trying to do, but as I got older I finally figured out that you were just trying to give me a reason to look up. I've spent every day for the last two months thinking about everything that I lost and how much I hurt, but I never stopped to think about you and what kind of pain you must have been in. I don't think either one of us will ever get through this if we're not the ones to give each other something to look up to while we're down.

Your loving daughter,

Angelita

Elena placed her face next to her father's. She wanted Romero to feel her warmth, to remember what life felt like. There were no rules or road maps; Elena was just making it up as she went along. There were no lessons on teaching a person to fight death. The best Elena could hope for was Love forgiving her and telling her what to do. Showing her and inspiring her. As she sat and held her father's hand, Love whispered in her ear that it was neither free nor unconditional. It was jealous and demanding, and most of all dependent on submission.

Elena continued to talk to her father, saying things that she had never said to him before. She talked about things like hope and reconciliation. The things that she said didn't magically become easier for her to say, just more and more necessary. She accepted that there were no easy answers. No clear and simple explanation why she had lost her son. The placement of blame was at best nothing more than a distraction. At worst, it invalidated the core tenets of what she thought she had come to believe and value. She wasn't sure when it had started. Her hypocrisy. She suspected that it began long before her son died. The only direct loss she had experienced was the overdose death of her son's father, Carlos. His reckless lifestyle had in many ways prepared her for that possibility. Unfortunately, his death came as no big surprise. The only other tragedy that Elena had faced in life had happened a lot earlier with the loss of Picasso, her beloved German shepherd, but at eight years old some of the impact had been lessened by her youth.

Her father brought her to church and taught her to fear and respect God. There was no doubt whatsoever that she believed. But she never had the need to scrutinize or question whether or not her belief was just something that had been handed down to her and regurgitated to her from her father and her father's father and so forth. Her spiritual convictions weren't necessarily born of independent thought. She believed what she was taught to be believe. Like most people, God was something that she inherited as a child. She never really made Him hers. By adulthood, He had become habit. She said all the right things and, as far as she was concerned, felt and did all the right things as well. But

Joaquin's death had exposed hairline fractures in the foundation of her beliefs. Tiny fissures of doubt and unanswered questions. Not having been truly tested before, her faith was more of a lifelong accessory than she could have ever admitted. As Elena talked to her father, she thought of Quincy and some of the conversations they had recently. If she was to be honest with herself then she had to accept that he had exposed her for who she really was: a part-time believer who put her faith to the test only at the most convenient of times. Quincy was right. It was hypocritical of her and his brother Liam to profess to believe in God but not believe in forgiveness. She started questioning how she could talk to him about the power of fate and destiny and yet hold her own father responsible for God's will. She thought it ironic that the man who believed the least in God was the man who was teaching her the most about God. In the quiet room at her father's bedside, Elena came to an irrefutable conclusion. That faith, true faith, was all or nothing.

64

As Quincy and Phee were bringing Maclin up to speed on all that had transpired since her abduction, Phee's phone rang. He looked at the caller ID and answered. "Hey, what's up, Brenda?"

"Did you find him?" she asked.

"We found Maclin, but Deggler was gone. Maclin is safe, thanks to you."

"Thank God. I, uh…I got some bad news."

"What is it?" Phee asked.

"Deggler has hacked into the FBI's files and they have no idea."

"How the hell did he do that?" Phee asked.

"Phee, he's one of the best I've ever seen. He's got emails, memos and even the eight profiles they did on him over the years. But that's not the worst of it."

"What do you mean?"

"He intercepted an interdepartmental email stating that all of the subjects were being moved to one location. The email just said somewhere in Jersey, but unfortunately it didn't say exactly where."

"Why the hell would Michaelson do something so stupid? If Deggler finds out where they are, he'll find a way to get to them," Phee said.

"He may have already," she said.

"Tell me," Phee said.

"Deggler's got a phone-tracking program connected to his system. He can reroute calls through his computer and then hack into their network."

"Okay, so what does all of that mean?"

"It means that forty-five minutes ago he tapped into Agent Michaelson's phone. Deggler may already know where they're moving the targets."

"Shit!!!" Phee exclaimed.

As Phee hung up, Quincy was finishing up a call of his own.

"That didn't sound good. What's up?" Maclin asked.

"Brenda just found out that Michaelson has moved the targets to one location and Deggler has found a way to not only hack into the FBI network, but he's even found a way to tap Michaelson's phone." Phee explained.

"So he knows everything we know and more," Quincy added.

"We've got to warn Michaelson," Phee said.

"We can't, not without tipping our hand. Deggler has no idea that we have this intel, or what he might be planning. I say we use that to our advantage," Maclin said.

Quincy jumped in. "I agree. Besides, if we tell Michaelson how we know what we know, we'll be locked up for the next thirty years. That was Alvarez on the phone. He just gave me a blow-by-blow of what happened at the dialysis center. I think I know who might be able to help us without tipping our hand."

65

gent Nguyen's father never trusted Americans. He and his family escaped Hanoi during the latter stages of the Vietnam War. Being from the north, they had to lie and forge papers and then serve out a short stint at a refugee camp at Camp Pendleton. From there they settled in Little Saigon in Orange County, California. After the senior Nguyen became an outcast for his pro-Communist views, the Nguyens moved to New York, where they opened a successful Vietnamese restaurant. The youngest Nguyen pursued a law degree before enlisting in the FBI. Tu Nguyen had always been at the top of his class. He had always been an overachiever and impressively successful in the majority of his endeavors. When Tu joined the FBI, his father warned him that he would never be allowed to be anything more than a token ethnic agent. Agent Tu Nguyen was determined to prove his father wrong and anyone else who doubted him.

As he sat in his office, Agent Nguyen turned the small family photo that he kept on his desk away from him as he heard the negative voice of his father in his ear. The day's earlier events kept playing over and over in his head, frustrating him and making it impossible for him to concentrate. What made it worse was that he couldn't talk to anyone about what happened. His colleagues were too professionally subjective and his family was too emotionally biased. He couldn't tell his wife or family that Michaelson had relegated him to being a desk jockey after his earlier mistake. He had worked his entire life to prove his overbearing father wrong. He wanted to show his father that his paranoia and xenophobia was outdated and irrelevant. He wanted to show him that even the son of a bitter Communist could rise to great heights in government in the Land of Opportunity.

As his cell phone vibrated in the inside of his suit jacket, he pulled it out and answered, "Agent Nguyen."

"You interested in saving your career?" the vaguely familiar voice on the other end asked.

Nguyen did as he was instructed and drove the short distance to Battery Park. As he drove up, he saw Quincy and Phee waiting for him. Nguyen exited his car as the two cops approached him.

"What is this about?" Nguyen asked.

"Did you tell anybody that I called you?" Quincy asked.

"No, I did exactly what you asked me to do. I didn't talk to anybody or say where I was going. You said this was a matter of life and death."

"It is," a woman's voice said.

As Nguyen turned around, he was shocked to see Maclin disheveled and dirty but still standing. "Agent Maclin??? But, I don't…"

"It's a long story that I don't have time to fill you in on now. We need your help, and we need it now," Maclin stressed.

"What kind of help?" Nguyen said, still confused.

"We know Michaelson has moved all of the targets to one location. You need to tell us where," Phee insisted.

"I can't do that. You're not even cops anymore," Nguyen responded.

"But I'm still an agent and you need to trust me. Deggler has found a way to tap into the system. That's why I haven't even told Michaelson I escaped. Deggler knows every move we're making," Maclin said.

"How do you know that?" Nguyen demanded.

"We can't tell you that right now. All that matters is that you trust me, because there are a lot of lives depending on whether or not you help us," she said.

"We heard what you went through today. Nothing you do can change what already happened, but the targets' lives and every agent that is watching over them is at risk," Quincy added.

"Then we need to call it in," Nguyen responded.

"We already told you, Deggler's in the system. As far as we know he's monitoring calls, emails and who knows what else. Listen to me brotha, we don't have a lot of time for bullshit right now. Do you want any more dead bodies on your conscience?" Phee asked emphatically.

As Phee stepped to Nguyen, the agent instinctively adjusted to a more defensive position. He remembered how quick and violent Phee's temper was. When Phee put up his hands in a conciliatory gesture, Nguyen decided that the cop had advanced on him more out of frustration than malice. Good or bad, it was Phee's directness that brought it all home for Nguyen. It was hard enough that people had died in part because of his having made a bad decision. Now he was being asked to go against everything that he had been taught and completely risk what was left of his suddenly anemic career. He was having more problems with what they weren't telling him than what they were. If they were wrong, he would be done; if they were right, lives would be saved. Nguyen told them what they wanted to know on the one condition that he be allowed to go with them. Deggler had become the all-elusive white whale at the Bureau that every agent wanted to take down. But to Nguyen, it had become much more personal. Deggler had taken lives on his watch, all but destroyed his burgeoning career and left him pervious to his father's cynicism. Stopping Deggler was all that mattered to him now.

66

There were six left. Deggler had successfully made it to the halfway point. The half dozen remaining targets had been moved to a nondescript facility that the feds sometimes used on the outskirts of Jersey. Some of the six knew each other in passing, but all knew of each other. They had all now been cast in the roles of degenerate clerics before the world. Most of them stayed in their designated bedrooms, but two of them watched ESPN in the common area with four of the nine agents assigned to watch over them. There was an uneasiness throughout the building. A palpable tension between hosts and guests. No one there wanted to be there. Not the agents assigned and certainly not the men who needed watching. The agents were professional but curt. The six targets were all overly courteous and seemingly sweet, grandfatherly types. But everyone in the building and beyond knew that they were all guilty of one unforgivable offense or another.

The red-brick building had been built in the '40s and located in a sparsely populated area in Englewood, New Jersey. It was sandwiched in between a plumbing supply facility on the left and a residence to the right. The feds had confiscated the building in a drug raid and now often used it for temporary housing of federal witnesses or agents in from DC. It was a secure, two-story building that was in the final stages of renovation. Some of the agents who had stayed there before had dubbed it "The Black Hole" because of the building's paucity of windows. The remaining renovations were much more external cosmetics than anything. An outdoor paint job and new roof were needed along with an updated HVAC system. The interior of the building was quite impressive. Although most of the original integrity and design of the building was intact, there were modern additions that had been effectively integrated. The building was retrofitted and designed to keep people out. There were three entrances: the front, the back and the adjacent garage, that were all steel-framed doors operated by an electronic key panel. The few windows that did exist were all powered and made of unbreakable Plexiglas. The security system and even most of the electronics and utilities were operated through a fiber optic central processor.

Deggler went into the FBI files and pulled up the original schematics of the building and even the proposed architectural plans of the renovations. It only took him twelve minutes to gain complete access to the electronic brain through his laptop. The first thing he did was change both the operating and override codes for the keypads to both doors and windows. Once in the system, he immediately overrode the existing program commands and recalibrated the system for his specific needs. He reversed the existing cell booster to jam phone signals. The building had been renovated to keep people out, but Deggler was using all of the technology at his disposal to keep them in. Forty-five minutes earlier he had accessed the roof from the adjoining building. As was the case with many of the older East Coast buildings, the air conditioning and heating units were on the roof. There were designs in the plans to relocate the units to the basement of the building, but fortunately for what Deggler had in mind, no such changes had been made yet. He quietly rigged the rooftop dual pack of the heating unit so that the combustion air was rerouted back into the building. He adjusted the flow of the air intake valve to expedite the influx of poisonous carbon monoxide. He calculated the chronological impact rate based on the square footage of the building and the amount of gas being released back through the venting system.

One by one, the occupants below started feeling the various symptoms. The effects didn't take long to register. Their red blood cells were absorbing the carbon monoxide far more quickly than oxygen. What was at first dismissed as cold- or flu-like symptoms quickly escalated to more serious effects. There was the weakness, the headaches and dizziness. Then the nausea and vomiting began. The oldest of the men even experienced chest pain and temporary dementia.

By the time the agents began to grasp what was happening, it was too late. They were unable to open windows or doors because Deggler had reprogrammed them. As they attempted to use their phones to call for help, they discovered that none of their cells had signals. They began to lose control of their motor skills and their resistance to gravity. The younger and stronger men fought as best they could, for as long as they could. Some of the older and weaker preachers seemed more ready to surrender. Disoriented and weak, they started to fall and made little effort to rise once they were down. By the time Deggler entered, most of the men were unconscious or barely mobile. An agent lying in the corner looked up to see Deggler in a filtered mask carrying two of the priests simultaneously over both of his shoulders. As the agent struggled to reach for his weapon, everything was in slow motion. The weight of the gun was much too heavy for him. As Deggler kicked the gun away, he stepped over the agent and exited to the garage with the two clerics in tow.

Deggler made two more trips and exited each time with two targets thrown over his shoulder like weightless mannequins. The last conscious agent was on the floor in a corner next to a large floor lamp. With all of the energy and strength he could muster, he reached for the socket that the lamp was plugged into and pulled the head of the cord halfway out just enough to turn the lamp off and on. In, out, in, out. On, off, on, off.

Phee and Nguyen were in the lead car as Quincy and Maclin followed closely behind. As they turned onto Linden Street, they could see the building directly in front of them a block away. A light in the window was flicking on and off in a coded distress signal. Phee immediately pulled out his phone and called Quincy.

"Are you seeing what I'm seeing?" Phee asked.

"Yeah," Quincy replied.

Maclin pulled out the spare gun that Quincy gave her and checked her clip as the two cars sped down the block toward the building. Just as they were arriving, Deggler came speeding out of the garage in a navy blue cargo van and crashed head-on with Phee's car, which caused Quincy to rear-end his partner. Phee and Nguyen's air bags deployed as the front end of their car was completely totaled. Quincy's car sustained damage as well but not nearly as much as his partner's. As both driver and passengers tried to shake it off, Deggler quickly threw the van in reverse, fishtailed it and took off in the opposite direction.

"You okay?" Quincy shouted to Phee.

Phee looked over to Nguyen, who nodded, and then shouted back to Quincy.

"You go after Deggler. Nguyen and I will take the building."

As Quincy and Maclin took off, Phee and Nguyen stumbled out of the car, shook off the cobwebs and moved in the direction of the opened garage door. Once inside the building, they saw bodies everywhere. The one agent who had sent the distress signal was barely conscious, but his hand was involuntarily twitching as it still held the lamp's cord. Phee noticed him first and crossed to him as Nguyen tried in vain to get a phone signal. Based on the symptoms he was starting to feel as well as the examination of the agents, Phee determined that they were all showing signs of gas poisoning.

"We gotta get these bodies out of here," Phee barked in Nguyen's direction.

As they each hoisted one of many fallen agents over their shoulders, they rushed them outside and placed them on the sidewalk in front of the building.

"How many agents were posted here?" Phee asked.

"Nine," Nguyen responded.

"You call it in, and start CPR on these two. I'll get the next one and we can alternate," Phee said.

As Nguyen pulled out his phone and dialed, Phee raced back into the building. The two men were able to get the remaining seven agents out in less than ten minutes. Fortunately all of the agents had a pulse and were showing varying signs of consciousness, even though most of them were very disoriented. Twelve minutes after Nguyen made the phone call, they heard the approaching sirens.

"I'm going after Deggler," Phee said.

"Go. I can handle it from here."

Phee searched the trousers of two of the agents until he found car keys. He pressed the alarm button and then hurried to the sedan parked across the street that responded. As Phee jumped in the car and sped off, he called Quincy to find out what his situation was and to inform him that Deggler had all of the targets in the van. When the first responders arrived on the scene, they were surprised to see one man hovering over the nine semiconscious agents. Nguyen would more than likely become a part of FBI folklore. The one agent who single-handedly saved nine. And even though that wasn't 100 percent the case, few of his colleagues would let the truth stand in the way of a good story. Legends were often born of much less accuracy and truth.

67

Maclin was quickly filling in Michaelson on the phone as Quincy was doing his best to stay up with Deggler's van. The cooling system on Quincy's engine had been cracked and compromised in the crash. Though the car wasn't running up to full speed, they were at least managing to stay on Deggler's tail. Maclin hung up the phone and turned to Quincy.

"Michaelson is sending backup and copters. Should intercept us in ten minutes."

"I hope we can hold out that long," Quincy said, referring to their damaged car. "Phee said the targets are in the van."

As Quincy pushed the car as hard as he could, Deggler crossed a small, two-lane bridge leading into a lumberyard. Quincy and Maclin felt the car dying as it struggled to cross the bridge.

"We're not gonna make it with this. I'll block the bridge.

Looks like this is the only way in or out. If it is, we just gotta try to hold him in," Quincy said.

"I'm not just gonna sit here and let that son of a bitch get away," Maclin responded.

"He's trying to pull us in so he can circle back."

"You don't know that for sure," Maclin protested.

"And you don't know that he's not."

"I know how he thinks, Quincy. Everything he does is calculated and thought out. He's not worried about us trapping him, he just wants us second-guessing ourselves long enough to buy him time. We've gotta move. He's got a van full of victims, and who knows what he has planned for them. Look, you can stay here if you want. I'm going after him," Maclin said as she pulled out her gun, exited the car and ran toward the lumberyard.

Quincy left the car in the middle of the bridge and then ran to catch up with Maclin. Even though he felt that they could be walking into a trap, not backing a partner wasn't an option. Quincy felt that he had finally come to a clearer understanding of Deggler. He understood how his mission was all that he lived for. How it consumed him and gave his life purpose. Quincy finally came to realize that the advantage Deggler had over him and Maclin was that he saw his mission as being greater than himself. Right or wrong, at least in his mind, he served a higher purpose. Higher than his own ego, fear or hatred. Something worth submitting to. There was nothing more dangerous or powerful than a person with a purpose greater than themselves.

The lumberyard was dark and quiet. Quincy caught up with

Maclin just as she entered the gateway. They used hand signals to communicate as they split up and both headed deeper into the yard. The aisles and piles of lumber in the moonlight seemed to stretch forever. Every corner was a hidden threat or potential danger. Quincy and Maclin both knew that Deggler could be anywhere. Quincy quickly turned with his gun pointed when a feral cat scampered across his path. They were throughout the yard, fed to keep the rats away. Quincy hated cats. The priest that had molested him had three, and one of them had badly scratched him when he was eight. Ever since then, he never trusted them. Unlike dogs, they were a much more difficult read. For instance, he was uncertain if the cat that was perched a foot above him would jump down and attack him or if it was staring at him because it wanted him to reach up and pet it. In addition to keeping a sharp eye out for Deggler, he made sure he was aware of the other animals in the yard as well.

As they walked down the main corridor of the yard, Quincy saw the front end of the parked van sticking out behind a pile of lumber. He threw a small rock at Maclin, who was eight yards away, to quietly get her attention. As she turned toward him, he pointed in the direction of the van. They approached the van from the north and south, Quincy on the front driver side and Maclin from the rear passenger side. Just as they got near the van, pieces of lumber began to rain down upon them. Maclin was knocked to the ground by a falling cedar plank. As Quincy rushed to her side, he caught a glimpse of Deggler running toward a wooded area.

"I'm okay. Go after him. I'll check the van," Maclin told

Quincy, who immediately took off after Deggler. As Maclin picked herself up and flung open the doors of the van, the look on her face was one of total and complete shock.

Quincy lost sight of Deggler as he reached the last lumber pile at the edge of the yard. He could only see the first row of trees in the black night. He could feel Deggler was in there, watching and waiting for him. Quincy went wide right and bolted into the woods. He chose what he thought was the most unpredictable course and navigated himself in a way that he wouldn't be an open target.

Deggler was a hunter. If Quincy was going to survive, he would need to try to use Deggler's instincts against him. He needed mother nature to be an ally. Quincy crouched low and listened without moving. He grabbed two broken branches and a baseball-sized stone in his left hand as he kept his gun pointed in front of him in his right hand. He threw one of the branches in the direction to his far left. He waited and listened. He threw the second branch even farther in the same direction. This time as he listened, he heard the faint sound of movement getting closer. He threw the stone farther than the branches to create the effect that he was moving farther away. Once again, as he listened, he heard the hunter coming closer. Deggler came into view fifteen yards away. Quincy watched him slowly move toward the sound of the thrown objects. Deggler was cautious and judicious in his movement. He never followed a straight line and constantly looked in every direction even as he moved forward. The trajectory that he was on would give Quincy his clearest line of fire in a matter of seconds.

Quincy felt the weight of the gun in his hand and kept it trained on Deggler's every move. Though he couldn't see Deggler's face in great detail because of the limited light, he was aware of Deggler's calmness and the cautious ease in which he took each step. One step, two steps, three.... Quincy fired, hitting his mark. Deggler staggered a little and then fell down a muddy knoll.

By the time Quincy reached the spot where Deggler had been hit, all that he found were a few leaves wet with blood. Quincy hurried down the decline in pursuit of Deggler. The forest was filled with magnificent evergreens with trunks thick enough to hide even someone as wide as Deggler. As Quincy carefully moved forward, he heard a sound to his right. As he instinctively turned and saw nothing, he knew instantly that Deggler had distracted him in the same way he had done only moments earlier. Without thinking, Quincy immediately turned in the opposite direction, just in time to catch Deggler plowing into him with his entire body. Quincy's gun fell at the base of the tree as the two men went down. Quincy got off the first punch with a right cross to Deggler's chin, but the large man seemed barely fazed. When he returned the punch, Quincy never remembered being hit so hard. Without his gun, he was outmatched and overpowered. He tried to make every swing and every move smarter than the last. As Deggler advanced and swung again, Quincy ducked and punched him directly in the solar plexus. As the air momentarily left Deggler's body, Quincy scurried back to the base of the incline in search of his gun. Just as he spotted the metal shining in the moonlight, Deggler grabbed him from behind and literally tossed him against a tree. Quincy landed and tried to rise, but Deggler was there behind him, grabbing him in a sleeper-chokehold. "Do you know the weight of your own soul?" Deggler whispered into Quincy's ear.

The next thing Quincy knew he was being dunked face-first into a stream that ran along the edge of the property. Quincy flailed about in the water as he was held under by the suffocating arms of the behemoth. As much as he tried to fight back, he only grew weaker with each second. Deggler knew that Quincy was dying. Despite the futility of the cop's resistance, Deggler knew it was the moment of fait accompli. He remembered this as being the same sensation he had felt ten years ago when he choked Willington to death. This close, without the extended distance of a weapon, he could actually feel the life ending in Quincy. He felt the desperation and flailing subsiding. The lack of oxygen was forcing Quincy's body to shut down. There was a moment just before death that Deggler found fascinating. It was the synchronized moment when the body, mind and spirit completely surrendered.

As he started losing consciousness, Quincy saw Elena. He also saw his brother and mother and even Phee. He saw them each as he remembered them most. Flashes and milliseconds of the people that had meant the most to him. He found an unexplainable peace in the midst of Deggler's violence. He submitted, but not to Deggler and not to death. Even as his body was overwhelmed and succumbing to Deggler's brute strength and force, he knew that this moment was neither his last nor the premature sum of his life. Quincy expected and demanded a miracle. Just before his body went completely limp, he heard the muffled sound of two gunshots and felt Deggler release him as he barely managed to lift his head and gasp for air. Quincy collapsed on the edge of the stream as Maclin approached and inspected the two bloodied holes in Deggler's back.

She picked up Quincy's fallen gun and checked Deggler for a pulse. When she found none, she rushed to Quincy, who was a few feet away. She laid his gun down beside him and quickly rolled him over and checked his vitals for signs of life. She saw his eyes flutter and then slowly open. She wasn't sure if he was in some type of shock, because he looked at her calmly as though he hadn't almost just died. She didn't understand why he looked at her as though he had always expected her to show when she did.

"You okay?" She asked.

"I'm fine. I'm…I'm good."

As he sat up and leaned against a stump, his hand brushed up against the cold metal of the gun on the ground beneath him.

"So I guess we're even," Quincy said.

"Only if we were keeping score," Maclin responded.

As Quincy tossed a weary smile in her direction, a gunshot rang out and they turned to see a bloodied Deggler lumbering toward them, with Phee several feet to the side of him. Both Quincy and Maclin raised their guns and, along with Phee, fired several shots into Deggler. Maclin emptied her clip into him even after he lay dead on the ground several times over. She then approached Deggler's corpse and patted his pockets until she located his wallet. She opened the wallet and then removed the photo of her and Willington and walked away.

68

As Maclin opened the back of Deggler's van, they saw that it was completely empty.

"But I don't understand," Quincy said.

"Neither do I," Maclin said.

"Come take a look at this," Phee said as he stood near the front of the van.

To their mutual surprise, the front end of the van was in perfect condition. Not a dent or scratch. Obviously not the same van that he ran into them with. As they stood by the van, cops, feds and copters were converging on the scene.

"How the hell did he switch vans?" Quincy asked.

"We lost visual on him for ten minutes max. Somebody had to have already been here waiting. There's gotta be another way in and out of here," Maclin said.

"Son of a bitch thought about everything. He played us to the end," Phee declared.

Maclin saw Michaelson arrive and walk toward them.

"Let me handle Michaelson," Maclin said.

Agent Nguyen drove up a minute later and joined the group as well. As Michaelson approached, he was surprised to see Quincy and Phee next to Maclin.

"What's going on here, Maclin? Where's Deggler and the targets? And what the hell are they doing here?" Michaelson demanded.

"Deggler's in the forest. He's dead, but the targets are not here," Maclin stated.

"Well then, where the hell are they?" Michaelson demanded.

"We don't know," Maclin said uncomfortably.

"And what about these two?" Michaelson asked.

"Detectives Cavanaugh and Freeman played a hunch and canvassed several abandoned churches in the city where they thought Deggler might be holding me. By the time they found me, Deggler had gone. We confiscated several weapons and whatever intel he left behind. I didn't notify you right away because while Deggler was holding me, he insisted that he had found some way to hack into our computer system and phones. Not being sure that his claims were real, but at the same time not wanting to underestimate him, I had Detective Cavanaugh contact Special Agent Nguyen and tell him that he might have some important information pertaining to the case…"

"And why didn't you call him yourself?" Michaelson asked.

"Like I said, if Deggler was in fact listening in, I didn't want to tip our hand that I had escaped," she responded.

"Of course not. Go on," Michaelson said sarcastically.

"Agent Nguyen just so happened to already be on his way to the safe house, so we drove out to meet him before he got there. As we all arrived on the scene, Deggler was just leaving, so we pursued him while Agent Nguyen answered the distress call from inside. Deggler must have had an accomplice waiting here, because the victims were no longer in the van. We're assuming it's Deggler's brother," Maclin finished.

"And you expect me to believe that this is how everything happened?" Michaelson asked skeptically.

"It's my report, sir," Maclin responded.

Michaelson turned toward Agent Nguyen and asked him, "As far as you know, is this all accurate? And I want you to think about your answer before you respond."

Agent Nguyen looked a little nervously in Maclin's direction.

"Don't look at her. I'm the one asking the questions," Michaelson warned.

"Yes, sir. To the best of my knowledge, that's exactly what happened," Nguyen said.

"You two, walk with me," Michaelson commanded Maclin and Nguyen as he walked off.

Quincy and Phee stayed behind, taking in all of the activity.

"How long do you think the targets have?" Quincy asked Phee.

"Obviously Deggler had something big planned for them, or he would have just killed them or left them to die back at the safe house."

"So the real question is how big and when?" Phee said.

"Yeah, exactly," Quincy agreed.

Maclin approached them, looking none too pleased.

"Doesn't look like that went too well," Quincy said.

"Even with all that's happened, he still doesn't want you guys anywhere near this thing. He threatened to have both of you arrested for interfering with a federal investigation if you don't back down," Maclin told them.

"What a piece of work. Six people are gonna be killed any time now, and he's more focused on being petty," Quincy said.

"So exactly how hard did you hit him?" Maclin asked Phee.

"Obviously not hard enough. He's still an asshole."

"You do know that we have every intention of seeing this thing through, right?" Quincy added.

"I'm depending on it. By the way, you're sure there's no way the guns can be traced?" she asked.

"Yeah, we're sure," Phee answered.

"Good. We passed a diner about a mile just before you hit the highway. Let me finish up here and call you when I'm leaving so we can figure out our next move. Hopefully I'll be done here in a few," Maclin said.

Just before Maclin turned to walk away, Quincy started laughing.

"By the way, you're a pretty good liar when you wanna be," he said.

"Thank you. I've learned from the best."

69

E lena went to the commissary to stretch her legs and break the monotony. She needed a distraction from the fact that there had been no change in Romero. She had tried Quincy a little earlier only to have gotten his voice mail. Even after she returned to her father's floor, she decided not to go straight into his room. As Elena sat in the hallway and picked at her salad, she noticed a nurse quickly exiting Romero's room and making a beeline to the telephone. As two other nurses rushed into her father's room, Elena panicked. It was the nurse's urgent sense of purpose that alarmed her and brought her running.

By the time Elena reached the doorway, the view of her father was obscured by three nurses surrounding him. Elena's heart dropped as she thought of her life without the benefits of love from either her son or her father. Her fear and mourning kept her frozen in the doorway. As one of the nurses cleared her eyeline, she saw then the reason for all of the urgency and commotion. It took her a beat to realize that Romero's eyes were opened and looking directly at her. Elena stood speechless, terrified that movement or words would somehow reverse her father's improbable return.

After Dr. Fong came and checked on her father, he pulled Elena just outside of Romero's room.

"Is he out of danger?" Elena quickly asked.

"He's out of immediate danger. We need to run a few more tests, but that's just more of a formality. He made a hell of a turnaround."

"Yeah, I guess he did," she said.

"I see things all the time in this profession that I can't explain. When they're good, I try less to explain them. We just take the win and keep on moving," Dr. Fong said.

"Can I talk to him?" Elena asked.

"The important thing right now is not to overstimulate his brain. He's had a lot going on today. I think we should let him rest, and you can come back tomorrow."

"Can I at least go say goodbye to him?" she asked.

"Only if you promise to make it short and sweet," Dr. Fong said warmly.

Elena quietly reentered Romero's room just as a nurse was changing an IV bag. Sensing his daughter's presence, Romero opened his eyes as Elena grabbed his hand and quietly spoke to him.

"The doctor wants you to get some rest. I'll be back first thing in the morning, okay?" Elena said.

Romero, who was still unable to speak, blinked his eyes once to show Elena he understood her. Elena wanted to stay. She wanted to take care of her father and protect him as best she could. Romero's brain wasn't the only one in jeopardy of being overloaded. Elena felt the lift, the weightlessness of forgiveness. Along with it came the rush. The need for immediacy. Selfishly, it was easier for her to ride the emotional momentum of all that had recently happened. She wanted to do it now. Whatever purging was to be done, Elena preferred that it be in this moment. Even if her father couldn't talk, Elena wanted him to listen. Elena wanted a million things and she wanted them all now, but when she looked at the peace on Romero's face, she settled for the promise and possibility of tomorrow.

"I was hoping that once you felt better, you and I could sit down and talk," Elena said.

This time as Romero blinked, Elena saw tears rolling down the side of his face. The last thing she wanted to do was upset her father in any way. Dr. Fong specifically said that it was important not to overstimulate Romero's brain. The irony was that if she wasn't careful, her forgiveness would potentially do more damage than the anger she had been harboring. She kissed her father gently on the forehead and crossed to the door. As she looked one last time at Romero, she knew all was good. Standing in the doorway, Elena saw her father's attempt at smiling and thought that, although long and uncertain, their journey of reconciliation would be like any other journey; it would require an ounce of faith and the tenacious ability to put one foot in front of the other.

On her way home from the hospital, Elena stopped at a bodega and bought some orchids. Even though Romero wasn't scheduled to come home for a couple of days, she immediately started making preparations for his return. After Joaquin's death, the apartment had come to represent darkness and depression. She needed the home to be filled with warmth, life and new beginnings. After placing a vase of orchids in Romero's room, Elena walked passed Joaquin's door. She turned back and gently placed her hand on the doorknob. It took her several minutes before she was able to turn the knob and enter. Elena found herself for the first time since her son's death in his room. In the two months since he died, she had avoided his room at all costs. It was the first time she felt strong and brave enough to put herself in a situation that she knew would completely envelop her in his memory. The simple act of being in her son's room offered a modicum of emotional progress and closure. On this day, Elena was attempting to be brave and proactive. The photos of her and Joaquin on the nightstand left her vulnerable and introspective. There were times she thought she still smelled her son. She thought she heard his laughter echoing off the walls of the small room. When the sadness came, she preoccupied herself with activity. She opened up drawers and went through his things.

Elena found the sketchpad that she bought Joaquin the day before he left Colombia. She sat on the bed and thumbed through the pages of sketches and doodles. She saw reminders of his potential as an artist. A potential that would never come to fruition. When she finally made it to the back of the pad, Elena saw a caricature of herself that her son had penciled. In the sketch she had a large head and small body. She was wearing a tiara and holding a dozen roses. She wore a swimsuit with a Miss Universe sash draped over her body. She smiled and then unexpectedly broke into laughter as she looked at the beat-up running shoes he drew her wearing. When he was alive, he used to often tease her about her obsession with running. Her laughter started small but soon ran deep and unstoppable. She laughed as a means of keeping the tears at bay. Her laughter was a choice. Elena chose to celebrate the presence of her child instead of continually mourning his absence. As she continued to look at the sketch, she was grateful for the simple things in life that Joaquin was teaching her even in death. Elena laughed in a way that surely made her son proud.

70

Quincy and Phee were drinking coffee and talking on their cells when Maclin entered the small trucker's diner. She signaled the server for a cup of coffee as she sat next to Phee, facing Quincy. Phee was the first to hang up.

"Quincy might have something and I'm waiting for Brenda to get back to us on a hunch," Phee said to Maclin.

Quincy hung up his phone and immediately checked its screen.

"I was talking to a buddy who runs the Port Authority. The easiest way out here from the city is to take the George Washington Bridge. I had them run Deggler's brother's image against the tollbooth cameras and they got a hit," Quincy announced.

As he downloaded a photo, there were two images: one was a close-up of the driver and the other was a wider shot of the SUV he was driving.

"This is him driving into Jersey. It was taken two hours ago at nine. No dark cargo van with damage to the front has been spotted going back to the city. Not over the bridge or through the tunnels," Quincy stated.

"Damn good chance he's still out here," Phee said as he checked an incoming text.

"Something that you said to Michaelson earlier got me to thinking," Quincy said to Maclin.

"What was that?" she asked.

"When you told him that we followed a hunch and checked the abandoned churches that we thought Deggler might be holding you in..."

"So you're thinking the same thing for the targets?" Maclin asked. "Makes the most sense. Like you said earlier, Deggler thought everything through. Always had a contingency plan. He wasn't gonna risk transporting them back to the city. He would have already chosen a place not too far from the safe house in case he caught some heat. He stayed at the lumberyard to keep us busy so his brother could get away with the victims," Quincy said.

"It's a damn good hunch," Maclin responded.

"Yeah, we thought you'd say that. Brenda just sent a text of the two closest abandoned churches in the area. Two miles from here in the same direction," Phee added.

The three of them sprang from their chairs and raced toward the exit.

The first try was a bust. The small church had recently been gutted by a fire and only had two standing walls left. The second church was a quarter of a mile from the first. It was off an isolated stretch of road with very few structures nearby. Quincy and Phee were in the lead car and Maclin trailed directly behind them. As they pulled into the long drive, they immediately saw the orange hue of fire coming from the church. As they jumped out, Quincy shouted, "I'll take the back. You two take the front." Quincy pulled out his gun and sprinted toward the back as Maclin and Phee charged toward the front. As Quincy rounded the rear of the building, he saw a man rifling through the opened back of a Navigator SUV which was parked next to the damaged cargo van. Quincy approached him with his gun pointed at him.

"Turn around and get on the ground," he shouted.

As the man turned around, Quincy immediately recognized him as Deggler's brother with an odd smile on his face. "I'm glad you're here," the man said.

Quincy saw the large knife in the man's hand and shouted at him again. "Drop your weapon and get on the ground."

"You don't understand. God told me to save them," the man responded.

Quincy stood between Deggler's brother and the back entrance to the church. As the man suddenly moved in his direction, Quincy fired once hitting him square in the chest. As he dropped to the ground, Quincy quickly kicked the fallen knife away and stood over him with his gun still pointed at him. The man was lying on his back looking directly up at Quincy. The sound of blood filling up in his lungs could be heard through his labored breathing. Quincy saw the resemblance to Deggler. A much smaller frame, but very similar facial features. The two brothers had the same blue eyes. Deggler's may have been a little more intense, but both sets were youthful but sad. Quincy hovered over him as the man lay harmless at his feet.

"I only wanted to help him. All my life that's all I ever wanted. Can you save…" he muttered just before his breathing stopped.

The gutted church was a large open space with a high A-frame ceiling. The fire was still young, but growing by the second. The smoke was thickening and beginning to suck the air out of the room. As Maclin and Phee made their way to the center of the church, they saw six men in a circle tied to ten-foot-high crosses facing each other. Each man had a noose around his neck that hung from the beams above. At the base of the crosses, each man stood on two bales of hay. They were positioned so that once the hay burned, the men would all be hanged on the crosses and their bodies burned in the process. Phee grabbed an empty oil drum to elevate himself high enough to untie the victim nearest to him. Maclin followed suit by grabbing a wooden workhorse and climbing it to set one of the victims free. Some of the men cried out painfully as the fires had started to burn them. The first freed victim crashed to the floor as Phee untied him. Phee immediately rolled the drum that he was using over to the next victim and did the same. Quincy entered from the back and helped as Maclin matched Phee, body for body. Then Maclin put out the small fire that attacked and burned two of the victims on the ground. After Phee and Quincy untied the last two men, they and Maclin started dragging and carrying the victims outside. The flames were fully roaring as they brought out the fourth and fifth victims. As parts of the church started to fall, Quincy moved to go and retrieve the final victim.

Phee grabbed him by the arm and stopped him.

"I'll go. I'm a lot quicker than you," Phee said. Before Quincy could protest, Phee offered a slight smile and bolted back into the burning building. As Maclin administered CPR to one of the victims, she looked at Quincy with concern for Phee. They suddenly heard the loud sound of wood cracking and failing. The front of the church collapsed and large flames swallowed large sections of the structure. Quincy immediately ran toward the church, but was physically knocked to the ground by a falling column at the entrance. Maclin stopped what she was doing and went to Quincy's aid. She dragged him as best she could, even as he protested and still tried to get back into the building. The church teetered back and forth a few times before completely collapsing. Quincy and Maclin looked on in horror, both speechless.

"I told you I was quicker than you." As they turned, they discovered Phee coming from the side of the building with the last victim thrown over his shoulder. Maclin smiled as Quincy looked at his partner, relieved and thankful.

71

Maclin, Phee, Nguyen and Quincy sat in the waiting room of the mayor's office. Since this was the largest case that the FBI had cracked in recent memory, the director of the Bureau flew into New York personally to thank the mayor and the key people responsible. Quincy's foot was in an air cast and Phee's arm was wrapped in burn gauze while Maclin sported a few scrapes and scratches of her own. Nguyen was spotless. Phee read an old *New York Post* that he'd confiscated from a janitor's cart in the elevator. The case had put each of their lives on hold in one way or another. The last few days, everything was all about Deggler. As consumed as they had been, Phee felt disconnected from current events, both local and global. Not that the *Post* was the greatest source of news, but it was a start. As he got toward the back of the paper, he saw a short blurb about the brutal murder of a cross-dressing sex worker who went by the name of Shay DeVane. Phee remembered that name as his brother's missing friend.

Agent Nguyen got up and started pacing. "Why does it feel like we're waiting outside the principal's office?" Nguyen said to no one in particular.

"Nguyen, have you ever in your life had to wait outside the principal's office?" Maclin asked.

"Actually, no," Nguyen said.

"I didn't think so," Maclin said as she and Quincy started laughing. Quincy noticed Phee was distracted by what he was reading.

"You okay, Phee?" Quincy asked.

"Yeah. I'm fine, just haven't had time to read a paper in the last couple of days."

"Too busy trying to save demons from the Devil," Maclin said.

"Now with all of the horrible stuff that's still coming out on the targets, kinda makes you question if it was worth going through all that we did to save them in the first place," Nguyen said.

"It's got nothing to do with who they are or what they do, we just do the job. Let their God sort out the rest," Phee commented without looking up.

Nguyen's phone rang and he stepped off to the side to answer it. Quincy caught Maclin staring at one of the old scars on her wrist. When she looked up, he offered her a warm smile and gently patted her knee.

"Are you two still quitting?" Maclin asked.

"All I know for certain is that I'm gonna take some time and do me for a change," Quincy responded.

"Ditto," Phee added.

"You'll both be back," Maclin said confidently.

"What makes you so certain?" Quincy asked.

"Because some people get to choose who they are and what they do, but for the rest of us, the choice is already made. The two of you are New York Blue, through and through," Maclin said.

"What about you? What are your plans?" Phee asked.

"When we're done here, I'm driving upstate today to go see a friend. After that, it's anybody's guess. I've got about ten years of vacation time saved up, so who knows? I may even try to get a life," Maclin answered.

"Well don't forget to drop an email once in a while to let us know how that works out for you," Quincy said.

As Phee continued reading the paper and Nguyen hung up his phone, one of the double doors leading to the mayor's office opened and Michaelson emerged. It was immediately obvious that whatever had just transpired behind the closed doors had left him pissed and defeated. He avoided eye contact and stormed off in the direction of the elevators.

"What's up with Prince Charming?" Phee asked.

"I just heard he's being transferred to Iowa," Nguyen said.

"I guess enough of the right people made formal complaints against him and his handling of the case," Maclin said.

"What do you mean 'right people'?" Quincy asked.

Maclin and Nguyen looked at each other conspiratorially.

"Let's just say there's no shortage of people that Michaelson pissed off. Half the agents in the field were happy when you hit him.

The other half were jealous that they hadn't done it themselves," Nguyen added.

As they all laughed, the mayor's assistant came out and invited the quartet inside.

Both the Bureau director and the mayor were very gracious and complimentary to the four, and made plans for a more formal citation ceremony in the next week or so. Quincy and Phee's captain, along with the chief of police, were there as well and privately pleaded with the two cops to reconsider their plans for early retirement. Maclin was offered Michaelson's vacated position and Nguyen was made second-in-command of the New York branch. Photos were taken and backs were patted and all of the attention and ceremony left the four a bit overwhelmed. As far as Maclin and Nguyen were concerned, this was just the kind of case that would jettison their career within the Bureau. However, for Quincy and Phee, it wasn't for accolades or promotion that either of them did what they did. It was simpler than that. Deggler was bad and needed stopping and it was their job to do just that.

After they left the mayor's office, Nguyen insisted that they go to his father's restaurant for an early lunch. Nguyen gave them all a quick tutorial on how the food was prepared and what were the best combinations. Although his pronunciation was horrible, Phee was the only one of the invited to have ever had Vietnamese food. As Nguyen's mother brought the appetizers out, Quincy and Maclin quickly overcame their initial tentativeness and, along with Phee and Nguyen, devoured the delicacies before them. As difficult as it was for him, Nguyen resisted the bánh cams, the deep-fried sesame balls that had nearly been his undoing. Nguyen had never brought people that he worked with to his father's restaurant. He had never felt connected enough to socialize with them, and his father had in no way ever encouraged him to do so. He proudly introduced his colleagues to his family and told them about their trip to the mayor's office. As they ate, drank and laughed, both Nguyen and his father were acutely aware of the ease and naturalness of the bridging of the two worlds.

72

After Phee left the restaurant, he ran a couple of errands and then stopped in Soho to pick up Brenda. They drove to his father's place in Connecticut. Clay had always adored Brenda. Not only was she the smartest woman Phee had ever dated, but he found her to be a sincerely kind human being. He was used to seeing his son with plenty of beautiful women from all backgrounds and walks of life, but Brenda was always the one that stood out as being special. Although Brenda and Phee had just been friends the last several years, Clay had always secretly hoped that his son would wake up one day and realize what he had in her.

They had just finished off three bottles of Amarone when Clay pulled out a flat, narrow, gift-wrapped box and handed it to Brenda.

"Phee called me this morning and asked me to have this waiting for you," Clay said.

"What is it?" Brenda asked excitedly.

"I think this is the part where you open it and find out," Phee said teasingly.

As Brenda opened the box, she discovered a rather plain looking letter opener. As she removed and examined it, she tried her best to hide her confusion. Clay and Phee held in their laughter at her attempts to remain diplomatic and tactful.

"Thank you...I could use one of these," she said, still a bit confused.

When Phee could no longer hold it in, he burst out laughing as he reached in his jacket pocket and handed her an envelope.

"Why don't you use it to open up this," he told her.

As Brenda used the letter opener to open the envelope, to her pleasant surprise she discovered a print out of two boarding passes. to the South of France. The attached note read:

I think we've kept Eze waiting long enough.

Brenda ran to Phee and hugged and kissed him with every-thing she had. Clay looked on and laughed. He was happy to see that his son had caught up to his own potential. Clay had always wanted both of his sons to have what he had in Dolicia. He had lost AJ a long time ago, but he still wished both of them unconditional love and happiness. Although Clay, Brenda and Phee were already tipsy, Clay opened a $20,000 dollar bottle of scotch that he had been saving for a special occasion.

73

Quincy had wanted to see Elena as soon as possible, but her father was having a bunch of tests done and she wouldn't be free for a few hours. Instead of just hanging around the hospital and waiting for her, she suggested they meet in the park around four. Since he had time to kill, he decided to drive up to the Heights to see his brother. Quincy's mind was still unwinding from the events of the last few days. The adrenaline and focus that was demanded of him had certainly taken a toll. His body was drained and exhausted, but his mind was still overactive and restless. He knew that, unfortunately, Deggler and "The Befallen" would stay with him long after their names were no longer spoken. They would occupy the neighboring states of his memory that his molester, Father Burns, had occupied for years. Hopefully not as dominant an occupancy, but an occupancy nonetheless. But for the first time in his adult life he had hope that such specters would be relegated to the lesser regions of his mind. His hope was predicated on a desperate variation of the laws of physics. Since it was a fact that no two objects could simultaneously occupy the same space, he was determined to make the same true of his conscious thought process. His focus on what was good in his life would leave very little room for his preoccupation with the bad. There were, however, a few things that still gnawed and pulled at him. Quincy couldn't help but wonder about Deggler's brother. Why for instance had the man seemed so relieved to see Quincy? And what exactly did he mean when he said he had to save them? Quincy had enjoyed a long and successful career based on hard work and good gut instincts. Something about his encounter with Deggler's brother bothered him, but he couldn't quite put his finger on it. The other thing that crossed Quincy's mind as he drove uptown was what Deggler had whispered in his ear as he was choking him. What exactly did he mean by knowing "the weight of your own soul?"

Quincy was deep in thought when he stopped at a light on 47th and 10th Ave. His reverie was broken by the sound of a hand slapping the hood of his car for protruding too much in the walkway. He looked up to see a tall African American cross-dresser with a platinum blonde wig, dressed in daisy dukes and knee-high latex boots giving him the finger. Despite the extreme makeover, Quincy recognized AJ from an old mug shot for solicitation that Phee had shown him a year ago. Quincy watched AJ cross the street and negotiate with the driver of a dark SUV. An irritated taxi driver blew his horn loudly as the light changed. As Quincy drove off, he quickly glanced back in AJ's direction. Little did he know that as the SUV took off in the opposite direction, he would never see AJ alive again. Little did he know that his partner's brother would soon be brutally murdered.

74

aclin loved the drive upstate. The beautiful landscape made her think of times long ago when she used to appreciate such things. She hadn't been to Albany since before the year Willington was killed. After she made her way to his tombstone, she sat on the cold ground and looked out on to the Henry Hudson. There were still a few boats out even though winter was quickly approaching. Despite where she was and her reason for being there, Maclin was more at peace than she had been in years. She talked to Willington as though he were sitting comfortably beside her. She told him about Quincy and Phee and how much he would have liked and respected them.

She laughed when she told him how little she still cared for Greek food. She shared with him as many random and insignificant things as she did subjects she deemed important. She told him things that she hadn't thought of in years as well as the new foods she had just tried at the restaurant of Nguyen's parents. There were quiet moments when Maclin just appreciated various memories of herself and Willington.

Maclin thought of how the majority of her disappearance had started the day that Willington died. The rest of it became a slower process. Her fading came with no blow horn or significant announcement. It was more of a daily erosion. She was less committed to navigating through life and the challenges it presented. She made no other investments or attempts at any meaningful connections. She was less present and attentive to anything that was not connected to finding Deggler. She had somewhere along the way begun to think of emotions as inconvenient choices. The only thing that bothered her was how little she was bothered by her inability to have an honest emotional response. This had become her disappearance. But as she sat by his tombstone and talked to Willington, she did what she hadn't been able to do in the last ten years. Maclin cried. The tears may have come unexpectedly to her, but in many ways she welcomed them. She welcomed the long, cathartic cry that reminded her of what it felt like to be alive.

75

Quincy sat in his brother's confessional as they casually spoke of more secular things than religious matters.

"…and I stopped by to see Ma yesterday," Liam said.

"Really???"

"Why do you say it like that? I told you I would."

"I'm just surprised, that's all."

"Yeah, well I like to keep you guessing."

"How was she?" Quincy asked.

"You know her better than I do, Quincy. She's always going to be the same," Liam said.

In the awkward silence between them, Liam played with a ball in his hand as was his habit when he sat in the confessional booth. He was happy when Quincy changed the subject and started talking about Elena. As Quincy went on about her, Liam heard in his younger brother's voice something that he hadn't ever remembered hearing. A lightness and peace.

"Trust me, you'll love her. She's special," Quincy said.

"She's gotta be. In all these years, I've never heard you go on about a woman like this. I'm glad for you. You deserve to be happy, Quincy. No matter what," Liam said.

"All of us do. What about you Liam? Are you? Happy I mean."

"I'm a priest. I don't know that happiness was ever in the job description," Liam laughed.

"It's a serious question, Liam."

"Well then, I'd have to say, just like with everybody else, it's a work in progress."

"But maybe even more so with people like you and me," Quincy added.

"Maybe. Some days are better than others. My kid brother telling me he's in love makes this a better day." Liam hesitated a moment, and then asked Quincy, "Does she know..."

"Yeah, I told her everything. And I'm glad I did. Don't you ever get tired of carrying this stuff around all by yourself?"

"Everybody deals with their baggage in their own way."

"And God and the Church is your way?"

"For the most part, yeah."

"When we were younger, I never understood how you could be so faithful to the Church that turned its back on us when we needed it most," Quincy said.

"That wasn't the Church, and that wasn't God. Those were

pretenders and weak men. Fortunately, in one way or another, they're all held accountable, even more so than most people."

"What happened to all men being judged the same?"

"I stopped believing that a long time ago. I think some of us have to be held to a higher standard. More knowledge brings more responsibility," Liam stated.

Quincy was quiet for a minute or two when the question that Deggler asked him crossed his mind.

"Do you think the weight of a man's soul is measurable or not?" he asked Liam earnestly.

Liam thought about it for a minute and then responded.

"You asking for a theoretical answer or more theological?"

"I'll take whichever one you're offering," Quincy answered.

"Well theoretically and even scientifically speaking, I gotta say yeah, 'cause even air weighs something. Now, theologically speaking, I guess you could make a good argument for it as well if you ultimately accept that we're all judged and measured by the impact we've made, both spiritually and tangibly," Liam said.

"Impact?" Quincy asked.

"Yeah, impact. The way I see it, the main thing that validates the existence of the soul is the impact and influence that it's had over others. Therefore, that's what it's measured by. Just my opinion though," Liam said.

As the two brothers continued talking about different things, Liam continued to absentmindedly play with the autographed Babe Ruth baseball from Father Conner's office. He thought back to the night before Conner's murder. Deggler had stopped by for confession and told him his plans for the pederast.

Liam went through the motions of dissuasion. Of all of the confessions that Liam had heard over the years, he connected with Deggler in ways that he was unable to do with anyone else. His own brother included. As he listened to himself attempting to discourage Deggler from committing a cold-blooded, heinous act, he realized that he was only doing so as a gesture. On the subject of murder, the Church's position was incontestable. Liam's conflict was that he was less and less convinced that the killing of a devil was a condemnable act. He felt that way when he stood in Quincy's precinct and saw photos of all of the murders that Deggler had committed. He remembered crying because he had never seen anything so beautiful. He felt a similar way years ago when he set the fire that burned his and Quincy's abuser. He thought then that his anger and pain would stop with that final act. He thought the hate in his heart would disappear. It wasn't until he first met Deggler that he realized he was wrong. As much as he tried to deny the darkness that had touched his soul, every confession that he gave to Deggler put him more and more in touch with his own iniquities. With the first two murders that Deggler had committed in New York, Liam had taken a much more passive position in his role as a hypothetical, spiritual mentor. But knowing the lineage of crimes that Father Conner was guilty of brought to the surface feelings that Liam had struggled to suppress. The truth was, not only did he not want to talk Deggler out of killing the priest, he wanted to accompany him and see it done firsthand.

On the actual morning of Conner's murder, Liam was surprised at how calm he was. It was the first time since he killed his abuser that he felt whole and empowered. As he watched Deggler methodically skin Conner alive, he found the whole experience much more liberating than he could have ever imagined. In fact, it was Liam's idea to burn the remaining six clergy. He thought Deggler was brilliant in many ways, but the one flaw he made was mentioning Liam's name as his confessor to his brother Noah when Deggler had called a day earlier to say his final goodbye. Somehow Noah had tracked and followed Liam to Jersey. He showed up with the intent of getting Deggler to repent and renounce the crimes of which he was guilty. Had it not been for Noah interrupting him, Liam was certain that he would have been able to bury his hatred with the six false men of God.

Sitting in his booth and listening to his brother talk of happiness, he wondered if he would ever find his own sense of peace. As Liam played with the baseball, he smiled and thought of why he had taken it in the first place. For many reasons, it reminded him of his baby brother. He wanted to give it to him as a present for his upcoming birthday. Although it was supposed to have represented a type of closure for Liam, he knew to Quincy it would simply represent a happier time in their lives, when their father lived, their mother laughed and both boys were free.

Epilogue

The sun was just setting and the air grew colder. Autumn was officially leaving and making way for what was expected to be a long, cold winter. Quincy saw Elena sitting on their favorite bench and made his way to her. He offered her a cup of chai tea and kissed her as she welcomed him. They each talked about their day and the climactic events of the past twenty-four hours. Quincy listened more than he talked. He liked the way she smiled when she talked about her father's miraculous recovery. He liked it even more when she teased him and told him that her plans for the future would include moving to New York permanently to be closer to the men in her life. As she grew quiet and sat with her head on his shoulder, Quincy rubbed her hands to keep them warm.

"Sunrise," Elena said with no explanation.

"Sunrise, what?" Quincy asked.

"The first time you spoke to me here, you asked me if I preferred sunrises or sunsets. I guess if I really had to choose, I'd take sunrises," she said.

"I'm just curious, any particular reason why?" he asked.

"Because one feels more like resolution and the other feels more like possibility. I like possibilities," she said as she stood and kissed him. She turned around and they both faced the water, taking in the final view. It was like glass, disturbed only by the random fish jumping just above the surface at low-flying insects. Just as they were turning to leave, they both noticed Forrest and his unsuccessful attempts at takeoff. It tried again and again with disappointing results. For the first time, Quincy actually found himself rooting for the large bird. The crane's determination warranted support and endorsement. Quincy and Elena stayed in the park longer, hoping that Forrest would find a way to lift itself high above the marsh and make its way south. He wasn't sure if it was only in his imagination, but Quincy thought he saw progress in the bird's attempts. Each time, it seemed as though Forrest rose a little higher and supported himself in the air just a little longer. Elena must have felt the same, because she ran around the park cheering the bird on as quickly and loudly as she could. Quincy had no idea whether or not the bird would make it or simply perish among the tiny piece of marsh that it had been inhabiting for at least the last week or so. Although both he and Elena had somehow become invested in Forrest's outcome, Quincy's definition of success in regard to the bird had altered. Maybe he would relearn to fly, and maybe he wouldn't. What impressed Quincy most was Forrest's unwavering belief that even in the face of overwhelming odds, flight was still possible.

As Quincy watched Elena cheer the bird on with total abandonment, he soon joined in and did the same. As they each laughed and did the best imitation they could of a flying bird, both Quincy and Elena performed the miracle that day that God had intended for them to do their entire lives. They each took flight. They both flew high above the limitations of their wounds and afflictions. One flew above indifference and faithlessness as the other flew above the inability to forgive and the underestimation of the power of Love.

Quincy accepted what Elena had told him when she said there were no coincidences. As he and Elena continued to move about the park like playful children, he couldn't help but wonder what would eventually happen to Forrest and if the bird would survive. Still, as certain as Quincy was of his own arrival, he grew certain that Forrest would also be successful on his long migration. It made no difference whether or not he and Elena witnessed firsthand Forrest's ascension, because Quincy felt in his heart that all things were possible. He didn't feel a need to wish the large bird luck, because he knew now that luck had very little to do with fate and predestination. In accepting the greater implication, Quincy did something he had never done before. He thanked God.

Read on for the gripping prequel novella to
Eriq La Salle's thrilling Martyr Maker series,

LAWS OF INNOCENCE: THE PREQUEL,

giving you a peek into the mind of a revengeful serial killer.

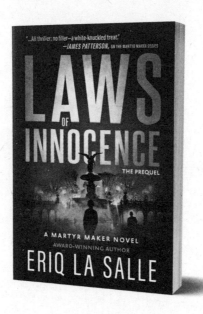

Ten-year-old Joaquin adored and worshipped his mother, his grandfather, and God. His life was blissfully sheltered and filled with love until the day he was tragically robbed of his innocence. But someone else was watching. Someone who was filled with a sense of retribution, compelled to take matters into his own hands. And all of New York would soon discover that vengeance and justice sometimes come from the most horrific and unlikeliest of sources.

1

Deggler already had thirty-six kills under his belt. Every ten years for the last thirty he murdered twelve targets then disappeared. Those that he killed were weak, vile and deviant. Regardless of what the police and the public called them, he never thought of his targets in terms of being victims. They were, each of them, "the befallen," and it was his God-given duty to remove them from the face of the earth. The cops and press dubbed him "The Martyrs Maker." Over the years Deggler had become quite proficient at killing. He honed his skills and elevated his game from when he first started. Deggler was patient and meticulous. He stalked his prey for months and learned as much about them as possible. Nothing he ever did was random or coincidental. The cops were predictably incompetent. Only once did they come remotely close to catching him. His three kill cycles took place in three different cities, which only added to their inability to predict his next move. He killed the first twelve in San Francisco, then Chicago and then Boston. Knowing that this would be the end of his mission he picked the perfect city for his crowning moment. By the time he was done, New York would never be the same.

———

As far back as he could remember, ten-year-old Joaquin was jealous of angels. He envied the winged cherubs' closeness to God and even more so their ability to fly. His mother Elena and even grand-father Romero instilled in him from the time he was two that angels existed and even played tangible roles in the lives of humans on a daily basis. The Catholic schools that he attended perpet-uated the notion through stern nuns and their dogmatic teach-ings. He was overwhelmingly liked by the sisters who taught him. They all saw him as a bright child whose mind and soul were malleable and receptive to the things they deemed most important. From the time Joaquin was five he proudly declared his love for his mother, grandfather and God. The young boy couldn't remember his father. Carlos OD'd on heroin when Joaquin was only two. The loss took years to register, and even then only incrementally. Only when strangers would casually ask about his father did he bother to think about the man he never knew. Occasional thoughts of Carlos were more or less a minor distraction in an otherwise happy childhood. Joaquin's mother more than compensated to fill any voids that she feared her son might feel. She couldn't love him more. Elena showered him with love and affection to the point of spoiling him. Romero did the same but also managed to slip in just enough discipline to make his grandson respect and fear authority. At first Romero didn't think it possible to love another human being the same way he loved his only child, Elena. From the day Joaquin was born he proved him wrong and constantly replenished the very thing that kept Romero feeling young and relevant as though he still had important things to offer the world. His love for art and water was in his blood, handed down to him from both Romero and Elena. The young boy constantly fished, swam and played on the banks of the Magdalena River. It was on the sands of La Boquilla beach that he first discovered his talent for drawing when at six years old he sketched a remarkable cartoon of his mother having fallen asleep while sunbathing. He inherited his talent from both his grandfather and mother, who were two generations of gifted artists. They were an incredibly tight-knit family until the summer of Joaquin's ninth birthday, when Romero accepted a teaching position in the States. "Why can't you just teach here?" Joaquin pleaded.

"Because the school in New York has better opportunities," Romero replied.

"But it's far, Abuelito."

"Yes, it is."

"Then can I go with you?" Joaquin asked.

"If you went with me, who would look after your mother? With me leaving, she needs a man looking after her more now than ever." As Joaquin lowered his head and poked his lower lip out in disappointment, Romero stifled a laugh and mussed the little boy's hair. It wasn't until he looked closer that he noticed the tears in his grandson's eyes. Romero knelt down so that the two of them were face-to-face. "Why are you crying, Mi Rey?" Romero asked. Romero had many nicknames for his grandson. His two favorites were ironically polar opposites in their meanings. The one that he used the most was Mi Raton, which meant "my little rat." This was the name that consistently made his grandson smile or giggle. In more serious times, Romero called the boy Mi Rey, which meant "my king." There were subtle changes in the boy's demeanor when his grandfather addressed him with the name. He stood a bit more erect and made a halfhearted attempt at stopping the flow of tears that now ran freely. "Please don't leave me, Abuelito."

Romero was temporarily winded by the pain he heard in his grandson's voice. "Listen to me, Mi Rey, when you love someone, you never really leave them because you always carry them right here," he said pointing to his own chest. "At the end of the school year, you'll come visit me in New York and I'll show you buildings so tall that you'll swear they scrape the soles of God's feet. We'll go fishing and eat giant hotdogs at the baseball games. Would you like that?"

"Yes," Joaquin said reluctantly.

"Good. Before you know it, this time next year you'll be with me. But in the meantime I want you to promise that you'll listen to your mother and take care of her. She needs you. One of the big things about being a man is putting the needs of loved ones even before your own needs. Don't forget that. Make me proud, Mi Rey."

Joaquin lived for his grandfather's praise. Nothing lifted the boy like a nod, smile or pat on the back from his hero. Romero palmed the side of Joaquin's face and lifted it up and told him, "Kings don't cry."

Even though he was brokenhearted, the boy attempted to put up a brave front and live up to the nickname his grandfather gifted him. The month leading up to Romero's departure, the two were inseparable. They often woke up at 4:00 in the morning to go fishing. They swam and ate whatever foods Joaquin wanted. They went to movies and museums and baseball games and soccer matches. Romero taught his young grandson how to improve his sketches. Joaquin spent the days trying to keep himself too busy to think about Romero's imminent departure, but on many nights, king or not, he prayed and then cried before he fell asleep.

Romero left for New York in the middle of summer. There was no way for either one of them to know, but Joaquin would never be the same.

Once Romero left, the shift in Joaquin was immediate. At first the changes were subtle. Elena knew her son was depressed, but she assumed that with a little time the two of them would be able to work through it. Instead he grew increasingly distant and detached. The more she showered him with attention and love, the more he seemed to retreat from her. Even though money was tight, she lavished him with things that she couldn't afford and took him places that suddenly lost their appeal to him. The only things they still seemed to have in common were their mutual loves for water and art.

As she did every Saturday, Elena took Joaquin to the beach.

She woke up at five and made him tuna sandwiches on homemade bread. She put dried cranberries, chopped walnuts and sweet celery in the tuna just the way Romero did. Elena made the bread the way her father taught her but somehow neither it nor the tuna tasted as good as the old man's. Shortly after noon, Joaquin stared toward the water and absentmindedly picked at his half-eaten sandwich.

"I think I was around your age when Papi first tried to teach me to cook," Elena said. "I made a bet with him. If I scored at least two goals in my next soccer match I wouldn't have to learn. I ended up scoring four." As she laughed at the memory Joaquin continued to stare at the water somewhere in his own world.

"Why don't you go in the water?" Elena asked.

"It's too cold," he said flatly.

"That's never stopped you before," she responded. "At some point, Joaquin, you're gonna have to stop moping around. It would break Papi's heart to see you like this, just like it breaks mine. I know you miss him and so do I, but right now I'm missing you even more."

Joaquin kept his head down as he watched a trail of ants making their way toward the tuna sandwich, which he had placed on the blanket beside him. He stared at the tiny insects marching toward him in unison, with a single purpose. Some hauled tiny crumbs in the opposite direction as others continued crawling toward his sandwich. He was much more fascinated by them and their collective efforts than the heart-to-heart his mother was trying to have with him.

"Joaquin, I'm talking to you," Elena's voice interrupted him.

Joaquin finally looked at his mother and saw the sadness that was pressing down on her. He wanted to lift it from her as much as he wanted to lift the weight of his own gloom. He grew jealous of the ants because they didn't have to feel the things that humans did. Their simple existence made sense to him. They were all interconnected and dependent upon each other for their very survival. He thought it strange that stupid ants needed each other much more than his grandfather needed him.

"Abuelito used to always say that when you loved somebody, you're always there for them," he said.

"And he was right," Elena responded. "But you can be there for people in other ways than physically."

"That's the only way that really counts." Joaquin said as he rose with his sketchbook and moved closer to the water.

Joaquin sat in the back of his class doodling in his sketchbook while his classmates recited their fourth grade multiplication table. It was a beautiful day in November and his attention was drawn much more to the foliage outside his window than to the monotonous drone of X times X. His view of sunlight was abruptly interrupted by Sister Rita Hernandez hovering over him. She stared down on him with a look of irritation and impatience.

"Joaquin, that's the third time this week. Since you obviously have no interest in what we're doing here, why don't you go sit in Father Augusta's office," the nun demanded.

As Joaquin got up and gathered his things, one of his classmates teasingly accused him of having ADD. When all the other kids laughed Joaquin rushed out of the classroom embarrassed.

Joaquin had never really been in a fight. His grandfather had always taught him that it took much more character to walk away from physical altercations than it did to engage in them. Some of the things that Romero had taught him no longer seemed applicable. The older boys in his neighborhood fought all of the time and they were highly regarded as a result. He wanted to be like them, admired and popular. He waited after school for the boy who teased him earlier. Nothing quite stirred the kids up like a schoolyard brawl. Joaquin shoved the boy and then got into a wrestling match with him. As the two tussled and rolled around on the ground their classmates egged them on like a hungry mob. The anger that Joaquin had been harboring for the past few months had finally found an outlet. He got the better of the boy and punched him repeatedly until he drew blood. As he looked down at the boy's busted lip, Joaquin felt immediately ashamed and remorseful but the sight of blood neither slowed nor deterred him. Every blow that he delivered left him feeling lighter and lighter. His grandfather had imposed standards and accountability that often weighed heavy on his small shoulders. He no longer had to be perfect out of fear of disappointing Romero. He continued to release his fury onto his nemesis until he had nothing left to prove. His classmates broke the circle as Joaquin stood and turned to exit. They no longer giggled at him as they had done earlier. Joaquin detected fear and respect in the way they stared at him. He walked away feeling different. For the first time in a long time, Joaquin felt like a king.

━━━━━━

"Bless me, Father, for I have sinned," Deggler muttered as he sat in the cramped confessional. He found himself staring at the folds in the heavy velour curtains that enclosed and separated him from the rest of the church. He never entered a space without taking in as much detail as possible—an old habit that had served him well. He studied the floor and even the veins in the stained oak walls. Deggler listened to the faint rustling of the priest on the other side of the partition as he shifted his body weight back and forth.

"What is the nature of your sin?" the priest asked.

Deggler smiled to himself at the thought of the question. He didn't consider the horrible torture that he had inflicted upon his targets as sin. Neither did he classify their brutal murder as such. The only thing that left him feeling guilty was the carnal feelings he often felt when torturing and killing his subjects. The more savage the killing the more aroused he became. In his mind this was his only sin.

"I'm often filled with lust," he responded.

"Have you indulged these feelings?" the priest asked.

"Yes, many times."

"You're obviously here because you feel that's the wrong thing to do, so the question is, do you intend to continue indulging yourself?"

"Have you ever had any desires or passions that you felt you had no control over?"

"Everyone experiences that at some point in their lives, but the Bible is very clear on what God's expectations of us are even when dealing with great temptation."

"Are those impossible expectations?" Deggler asked matter-of-factly. "After all, we're born flesh and blood with all the weaknesses that accompany that condition."

"Our human weaknesses are not to be used as an excuse for a

lack of discipline. God would not have imposed such demands if he knew it was impossible for us to meet them."

"So how do you live up to them, Father?"

"We're not here to discuss me."

"Of course we are. Doesn't God put the highest demands on our religious leaders? Aren't they charged with leading by example and not just recycled rhetoric? I'm just asking you man-to-man how to deal with weaknesses and temptation."

The priest was silent for a moment, a bit taken aback by the man's assertiveness. In confession people were usually more demure, burdened with the weight of shame and embarrassment in verbalizing their darker secrets. There seemed to be no such hint of shame in the voice on the other side of the partition.

"When I'm faced with any type of challenge, whether it be great temptation or general flaws in my character, I turn to the Lord and He alone strengthens me."

"So you're saying that you're able to resist temptations and weaknesses by simply turning to God?" Deggler asked.

"Turning to God isn't always a simple thing. But yes, God saves me from myself on a daily basis. It's my faith that gives me salvation. If you dedicate and give yourself to the Lord and His word, you'll know His power and Grace the same way I do."

"Can a man who's done horrible things in his life make it into Heaven, Father?"

"If he genuinely renounces what he's done and repents. Are you here to repent?"

"What if there were things that not even God could forgive?"

"There is nothing that God can't forgive."

"Even the charlatan, the man that pretends to be everything that he's not? Even in the name of God. Are you saying that even that man is worthy of Heaven?"

The priest grew indignant as he actually heard Deggler laugh. "If you're not going to take what I'm saying seriously then there's nothing I can do for you."

"Trust me, Father, I take what you say more seriously than you can imagine."

As Father Conner assigned him a few Hail Marys and mapped out the requirements of his repentance, Deggler's mind drifted. He thought about the things that he secretly knew about the priest. Deggler had kept close tabs on the priest over the last three months. He witnessed firsthand the cleric's penchant for prostitutes. The priest indulged himself with dirty whores once or twice a month. Deggler knew his weaknesses. He knew his hypocrisies. Most of all, Deggler knew that the priest would be his first New York kill as soon as he finished compiling his list of eleven more targets.

2

Although it broke her heart, Elena had no choice but to send Joaquin to live with his grandfather after it became unassailably clear that he was getting more and more out of hand. He was getting into fights or some other form of trouble on average once or twice a week. By the time he started sneaking out of the house to hang with some of the older boys in the neighborhood, she knew he was in danger of getting into serious trouble. She had lost his father to drugs and the streets; she was not about to lose her son as well. He was at the age when the presence of a strong male was obviously more necessary than ever. She decided to let him go and live with Romero, with the plan of her joining them in about six months.

Joaquin had never been on a plane before. It was ironic that his first flight was alone. Elena couldn't afford to fly with him or take the time off from work, so she put him on a nonstop flight to New York and begged one of the flight attendants to keep a close eye on the boy. Even though Elena couldn't stop crying as she said goodbye, Joaquin hid his anxiety well and pretended to be calmer than he was. From the time the plane took off, he stared out the window for the majority of the five-hour flight from Cartagena to JFK. The boy had always wanted to fly. Not just in a plane but to literally fly under the power of his mind. He dreamed of the feeling of his feet leaving the earth and hovering far above the pull of gravity. To fly like the angels he so passionately envied. When he was five and his grandfather asked him what he wanted to be when he grew up, Joaquin proudly stated that he wanted to be an angel.

When the plane started its descent Joaquin was left wide-eyed and speechless by the million buildings and endless acreage that New York welcomed him to. He closed his eyes and braced himself against the bumpy landing. Even after the plane had completely stopped, Joaquin still had the sensation of flying. As the flight attendant escorted him off the plane, the first thing he saw was the sign in Romero's hand that simply read: Mi Raton. Joaquin forgot the months that he had been apart from his grandfather. He forgot about the feelings of anger and abandonment that started overtaking him the day Romero left. He no longer felt the need to fight or impress anyone. When he ran to his grandfather's outstretched arms, he only thought how happy he was to be reunited with him once again. He kept his face buried in Romero's midsection to try to hide the fact that he was crying. The last thing Joaquin wanted to do was disappoint his hero.

The taxi ride from JFK was the most fascinating trip Joaquin had ever taken. His head whipped in different directions as the sights and sounds of the city called and demanded his full attention.

"Careful, Mi Raton, if your eyeballs fall out we'll have to glue them back in. I have a surprise for you," Romero said teasingly.

"What is it?" Joaquin asked enthusiastically.

"On second thought, maybe you won't like it. Just forget I said anything."

"Please Abuelito," Joaquin begged.

Romero patted his pockets as though he were searching for something that he couldn't find. Always the showman, he played out the charade until he knew Joaquin was close to imploding with curiosity.

"Ahh, here they are," he said as he pulled out two tickets from his breast pocket. "If you're not too busy tomorrow, I was thinking maybe we could catch a Yankee's game," he said as he handed the tickets to Joaquin.

Joaquin's eyes grew even bigger, and for a second or two he forgot to breathe. He stared at the tickets as though they might magically transport him to the game right away. Tomorrow wouldn't be able to arrive soon enough. It took him a moment or two, but eventually he remembered to thank Romero. He leaned over in his seat and hugged his grandfather tightly.

The game was a good one from the start. Yankees were hosting the Anaheim Angels and the crowd was loud and passionate. Joaquin had never been in a stadium as large as the "Yankee's house." Their seats might not have been great, but they were the best he ever had.

"Hot dogs, pretzels and chips. Hot dogs, pretzels and chips," a passing vendor chanted as he walked by scanning the crowd for hungry fans.

"You want a hot dog?" Romero asked.

"Yes, please."

Romero handed him a ten-dollar bill and told him to get the vendor's attention.

"Excuse me. Excuse me," Joaquin called after the man unsuccessfully.

Romero laughed as the vendor kept going. "Mi Raton, this is New York. When you want someone's attention you've gotta really get it. YO, HOT DOG!!!" Romero bellowed, startling Joaquin in the process. Sure enough the hot dog vendor turned around and headed back in their direction.

"Who wanted a dog?" the man asked.

Romero nudged Joaquin, who raised the ten-dollar bill in the air and managed an impressive bellow of his own. "Yo, I want a dog." Romero winked at Joaquin and laughed as the dog was handed to the boy and he stared at it as though it were the biggest hot dog he had ever seen.

By the time the ninth inning rolled around, Joaquin had successfully woofed down two hot dogs, popcorn and a large Mountain Dew. It was a matter of time before he crashed but right now he was flying high on sugar and adrenaline. He took in the crowd as much as he took in the game. Joaquin worshipped every moment and detail that he could. He hadn't been happy in a long time, but sitting next to his grandfather watching the Yankees and stuffing himself on concession food, he couldn't conceive of life getting much better. But in that moment it did. Derek Jeter stepped up to bat with the Yankee's last chance to tie. On his very first swing he hit the ball so hard that it looked like it might end up in New Jersey. It was a high-arcing ball that was destined for a highlight reel, until out of nowhere the Angels's outfielder Torii Hunter, who was nicknamed "Spider Man," jumped higher than Joaquin had ever seen anyone or anything jump. Hunter seemed to hang in the air forever and looked like a large predatory bird zeroing in on its prey as he snatched the ball out of the sky and prevented the home run. The Yankees lost by one and Romero was greatly disappointed, but Joaquin was happy because the end to his perfect day was punctuated by watching an Angel fly.

Romero held Joaquin's hand tightly as they moved with the sea of people toward the exit. As Joaquin floated along, all he could think about was how the Angels's player had now validated his own fantasies of flight.

"Romero," someone from the crowd called out. As Romero stopped and turned around he saw Father Conner with three boys that were all around Joaquin's age. Father Conner was the Catholic priest at the church Romero attended. He was hugely popular and highly regarded by those that knew him personally as well as those that knew him by his generous reputation. "I thought that was you," the gregarious priest said as he warmly greeted Romero. "What a game. I guess God was a fan of the Angels today."

"Just for appearance's sake. I'm convinced He still has a soft spot for the Yankees," Romero retorted. As the two men laughed, Father Conner pointed at Joaquin. "Who's your bodyguard?"

"This is my grandson Joaquin. He just got here from Colombia. He's going to be living with me for a while. Joaquin, say hello to Father Conner."

"Hello," Joaquin said shyly.

"Welcome to New York, Joaquin." Conner looked over at the boys who were with him and gestured toward them. "These future Hall of Famers are some of my boys from church. Looks like we have another young soldier for God. Boys introduce yourselves."

Alberto, the smallest of the three boys, was the first to step forward and introduce himself to Joaquin. Within seconds the four boys were giggling and recounting the highlights of the game, particularly the amazing catch at the end.

"Which way are you headed?" Father Conner asked Romero.

"To the subway."

"Nonsense, we've got room in the van."

"I wouldn't want you to have to go out of your way."

"Don't be silly. I could use some adult conversation, besides it'll give the boys a little more time to get to know each other.

"Thank you, Father," Romero said as they all walked in the direction of the parking lot.

Twenty yards back Deggler followed and watched the group intently. This was actually the part of his mission that he liked most. It was the selection process and he was quite good at it. It was neither accidental nor luck that he had killed and escaped capture for thirty years. His amazing success was attributable to his patience and meticulousness more than anything. Deggler took the time to study his prey. He never started a kill cycle until he had selected all twelve targets. He was currently at eleven. Once he was satisfied with his twelfth choice, the killings would begin.

3

Joaquin and Alberto became fast friends. They lived a few blocks from each other and attended the same school and church. Alberto's family was from Guatemala and was a very quiet and unassuming clan. There were four of them that lived in a cramped two-bedroom apartment. Joaquin never met Alberto's father because the man worked three jobs. Alberto had a ten-year-old sister named Esperanza who always made Joaquin nervous because he had never seen a girl so beautiful. Before her he had only viewed girls as annoyances—pesky creatures that boys were forced to tolerate. Whenever the three of them played together he often found her staring at him as though he were some type of alien that fascinated her. Alberto's mother watched Joaquin whenever Romero was held up at work. She was a petite, religious woman that prayed often and was rarely seen without her rosaries. When she laughed it reminded him of Elena's laugh, and it made him realize how much he missed his own mother and wondered how she spent her time now that he was gone. Joaquin was incredibly close to his grandfather and worshipped the ground he walked on, but it took him being away from Elena to realize how much he loved and missed her as well. He thought a lot about the last time he saw her and how she couldn't stop crying. In the evenings that Romero called Elena and let him speak to her, Joaquin never knew how to let her know how he felt about her. When prompted he said the prerequisite "I love you," but anything beyond that left him feeling incredibly awkward and inarticulate. Just before Romero left Colombia, Joaquin overheard him warn Elena not to turn him into a mama's boy. Joaquin was careful and tried his best to make sure Romero never thought of him that way.

Romero wasn't a deeply religious man, but he was devout enough to attend Mass regularly and to want his grandson to know God and the sacrifices Jesus Christ made for the world. He also used church to give Joaquin even more structure and discipline.

Alberto and Joaquin helped out at the church twice a week after school. They did odd jobs and helped keep the church pristine.

"Cleanliness is next to godliness," Father Conner constantly told the boys. He consistently lectured them not only on the upkeep of God's house but on their personal appearance as well. And even though they were as rambunctious as any of their peers,

Alberto and Joaquin were always two of the neatest fourth graders one could meet. Father Conner was unique. He was the only adult that the kids ever knew who, no matter what, left them feeling that he was a genuine friend. He always let them know that they could come to him at any time and talk to him about anything. The first day Joaquin attended church, Father Conner had a sketchbook waiting for him neatly wrapped with a small red bow on it. It was Father Conner that Joaquin talked to about his confusing feelings for Esperanza.

"Can I tell you a secret," Joaquin asked uncomfortably.

"Of course you can," Father Conner encouraged.

"I don't know what to do. Sometimes when I get around her my stomach hurts."

"Joaquin, trust me there is no medicine on earth that can ever cure how she makes you feel," Father Conner laughed. "I usually tell the boys around here that you all are much too young to start thinking about girls, but I have a sneaking suspicion that you may already be beyond the warnings of a feeble priest. So I'll give you a little advice instead. First and foremost, always remember, God sees all so act appropriately. Second, every girl wants to be thought of as a princess. The first boy to figure that out is usually the one she falls for."

"Am I always gonna feel sick when I like a girl?" Joaquin asked.

"Only if you're lucky enough to like the right one," Conner smiled. "Go grab your pad and your jacket so I can take you and Alberto home."

"You gonna tell my grandfather that I like Esperanza?"

"Not unless you want me to. Whatever is said in this room stays in this room."

"Thank you, Father."

———

Deggler fell in love once. Just once. It happened ten years ago when he was living in Boston. He never touched her, never held her; he never even officially met her. But he fell in love with her nonetheless. He found a picture of her in the wallet of an FBI agent that he was forced to kill when the agent came close to apprehending him. Although Deggler didn't even know the woman's name, he fell for her when he saw the infinite love in her eyes. The type of love he had been missing his entire life. As she posed for the picture alongside the agent, Deggler could literally feel how happy she was. She radiated a deep, impossible happiness that had eluded him his entire life. Every time he looked at the photo he wondered what his life might have been with a woman like her.

Years ago, when God first spoke to Deggler and charged him with his mission, the killings immediately gave him purpose and validation. It was at that point that he dedicated his entire life to killing for God. Even though it was an anointing that only God's chosen few were blessed to have, there were times that Deggler pondered the simplest of things like peace, normalcy and the love of a good woman. Deggler sat in his van and watched as Father Conner exited the church with Joaquin and Alberto in tow. He listened to the boys' shrill laughter as they headed down the block accompanied by the older priest. For reasons that he didn't fully understand, Deggler was drawn to Joaquin. Not unlike the woman in the photo, the boy made him think of the deep voids in his life. He sat in the van and wondered what it felt like to be constantly surrounded by the sound of a child's laughter. He thought about what it might have meant on a daily basis to be rewarded with the unconditional love from the son he never had. Even though Joaquin didn't look anything like him, Deggler still fantasized about the boy being his son. It was more so because the boy reminded Deggler of the innocence that he himself was never afforded. His entire childhood had been a series of unimaginable abuse.

Before each kill cycle, Deggler usually found himself much more reflective and introspective. He was filled with "what," "why" and "how." Once the killings started though, all questions and self-examination were pushed aside. Once the killings started all he thought about was fulfilling God's will.

As soon as Father Conner and the boys disappeared up the street, Deggler grabbed some surveillance equipment from the back of his van and made his way around to the back of the church. After he jimmied the lock he made his way to Conner's office. If the preliminary homework that he had done on Father Conner paid off, then not only would the priest be added to the kill list, Deggler would make sure that he was one of the first to die.

4

All week long Joaquin thought about what Father Conner said about all girls wanting to feel like princesses. He waited until Alberto went upstairs to use the bathroom before he reached in his pocket and handed Esperanza the present he had gotten for her.

"What's this?" She looked at him confused.

"Open it," he urged her, hoping that Alberto wouldn't come back prematurely. When she opened the crudely wrapped present she discovered a miniature Asian figurine, made of porcelain.

"Where'd you get this from?" she asked.

He fidgeted nervously trying his best to get a read on whether he had done something good or bad. He panicked and wished he could take it back. Not just the present but also the entire moment. He wanted to disappear before she laughed at him and made him feel smaller than he already felt. In a split second he thought of his doomed fate. He thought Alberto would either tease him mercilessly, or maybe he would be angry and not want to be friends with him anymore. What if she told her mother and her mother in turn told his grandfather? Joaquin had taken the figurine from Romero's extensive collection that he started when Elena was eleven and bought the first one for his birthday. Every year since then for Christmas or his birthday, no matter what featured present she got him she always added another of the figurines. At last count the collection was up to thirty-eight that Romero kept in a display case in the corner of the living room. Joaquin was certain that Romero wouldn't miss just one. He remembered how his mother smiled when she looked at the figurines. All he wanted was to make Esperanza smile the same way.

"I got it for you. I just thought you would like it," Joaquin said.

"I do; it's pretty," she finally replied.

"I think she's a princess or something," Joaquin added.

In that moment he saw the thing that he wanted most. Esperanza kept her eyes fixed on the figurine and smiled. The dimple on her left cheek hung lower and ran deeper than its twin on the right side of her face. She had beautiful dark brown eyes that reminded him of chocolate. When she finally looked up at him, he thought about how much his stomach hurt and wondered why his hands trembled a little.

Esperanza looked around and made sure no one was watching and kissed him on his cheek. The kiss completely caught Joaquin off guard and left him flustered and awkward. By the time Alberto finally came back downstairs he couldn't help but wonder why his friend was acting so strangely.

From the time that she kissed him, Joaquin could barely think of anything else. All of the boys he knew, both in Colombia as well the ones he had befriended in New York, complained about how gross girls were. They had been right for the most part, but Esperanza was different because everything that she said and did made him disagree with his peers. Alberto and his mother walked him home at 6:00. The two boys played in his room while Alberto's mother talked with Romero. After they left, Romero called Joaquin out to the living room.

"I need you to help me find something," Romero said.

"Okay. What are you looking for?"

Romero looked on the floor in the corner as he talked to Joaquin. "I can't find one of the figurines your mother gave me. I could have sworn it was here last week when I cleaned them. You haven't seen it have you?"

"No," Joaquin panicked.

"If you were playing with them and something happened to one of them, you would tell me, right?"

"Yes." Joaquin was in a completely foreign place. He had never lied to his grandfather, but he was too scared and confused by the truth to tell him that he had taken the precious figurine for a girl. It was one of the times he wished he could fly. He wanted to elevate himself to distract Romero from interrogating him. Instead of flying, all he could do was stand there battling nausea from his sudden onset of vertigo.

"So maybe it just flew off the shelf and out the window all by itself, because you haven't touched them at all, right?" Romero continued questioning him.

"No," Joaquin lied again.

"And you're sure?"

"Yes, Abuelito," Joaquin said getting sicker by the moment.

Romero reached in his pocket and pulled out the small figurine. "Well, that's odd that you say that because Mrs. Guzman just told me that she found this in her daughter's room and when she asked her where she got it from, Esperanza said you gave it to her."

Joaquin just lowered his head and studied the floor. Romero's tone completely changed. There was nothing warm or gentle about it. His voice was deep and heavy with disappointment.

"You stole and you lied. Two of the worst things a man can do. You lose somebody's trust, it's a hard thing to get back. I don't even know what else to say to you right now. Go to your room, you'll be spending a lot more time there. When you're not in school or church, that's where I want you, do you understand me?"

Joaquin couldn't bring himself to look at his grandfather. The best he could do was nod his head and numbly walk back toward his bedroom.

Joaquin always felt a bit intimidated when he was alone in the large church. He constantly saw shadows or heard noises in the corners of the gothic hall. Ironically the church made him feel small and much less connected to God. At night when Joaquin knelt by the side of his bed and prayed, he actually felt the presence of his Lord much more. He felt like he could tell God anything. It was always different when he attended Mass because he felt it was more out of obligation and assignment than his genuine connection with the Almighty. He didn't understand why God felt so real to him in private but was somehow lost and diminished in the routine of public worship. Joaquin loved God but hated church. Despite the prayers and various rituals during service, Joaquin was never wholly convinced that God felt the need to actually make an appearance in the house of worship.

He was sweeping between the pews when Alberto came from Father Conner's office. Joaquin couldn't understand why his friend avoided eye contact with him and was being so distant. Alberto looked sad and as though he had possibly been crying earlier.

"You okay?" Joaquin asked.

Alberto ignored him and began sweeping on the opposite side of the church. Joaquin crossed over to him and tapped him on his shoulder.

"What's wrong?"

Alberto recoiled from Joaquin's hand as though the simple touch had somehow burned or otherwise wounded him.

"Don't touch me," Alberto hissed at him.

"What...?"

"Just leave me alone, all right!" Alberto quickly walked away with his broom, leaving Joaquin totally confused.

5

Father Conner always had the best candy in his office. There were two large glass bowls on his bookcase filled to the brim with an assortment of sweets. He knew how hard it was for most of the children that sat across from him to concentrate on anything until he gestured toward the bowls and offered them the candy of their choice. It was this type of thoughtfulness that endeared Father Conner to the kids and parents alike. He was a pillar of the community. In the eyes of many he was the Hand of God. Father Conner was both learned and kind. His life was dedicated to the service of others. Aside from being a great spiritual leader, he often took some of the boys from church on field trips and even had sleepovers at his home. He was a big believer that the souls of the youth needed early intervention to better their chances of living up to their spiritual potential.

"Is your grandfather still upset with you?" Father Conner asked Joaquin as the boy nibbled on hard candy.

"I think so."

"Are you still on punishment?"

"Yes."

"He'll come around. At one point or another, every man has been guilty of doing something crazy for a girl. They're born to make fools of us and we're born to oblige them." As Father Conner handed Joaquin a brand-new sketchbook, his eyes lit up and he thanked the priest.

"I think the thing that really bothers him is the fact that you were able to steal so easily and then lie about it just as easily. Can you see how that would disappoint and upset him?"

"Yes, but I'm sorry."

"I believe you, and at some point you need to show him that. Have you ever stolen before Joaquin?"

"Yes, but just once." Joaquin's voice was nervous and insecure.

"When?" Conner tried not to sound too authoritative.

"I took some money out of my mother's purse the day my grandfather moved here."

"Did she ever find out?"

"I don't think so."

Father Conner leaned back in his chair and rubbed his eyes as though he were both tired and burdened by the revelation.

"I have to be honest Joaquin; that does worry me. Taking something to give a girl, although not right, is one thing. You stealing money is another. What is the root of all evil?"

"Money," Joaquin mumbled.

Joaquin inadvertently let the sketchbook slide from his lap as he started crying. "Please don't tell my grandfather. I don't want him to be mad at me anymore." Father Conner grabbed some tissue as he got out of the chair and crossed over to Joaquin. He knelt down beside the boy and spoke very softly as though the sound of his voice alone could make him feel better.

"You don't have to cry, and you don't have to worry. I've always told you that whatever we say in here is our secret. Okay?" Father Conner used the tissues to gently wipe away Joaquin's tears. He then gingerly cupped the boy's face in his hand and kissed him on the forehead. "See, don't you feel better already?"

"Yes."

"Good," Conner said still holding Joaquin's face in his hands. He caressed his cheeks and looked at the child as though he were absorbing everything he could. He leaned in again but this time he slowly kissed Joaquin on his lips. Joaquin pulled back in surprise but Father Conner wouldn't let go of his face. "It's okay, Joaquin, you do trust me, don't you?" Joaquin nervously nodded his head once.

"You don't have to be scared of anything. I'll protect you." Father Conner leaned in and kissed Joaquin again on the lips. This time, longer and with more intensity. Joaquin had no idea how to process what was going on. Elena had drilled in him that if an adult ever touched him inappropriately to run away and let her know immediately. She told him that there were bad people in the world—dirty and perverted. But obviously she wasn't talking about

Father Conner because he was a priest, mentor and friend. She couldn't have been talking about him because a lot of grownups said that Father Conner was the Hand of God.

On the walk home Father Conner talked to Joaquin as though nothing different had happened between them. Joaquin was confused and hurt, both emotionally and physically. He couldn't understand why Father Conner did the things to him that he did. Even when he cried and asked him to stop, the priest just kept saying, "Trust me." When they finally reached Joaquin's doorstep Father Conner placed his hand firmly on the boy's shoulder and said, "Just like I've kept your secrets, you have to keep everything between us a secret as well. I don't want your grandfather angry with you and sending you back to live with your mother. I care about you too much, Joaquin, and I know how much that would upset you. I only do what God tells me to do. He tells me how to love his children. Just like God doesn't want me to tell anybody your secrets, he doesn't want you telling anyone about what we did. We all have to obey God's word. Do you understand that?" Father Conner asked as he handed the boy the sketchbook.

Even though he didn't, Joaquin did his best to try to understand. He nodded weakly and answered, "Yes, Father."

Romero was in the kitchen cooking when Joaquin came in and went directly to his bedroom. In the two weeks that he had been on punishment and exiled to the confines of his room, he sketched images of Esperanza and his mother as a means of escaping the boredom. Tonight he was much too depressed to do anything but lie on his bed and hope that sleep would numb him from the things he was feeling. He didn't eat that night. He didn't sketch in the new book that Father Conner gave him. He didn't read. He did nothing. Even though he lay curled in the fetal position on his bed he was unable to sleep and escape the horrible thoughts and images that bombarded his mind. He listened to his grandfather going about his evening without him. He heard the sporadic sounds of pot lids clanking with pots. There was twenty minutes of silence that he assumed was the time Romero read the paper and quietly ate dinner. On top of everything else that he was feeling, Joaquin was additionally pained that tonight he was in no way a part of Romero's routine. Joaquin wanted to go to his grandfather and tell him everything but he was scared Father Conner was right. Romero would be even more upset with him and possibly send him back to live with his mother for spreading lies about the good priest. If he told anyone, who would believe him over Father Conner? Everyone loved Father Conner and Joaquin was nothing more than a proven thief and liar.

When he did eventually fall asleep, Joaquin had an amazing dream. He was in an abandoned building that he and Alberto had recently discovered. The building had a large hole in the ceiling that let in endless sunlight and the bluest skies. Father Conner was standing in a corner of the building hidden by the shadows, but Joaquin was able to see him nonetheless. In his dream Joaquin saw a giant, invisible hand that only he could see, descend from the sky and squeeze into the hole in the ceiling.

When the hand reached in and lifted him he no longer felt sad or confused. Joaquin knew he didn't have to fear Father Conner anymore. Instead of feeling the need to run, he just let the hand lift him and teach him to fly. He levitated and watched his feet leave the ground, disengaging from gravity and all that held him earthbound. Joaquin rose through the roof of the building and then beyond. As he looked down, Father Conner became an indistinguishable speck. Joaquin flew by Alberto's apartment building and saw him and Esperanza playing outside. They both looked up in the sky and saw him overhead. Joaquin slowed down enough to watch them running after him, all the while waving and smiling at him. Just as Joaquin flew over the street that he lived on, he saw Romero rounding the corner with two bags of groceries. His grandfather looked up at him and laughed while he dropped his bags and waved enthusiastically. Joaquin flew higher and faster and in no time he was hovering over his mother, who sat in their favorite park staring out at the water. At first she was sad but when she saw Joaquin smiling down at her she stood up and cried with joy. Joaquin flew above her for a while until he knew she was happy then he ascended past the clouds and even the sun. He always wanted to fly. He knew deep down he had the power and ability. Joaquin thanked God for finally showing him how.

The next day when Joaquin woke up he put on his usual Catholic school uniform, had his usual breakfast and had a usual day in school. At 3 o'clock when he was supposed to report to Father Conner at church, he instead went to the abandoned building that he dreamed about and hanged himself from an overhead beam in the center of the room. The last thing that he saw was his feet bathed in amber sunlight dangling above the ground below.

It was his eleventh birthday.

———

Deggler learned a long time ago not to kill with emotion. The only exception to that rule was when he was still in his early twenties and he murdered his father. Even though he had now killed well over thirty men in his life that was the only time he allowed himself to be ruled by his rage. His killings were all deliberate and well thought out. Although he hated what his subjects represented, he remained emotionally detached and focused on his overall mission. God had chosen him to do His work, and nothing, not even his personal feelings, could in any way compromise or jeopardize the importance of his calling.

When he read about the boy's suicide in the newspaper, Deggler actually cried. He thought about how beautiful and innocent the child was. He thought about how Joaquin had made him regret not having a son of his own. Deggler felt the loss as though the boy was directly connected to him. He sat in front of one of his many monitors and played back the surveillance footage he had on Father Conner. He saw the horrible things the priest did to Joaquin. He made himself watch it over and over, and each time he felt his hatred deepen. Deggler prayed for the strength and discipline that he desperately needed so that he wouldn't kill Father Conner before the designated time of reckoning. For thirty years his kill cycle had always begun on the exact same date, but unfortunately that was still two months away. As much as he wanted to kill Conner right away, he couldn't veer from his course. This would be his final cycle and he needed it to be perfect and pleasing to God. The one thing that gave him patience and strength was the fact that he had two months to plan how to kill the priest. He would enjoy this kill as much as he did when he killed his own father. No matter how gruesome a fate awaited the other eleven targets on his list, none would be more painful and methodic than what he would come up with when it was time to kill Father Conner.

Acknowledgments

First and foremost God always gets top billing in my book. For those of us that are foolish enough to chase what others deem unrealistic dreams, God often populates our paths with angels that encourage us in our pursuits. These are my angels.

My agent Rockelle Henderson. The road for an artist is a bumpy one littered with countless rejections and disappointments. I have to thank you for being my North Star. Not only have you guided and inspired me but you have even on occasion given me just enough of a ki-ck in my ass during my "woe is me" periods. You've been with me on this journey to land a good publisher for almost a decade and seeing how you never gave up on me definitely helped me not to give up on myself. It means so much to me having a Sista like you (and your mother) in my corner.

My project manager Annalisa Rinetti, aka "The Crazy Italian."

You were the heart and soul of the Dream Team, which you assembled to help promote the Laws Series. I can't count how many hats you've worn. You not only thought outside of the box but you constantly challenged us to blow up the box altogether. I especially loved the group meetings at my house complete with intense strategizing and of course, authentic Italian cooking. Words could never adequately express my immense gratitude for having you as the team's captain.

Sherri Saum, aka "The Angel Faced Assassin." You are the first to read anything I write, and the first to let me know if it's half as good as I hope or twice as bad as I fear. You have single-handedly spared the world from my misguided attempts and indulgent musings. Your critiques have been spot-on, even when I wished you were wrong because I knew it would mean more work for me. You've cut me so eloquently when I needed it most that I wasn't even aware I was bleeding. Thank you for always demanding more of me.

Toni Ann Johnson, aka "The Lit Ninja." From the time we both started out as actors you've been like a baby sister to me and I've always been so proud of you blossoming into not only an incredible writer but someone who truly understands both the craft and soul of writing. Thank you for always taking the time and so graciously sharing with me the technique of becoming a better author. I'm still working on cutting down on my usage of double adjectives, so please be a little patient.

Lisa Bellamore, aka "Crazy Legs." It always amazes me that you and I ever get any work done because we spend the majority of our interactions laughing hysterically, pretty much about any and everything. Hector Lavoe!!!

Christie Mikki Dawson, aka "The Social Media Guru." It's been quite the accomplishment convincing a technosaurus such as myself, that tweeting, posting and hash tagging, weren't incurable diseases that would make my fingers fall off or lead to blindness. You really are a pain in the ass, but just the right kind, and I adore you for it.

Penni Wasserman, my assistant. I appreciate you being a great go to sounding board. Thanks for never laughing when you enter into my writing space and somehow manage not to laugh even when you catch me in the middle of being animated or talking to myself while trying to work through some bumps. Trust me, I know it ain't always pretty.

I would also like to thank my tribe. The close group of people in my life, who loyally read my first drafts and offer honesty and insightfulness that always elevates my writing.

Elisha Wilson Beach

Elke Tegler

Ken Baldwin

Adai Lamar

Deborah Taitano

My favorite cuz Shelly Sheppard

My nephew Eugene Haynes IV

Audrey Dees Sims

Shelley Robertson

Thanks to Lavaille Lavette Books and Sourcebooks for not

only giving me a home but also honoring me with the opportunity to be one of the very first authors selected to help kick off your incredible collaboration.

Thanks to the fans and critics that have shown so much love. You guys encourage and empower artists in ways that you may not even know.

Last but by no means least, I'd like to thank Nana Danquah, Jennifer Pooley and Ivy Pochoda for being great advisors and supporters who have always generously shared their vast knowledge and experience of the publishing industry with me.

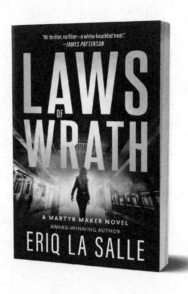

LAWS OF WRATH

A MARTYR MAKER NOVEL

AWARD-WINNING AUTHOR

ERIQ LA SALLE

The butchered body of a transgender woman is found in a dumpster in Chinatown, New York. Nothing out of the ordinary for the NYPD, except the victim just so happens to be the brother of Detective Phee Freeman. At first the slaying looks like the random act of a vicious killer, but when it is discovered that there are similar ritualistic murders throughout the city, Phee and his partner Quincy Cavanaugh, along with FBI Agent Janet Maclin, have no choice but to join forces with Dr. Daria Zibik, a brilliant but deranged Satanic cult leader. Phee and his partners must do everything they can to stop the bloodshed and determine if the evil they are hunting and the psychopath they are trusting could actually be one and the same.

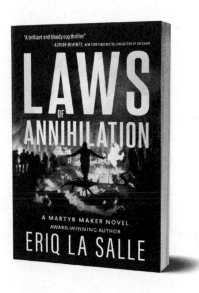

Shortly after being diagnosed with terminal cancer, FBI Agent Janet Maclin is facing her toughest case yet. She is assigned to help NYPD detectives Quincy Cavanaugh and Phee Freeman, who are investigating a series of gruesome hate crimes that threaten a city on the brink of a race war. As the body count mounts, time is running out for Maclin—in more ways than one. Adrian McKinty, New York Times bestselling author of The Chain, calls this thrilling conclusion to the Martyr Maker series "a brilliant and bloody cop thriller that Ed McBain himself would have been proud to have penned."

About the Author

© Lori Allen

Actor/director/producer Eriq La Salle is best known to worldwide television audiences for his award-winning portrayal of the commanding Dr. Peter Benton on the critically acclaimed and history-making medical drama *ER*. Educated at Juilliard and NYU's Tisch School of the Arts, his credits range from Broadway to film roles opposite Eddie Murphy in *Coming to America,* Robin Williams in *One Hour Photo*, and Hugh Jackman in *Logan*. La Salle has maintained a prolific acting career while at the same time working steadily as a director, taking the helm for HBO, Showtime, NBC, Fox, CBS, and Netflix. He remains a staple in the Dick Wolf Entertainment camp after four years as Executive Producer and director on *Chicago PD*, as well as directing episodes of the reboot of *Law & Order* and *Law & Order: Organized Crime*. In addition to acting, directing, and producing, in 2003 La Salle wrote an episode of *The Twilight Zone* entitled "Memphis," which made WGA's list of 101 Best Written TV Series. He lives in Los Angeles, California.